THE RECKONING

By

ERIC
ENCK

Library of Congress Control Number: 2006938593
ISBN: 0-9772034-7-6

Printed in the U.S.A.
First Edition February 2007

BLUPHI'ER
PUBLISHING

Blu Phi'er Publishing
Shreveport, Louisiana
www.bluphier.com

Other Books by Eric Enck:

Tell Me your Name (Available on Amazon and book stores)

The Work (Available on Amazon and book stores)

Please take the opportunity to read the following books from Blu Phi'er Publishing:

Negro in Nam: My Father's Tale
By Michael L. Bernoudy, Jr.

Humanity's Edge
By Tamara Wilihite

True to Self
By Tilisha Alexander

Precedent of Justice
By Patrick Raley

The Chronos Project: A Race Against Time
By Marc Anthony Rios

Also, be on the look out for the following titles from Blu Phi'er Publishing:

Stained Glass Window: Memoirs of a Cheater
By Michael L. Bernoudy, Jr.

Tales of Love and Woe
By Lawrence Strickland

A Mambo Duet
By Eugene Rodriguez

The Renegade
By Jane Timm Baxter

ORDER BOOKS AT WWW.BLUPHIER.COM

To all the women in this world...

You are not alone.

To Bram Stoker. Author of Dracula...

You were right.

I dead-icate this book to all my fans, and I hope this novel finds you well and endowed in evil. To all the lovers of vampires, this is my homage to you and the beautiful creatures of the night.

I hope the devil never whispers in your ears.

ERIC-

To

Courtney.

May your Days
Ahead Be Bright
And full of Magic

Love you.

4/14/07

PROLOGUE

FROM THE CARPER FALLS HERALD:

Between September 1999 and December 1999, six Maryland teenagers were slaughtered in a grisly string of homicides that have remained unsolved. No positive connection in the cases was deduced, but they have entered modern folklore as a series and are so considered here. The evidence required to prove-or disprove-a connection, like the killer, has remained elusive.

On September 30th 1999, Ted Simmons, age 13, went bowling at Brewser Lanes with his brother Antin, age 11, and a neighbor, Douglas Peters, age 14. They never made it home that night, and a search was launched, resulting in a grim discovery two days later. Bikers found the remains of their naked, battered bodies in a ditch near the Callson Creek, in the Carper Valley Woods Preserve. An autopsy showed that the three boys were dismembered, but police have no other clues.

A month later, on November 28th 1999, Jennifer Gibson, 15, and her sister Patricia, 13, failed to come home from a neighborhood theater. Reminded of the triple murder, still unsolved, Maryland panicked. Carl Tolbert, lead singer for the rock band GOLDEN HEART RULES, made a public appeal for the girls to go home. On December 1st 1999 a motorist in Worcester County spotted the victims in a roadside ditch off of Route 13, their naked, frozen bodies lay out side by side. Both sisters had been beaten with one girl's head crushed. Sheriff Harrison Turner and his men stubbornly refused to comment on the reports that Jennifer and Patricia had been mutilated, with the lips of one girl sliced away.

On December 10th 1999, Judith Longwind, 17, went missing on the one-mile walk between a friend's house and her home. There was no doubt about mutilation a week later, when her dismembered remains surfaced in two 55-gallon drums, floating in the River Bridge Canal. One barrel contained the girl's head, with four .32-caliber slugs in the brain. The other barrel contained internal organs. The *evidence discovered by the Police was marginal at best. The gun used was not left behind. Local papers read: The Maryland psychopath dubbed the " Violator" is at large selecting teens as victims.*

Sheriff Harrison Turner of the Carper Falls Police Department lowered the newspaper and looked out his office window at the silent street. This town wasn't prepared for what was coming. As children slept and parents made love, the moon centered the night sky like an omniscient eye of doom. In a few days, there would be nothing left for Harrison Turner to keep him here. In a few days, blood would rule the streets like the days of Rome and coroners would perhaps whistle while they worked.

I.

Unforgiving nights allow sanctity. Stepping slowly over the threshold of the apartment door, it wants it again. It wants to smell the blood like most want to smell flowers along a romantic yearning. The irony of darkness was here in the midnight hour. It saw things much clearer for what they were. It didn't care about getting caught. It cares about the moment, the purpose, and the knife clutched in its hand wants retribution. It wears a mask that would give madmen troubled nights. It needs to feel the blood of the innocent because no one is innocent. When the Violator opened the bedroom door, it observed the ghostly moonlit walls, the hardwood floor creaking with witness, and the crib in the corner.

Carper Falls, Maryland is the beginning of all things sacred, and like all things sacred, a mass murderer such as this one must go on with respect. Clear sightedness always guarantees a perfect illusion. The locals don't know what is true below the sleepy drifting terror entering the hearts of many. The town is one of the greatest of old communities. It's a place where a business district claims true through old fashion mixing with the new. Carper Falls is a rest area for tourists and outsiders. Many of them drive along roads they know little or nothing about. The magic found within memory is not instituted here in Carper Falls. It is maintained, because it is as cherished as Romanian wine.

Brenda Dejour, a young woman with callous thoughts about her life, packed her book bag full of notebooks and photocopied drawings concerning the occult and vampires. Her curiosities went far beyond school. She glanced out the window of the public library towards Baker Street, and saw how dark it was getting.

The sky remained slashed open with a murdered sun and left no remorse for the twilight to follow. She stood with her young eyes open towards destiny and thought about what was happening to her town. Something she knew. Something she could not control. A serial killer was eminent. One that was responsible for several murders in the district. The police had found no clues, and as unintelligible as it may

1

seem to those that hold their curtains open with possible suspects in mind, no one really knows. And no one will *ever* know why.

Originally the town was found in pre-colonial times, when more of the surf that beckons the eyes of the old and wise prevailed without pollution. That was long ago, and in the lesser years of consumed with simplicity and gratitude.

The locals like Southern Gale who was older than legends and Freddie Hurst, his partner, watch with unsuspecting eyes, as people and seagulls pass by. Southern and Freddie own a gas station out on Route 50, just before the bypass onto 13. Here, Carper Falls comes to its last chance. The roads are flat, tasteless for a whim. It's here where many common folk live. There is a post office and a police barracks, ran by Sheriff Turner, who receives his coffee for free every morning from the local Donut Connection.

He has a few deputies that care more about their lotto tickets than their badges. There are small pizza joints, a FOOD LION, and a downtown plaza where one can buy Lottery tickets spend whatever earnings claimed on the second hand clothing stores pretending to sell first hand items. (Unless one were to be lucky enough to be part of the percent that wins *really* big: and then they could get a one-way ticket out of town and move to a better area of Maryland; or perhaps Dodgeville, where the New England Carnivals that pass through never seem to leave).

Small towns love emulating large cities. People go about their daily lives in areas that could pass for suburbs of major metropolises. Yet at the same time it's almost bizarre in a way to see the moments of unforgiving time dwindle down into boredom along lost roads, like Border Street or Main.

During the summer, most of Carper Falls is a tourist extravaganza. The roads are packed with cars like a bad heart full of congestive failure. But now, like every winter, the suburb of Maryland stuck between the old sections of Ocean City, where the beach never let's go of you, has become desolate with silence.

The locals have become aware that the town's first serial killer is now in their mist. Through the eyes of youths on the playgrounds, the streets, the sandy beaches where the afternoon sun touches the ocean's current trying to warm the water of a winter's grip, sadness can be seen. The unpretentious houses lining the surrounding streets with dormered and gambreled roofs are homes to unsuspecting youths that watch the uncomfortable skies above. Sometimes gray and deep with the hint of snow, other times, blue, reminding most people to pray for better times that hopefully lie ahead.

Brenda Dejour gathered what strength she had inside of her and headed for the long walk home, where at least during her walk she could contemplate on her project for school. The horizon hovering over the breaking waves along the coastal surf would perhaps help her think. After all, she had a lot to think about. She was a young woman in a cruel world where perhaps men were no longer understanding of what society wanted from women. Brenda had a moment of clarity that lit her with a delicate intricacy. Perhaps that was how serial killers were born. Perhaps in the dark corners of all minds, it is safe to assume everyone has a dark side. It's those that all that realization to manifest itself in to actualization that find themselves immersed in their bloodletting.

As it so happened, vampires interested her.

Not like they would most people. The Hollywood stories and the books by famous authors only captivated her mind with arousal for the occult. Brenda's yearning was full fledged and full throttled. She was interested in the history of vampirism, ever since things went bad at home.

On a Wednesday morning, Southern Gale, a local gas station owner, came to work still surprised about what he saw on television. If anyone new better, they would see worry in his old eyes. Never in all the sixty-five years of his life has he encountered such horrifying bewilderment. The police were on a search, mainly in the wooded areas of what many called " The Valley". Six teenagers were recently killed within a time frame of only a few months. Southern stepped out of his new Pick-up truck and walked into the station, arthritis made the short journey painful. Behind the counter a 32-year old high school drop out named Veronica sat reading the latest issue of Entertainment Weekly. Popping her bubblegum, she looked up when Southern entered.

"Hello boss."

"Top of the day Veronica."

"I guess."

"Anything new?"

Southern asked, taking off his vest and draping it over the side counter. His huge gut peeked slightly out from under the company shirt he wore. He observed the stack of newspapers lying on the floor bundled with twine. Leaning down as his knees popped, he cut the twine with a pocketknife.

"Nothing much South. My Soap operas are coming back on."

"That's great Veronica." Southern said, rolling his eyes. "My wife watches those things, they're not very real you know."

"I don't care." Veronica said. "They're still fun to watch, and besides, half the crap you read in the newspaper isn't real either."

South glanced at the girl behind the counter.

"He's real."

"Who?"

"You know who, that maniac killing kids. I heard from a Deputy they didn't put everything in the paper. They never put everything in the paper."

"Sometimes it's better to leave some stuff out boss." Veronica said softly.

Southern pulled the top copy out of the stack of fresh newspapers. His eyes widened as if all the surprises in the world were now his, and his alone to cherish.

"I'll be goddamned." he said.

Standing up, Veronica leaned over the counter to see what her boss was doing.

"They even gave this son of a bitch a name."

Southern read the headlines of the front page, his old tired eyes wandering side to side. A cowboy hat with a turquoise jewel in its center sparkled in the morning light.

"He's a sick son of a bitch." Veronica said.

"He's killed six teenagers in the past few months. Just came out of nowhere, although the cops think he's local."

"Probably is." Veronica agreed. "I don't doubt it at all, remember back in the early eighties that woman who killed her kids and then called 911 singing about it?"

"Veronica." Southern said. " That was Baltimore, you'd expect something like that out there, and this is the valley for Christ sakes. Tourist trap, this is a small town where nothing ever happens."

"Something happened near here though remember last summer?"

"What are you talking about?"

"Oh man" Veronica said. "You really don't remember? The woman who was found dead in traffic?"

"Sorry." South said. "It doesn't ring a bell."

A car suddenly came across the bell strips for the gas pumps. Veronica turned and saw the vehicle, but South didn't deter from the newspaper.

"Rumors were all over Ocean City. Some old woman in Baltimore was in Center Square. The cops told reporters she was leaving the bus terminals. She was in a station wagon. When the lights went from red to green her car came out into the intersection first and then just slowed to a stop right there, like she was coasting or something."

"Go on." South said.

He pulled a cigarette from his shirt pocket and drew a match to light it.

"The car gets halfway across the road and the tires turn to the right which was good, because it was a right turn only lane and stops right there in the middle of traffic, cars blaring their horns behind her and everything. Some lawyer on his way to a vehicular homicide trial of all things gets out of his Mercedes and goes over to help the lady. He figures maybe her car stalled or something, and she can't get it started."

"What happened?"

"Well, the lawyer knocks on the old lady's window, asks her if she's okay. Keep in mind this old bag is still holding onto the steering wheel, but they say her eyes looked like shiny marbles in her head.

5

When the lawyer knocked on the glass, the bitch fell over in the seat, and the way she fell made the lawyer and a few other people standing behind him freak out. He started calling the other cars behind him to help."

"She died?"

"Yep." Veronica said. "Right there in traffic. She made it halfway through the light and I still believe it was from the car coasting. The lawyer and some other guy opened the car door, and they knew right away that she was dead. Strange thing was that there was blood all over the seats, some of it not hers."

"What?" Southern asked dismayed.

"But that's not all. That afternoon, they took this woman down to the city morgue; they identified her as Margaret Hither. I'll never forget her name. Some things you read in the newspaper you never forget. She had moved to Baltimore of all things. The blood they found on the seat was not hers, Police still don't know who it belongs too."

Southern stood quiet.

"And not only that, there were wounds found on Margaret, mostly in her neck, although under the coroner's speculation they were thought to be some sort of animal bites. When they did the autopsy on the old hag they found odd things."

"Like what?" Southern asked.

"Well." Veronica started. "Her body never entered rigor mortis, which I'm told is a normal phase during the dying process. When you die, you stiffen like a damn log, and then you reshape. This is part of decomposition. They did the autopsy anyway and embalmed her. Although the embalming fluid kept coming out."

Veronica paused, looking out the window; she observed no movement from the dark car that was parked across the bell strips.

"Get the hell out of here." South said. "Next you're going to tell me she came back to life."

"I'm serious." Veronica said. "It was in the papers. They placed the lady in the Morgue drawer and all, and that evening when they went to try to put more embalming fluid in her, the Chief Medical Examiner pulled the morgue drawer out and Margaret Hither was sitting up, like she was still alive or-

"You're making this shit up." South interrupted.

"I swear, Christ South, unexplained shit happens all the time."

"I don't believe that. There's always an explanation Veronica. I've heard of dead bodies sitting up on their own before, but it's a nerve thing. It's caused by gas leaking through an orifice. My mother used to work at a nursing home, and when the old people would die they would sometimes flagellate, sometimes more than once. It's air escaping, that's all."

"Well." Veronica said. "I don't know about any of that, but what I do know was the Chief Medical Examiner must have never experienced it before because he was found dead of a heart attack a few hours later. The cameras in the room showed the police everything that happened; even they think it was eerie. Some think Margaret was bitten by a-

"Veronica." South said.

"What?"

"You're weird."

Veronica shrugged, and then looked outside.

"Nice car." she said.

Veronica saw it first hand. It was a massive black muscle car idling at the pumps, before the driver behind the dark tinted glass shut the vehicle off. Southern looked up, but briefly.

"1970 Shelby Cobra Mustang." he said. " My cousin had one restored in the eighties. Goddamn deathtrap. He died in it crossing the Susquehanna Bridge in Pennsylvania."

Southern took a step closer towards the window forgetting momentarily about the newspaper in his hand and the giant black letters scrawled across the headlines that spelled out the word-

VIOLATOR

"That's really odd." South said, finishing his cigarette.

"What's that?"

Southern blew out smoke, hesitated, then turned towards Veronica.

"My cousin died in a car that was just like that one, same color and all."

"That is weird." Veronica concurred. "I bet you have gooseflesh."

"I do."

The driver's side door opened, and Veronica watched the tall man emerge from its confines. His shoulders were broad and his legs were long. He moved rhythmically as if all his notions were behind him and all he has done way out in front. He wore black sunglasses. Aviator Ray bans. Veronica could tell they weren't the cheap kind either. Not like she had for sale on the spinning rack in the gas station. The man wearing shades reached out grabbing the door as the bell above chimed.

"Ah" South said. "First customer of the day."

The stranger smiled, and it was a warm smile that fit him well. Too many people don't know how to smile anymore, especially in this day and age.

"I hope to not be your last." the stranger said.

Southern smiled, then turned to walk away to his office. In truth, memories of his cousin all came at once, and perhaps it was a bit much to bear. The car wasn't the only thing that reminded South of his cousin, Chad Boddly. It was the stranger's smile as well. He didn't want Veronica to notice his depressed ambiance. And perhaps she would never guess he was that way. South didn't like telling people his problems. Especially to people he didn't know. Some things are better left unsaid, and unnoticed. Veronica's story would stay with him however. All the way to his office, South thought of Margaret Hither sitting up on a shiny death table smiling. He even thought of her whispering his name in the dark. It's sometimes better to not know what nightmares look like, then to have to remember them.

"It's a fine morning isn't it?" South heard Veronica ask the stranger, as her voice faded to the close of his office door.

"Yes." said the owner of the Mustang. "So far, it's a terrific morning."

"Especially for a ride in such a beauty." Veronica said.

The stranger smiled once more, as he withdrew a twenty from a chain wallet. Veronica observed the stranger's left hand.

"I like your rings."

The stranger paused, then pushed his dark sunglasses further up the bridge of his nose.

"Thank you." The stranger said. "I like your gas station."

"It's not mine." Veronica took the twenty and opened the register.

"Although I wish it were, I wouldn't have to work so much."

The stranger looked around, then back at Veronica.

"When you own a business of your own, you'll find you have to work twice as hard to keep it alive."

"I guess you're right." she said. "From around here?"

The stranger closed his wallet.

"We're all from around here."

Veronica giggled. She thought this guy was too cool, and God did he smell good!

"I actually just moved into a house on Main Street."

"You'll like it here, not much to do in the winter time though, and the summers are so packed with tourists."

"I like tourists."

Veronica paused, then leaned forward.

"Well do you have a name?" She asked.

"I do." the stranger said as he grabbed the door and the bell above chimed. "It's Robert."

"Well good day to you Robert, come back again."

"Oh I will Veronica" Robert said, and left into the morning sun brightening the store glass.

Veronica went back to the magazine, reading an article about baby names. It was when the Mustang purred to life, rolling away from the gas pumps a thought suddenly hit her like a blood stained hurricane. She took her left hand and pulled her smock free from her left breast, realizing she had left her nametag on the dresser at home.

How did he know my name?

She didn't tell the stranger her name did she?

Did I?

9

II

The demographics of Carper Falls was destroyed by a hurricane back in 1969, right before Shelby Cobras were made. Never again has the town suffered such disaster. In 1976, the year the vicious killer everyone that Wednesday morning was reading about had come to be born, another storm hit the East Coast during the winter. A snowstorm dumped over 14 inches on the entire mainland in Carper Falls freezing itself into the memory of everyone in the region. Sylvia Dejour, a quiet profound and internally darkened horse trainer remembers it well, although her daughter Brenda was much too young at the time. Sylvia was the typical female of this world, and a better mom than most. She wanted the best for her daughter and what could be wrong with that?

Her daughter was now twenty years old, with the firm belief the killer abducting children in Maryland would never be caught. She had good reasons for these beliefs.

Her parents raised her to be a fine outstanding member of the community, despite the fact oppression and anger has more or less consumed the young girl. Her eyes often looked at the ways of the world with a deep set blue of mystery. Her parents have done nothing but fight for the past several years. Her father recently turned into a raving alcoholic. A control freak which has done nothing but degrade his wife, to the point of no return. It was no surprise that Brenda developed a taste for dwelling in the dark room beneath her mind. How long could she remain under the roof? And how long could she watch mom being abused? How long could she stay away in college knowing what mom was going through? She watched her father beat mom almost to death with a baseball bat last Christmas while the Maryland parade danced through the town.

But yet, she never called the police on him. Most people would call this crazy. Sylvia called it survival. Brenda sunk into the interest of the macabre, starting with horror movies. At first, she'd venture to the local theatre where those two girls were viciously attacked a few months ago. And then later, Brenda developed a fixation with the vampire. This was her way of dealing with what's been going on behind locked doors.

The libraries were filled with stories many people heard with attuned ears as children. All the experts believed that vampires didn't exist. There are however killers in our times. Modern Dracula's that murder but don't drink blood, at least for no reason other than a perverse escapade. If Dracula were to live today, he would own a house near the beach, at least to the young student's opinion. He would have a car in this modern time as well, perhaps, a Mustang. Brenda loved Mustangs, especially the newer ones. The few friends she had owned them, and Brenda yearned to own one soon enough. Brenda imagined Dracula driving away from the lowering sun in a car much like one she would one day own, the seats covered in blood, festooned with bits of bone and a legacy of gore.

Except Dracula, perhaps rode upon a horse into the welcoming arms of moonlight during those times Brenda so enjoyed reading about with a steady bemused concentration of a scholar. Theories like these always kept Brenda's resourceful mind occupied and free of thoughts that she may come home one day and witness her mother dead on the floor. Brenda was no more obsessed with vampirism than the average person was consumed with evil pursuits. People look away from evil, but the truth is the nose and eyes want more of it. There's nothing wrong with that. There's nothing wrong with admiring the horrors in this world. Or when you are driving by a car accident and wondering what the dead people inside look like. Were they dead on impact? Or did they die much later? Was the bloody head in the back seat's whose last thoughts stuck on a prayer?

Brenda decided unknowingly, that her purpose on this world was not yet discovered. It would be discovered in Carper Falls.

Brenda Dejour opened the novel she has been coming to the library for since late summer. Francine Bowry, the library attendant thought it odd; she never signed the book out. She rather came to Carper Library to read.

FROM CHAPTER 12 VIOLATOR (As dictated by Barnabus Nodsley Vampire Hunter 1776):

What is a razor to the wrist, an invitation to more answers needed? Are not the most questions answered before they ever leave lips? Even the undiscovered ones of the night are asked before suicide. How many mortals have done something mundane and true before committing atrocities on themselves? The local father who cooks dinner for his family before going out to the horse's stable and hanging himself by the swing of the rope does not hold a tie for an explanation. But one often wonders inexplicably, why make the dinner at all? Do you believe any normal family member would want to eat the food when the first thing that comes to a view from opening the stable door is your significant other's feet swaying in mid air? Maybe seeing the face of all that you are bloated and stretched by the hang of the rope?

Brenda looked away from the book for a moment. She read Bram Stoker's Dracula four times and studied countless stories and videos on the fascination with vampirism since Jonathan Dejour started hurting Sylvia. Her mother has never been the same since she miscarried the baby and, despite the recent teenage killings in Carper Falls, she has tried to live a normal and oblivious life.

Sometimes, reading is an escape from what surrounds people in the real world. Her eyes followed words like piranhas follow a naked body to the bottom of the ocean, as she read on in a book by Barnabus Nodsley, known in the novel sometimes as Nola, a supposed vampire hunter. The book was called VIOLATOR. It was also what the cops have been calling the serial killer who seemed to be hiding somewhere in Maryland. The book was Brenda's escape, while others her age partied and hung out with boys. Brenda enjoyed her boring town, because underneath it all, was a vast world of things a person can entertain their time with, not like big cities which are filled with stereotypical insight, and fashion. In truth, who really cares about that? It's what's underneath the human soul people care about, or should. It's those promises for better days and those whispers in the dark that allow us to remember why we're alive to begin with. No matter what went on in the world Brenda's escape was the local library, and every book inside spawned an idea so prolific and insane than the idea before it.

FROM CHAPTER 13 VIOLATOR (Barnabus Nodsley: Castle Keeps Well, Forest Hill Cemetery):

I took a rack of rope, hoping to purport on such a night, and just in case my tidings would run dry with hope. I will use the rope to hang myself before they would ever get to me. I have many pieces of wood sharpened to points on both ends, and many sharp knives that made them this way. The villagers of old have commented it wrong considering the dead that will rise again...to feast.

You must take their teeth, and if you cannot, you must take the vampire's head. You must burn them alive while they remain disfigured from hell's grip. You must enter the domain and smell the horrid gone over odor of flesh, and only then will you know you are close. I suggest an ax, or a splitting maul, perhaps a steed to accompany you to slay the vampire. Because one is many and they are all violators. Take forwards with you a mustang. A horse of better days, and see to it your steed does not gallop from the jagged smile of evil.

Brenda smiled as she read, and flipped the book to the last page for its bibliography content. Her thoughts were far away from reality when she left that morning. Brenda suffered from a limp since she was eighteen, but has since learned to live with it. Her motorcycle hit with such an impact and force, her helmet caved in. The Doctors said she was lucky to be alive much less walking again. It was shortly after that; Brenda remembered her father's abusive voice. She began to do things. A wind of change swept her, and as the cocoon of sadistic serenity formed inside of her.

Brenda began to set fires. At first, it was to large piles of leaves. She would sit outside in front of the burning bush and watch the flames dance. Brenda imagined jumping in the flames. She imagined her father being thrown in their and burning alive.

She would glance at the surroundings in the dark that illuminated at night, and there, fantastic voices were born calling from the trees. She could hear the voice of her unborn sister. She knew her name even. It was one Mom never thought of. Dad had beaten Mom so bad she miscarried, and that was all it took for Brenda. She lost her mind that night, and ever since, the voices have grown louder.

The fires started with leaves, but then escalated to other things, greater things. She would kill small animals and throw them in the fire and watch them burn. But that wasn't the same as hearing them burn to death. The voices grew stronger, and they wanted to hear the animals scream. So Brenda would capture neighbor's cats and dogs and throw them alive and screaming in the fire.

But soon, the voices wanted more. They grew tired of the animals. During her senior year, blue-eyed blond haired Brenda Dejour had no problem getting boys to like her, but performing sexually with them was a whole other matter. Brenda wanted to kill every young man that bedded her. After sex she felt ugly and didn't understand why. Brenda never told her parent's her problems because she believed they had enough of their own.

The books she read in college during psychology told her the root of a bad sexual experience was perhaps caused by her own repressed anger. She couldn't help but think about this when she let Victor Colt ram his manhood inside her. But Victor took things too far. He liked to tie her up and bite. It can be truly said Victor Colt was Brenda Dejour's first victim. She took her turn with the handcuffs one day when Victor's parent's weren't home and preceded to poison him with rat killer.

She buried him under the porch at the house in Dobson which was a small Pennsylvanian suburb of Lancaster County near her attending college. Victor's parents never suspected Brenda. In fact, they never knew of her. With no one to blame and no motive, leads ran as cold as hanging meat in a blood locker.

At home, problems progressed through college. Once, Brenda nailed her bedroom door shut to stop her parent's screaming. She was preoccupied with any sign that something was wrong with her. Brenda wanted her sister to be alive. She wanted to take back killing Victor Colt and burying him under the porch bordered by white latticework. She cut his throat open with a pair of scissors just to see what it was like, although he'd been dead for several minutes from the Rat Killer. She remembers his eyes. They were listless orbs of what used to be. They were the eggs of ignorance. They were closed windows to a wrecked soul and a torn dream.

Brenda often got angry with her parents and imagined killing them in ways the normal mind and psyche couldn't imagine. One day, scientists will be able to enter the mind of a serial killer and film their dreams, until then, we have to see what they do. For a killer's thoughts come to life for us who are innocent to witness. What we don't realize, is that no one is innocent. Brenda often wanted her own heart to stop beating. She wanted to know what the world would sound like then. Would it be clear to her that the fires were extinguished then? For the past four years her life grew increasingly slovenly, and she submersed herself into the knowledge of vampirism.

When she observed her father brutally rape her mother over a drunken fit one night on the sofa, did Brenda finally snap, this time, the whole way. Brenda began to catch animals again, mainly rabbits. She would disembowel them, sometimes eating their entrails raw. This was retaliation against her feelings. Sometimes, Brenda would wait for her parent's to leave for work and go down to the kitchen, placing the insides of dead animals in a blender, drinking the concoction, believing if she did that, the voices would keep her father from hurting mother. And better yet, keep her from hurting them both. Brenda started keeping a journal of all her thoughts, as if she could go back and look into them maybe to recollect on darkness.

If people knew the real Brenda Dejour, who suffered from somatic delusions, a form of schizophrenia that was never diagnosed, they'd say she needed to committed. She told the kids at school her nickname was "ENOLA". She sometimes would kill birds and drink their blood to stop the voices in his head. Voices that told her to kill or "they" would hurt mother. When Brenda turned nineteen, she captured neighborhood pets again. This time mostly dogs. She'd often cut off their heads with daddy's chainsaw and drank the blood. Two days after Christmas of that year she conducted target practice on rot weiler puppies she saw at a kennel during a late night walk. She brought her father's pistol down to the kennel and looked into their eyes. She could hear her mother screaming. She could see a crib in the corner of a dark room where her sister should have been but never was. She shot each dog dead under the midnight eyes of God.

She walked to the kennel and dipped her fingers in blood smearing it all over her face. She walked home feeling the cold night air coagulate the blood on her face. This is something a vampire would do. This idea excited Brenda. It seemed killing animals was not enough. It seemed Victor Colt was only an appetizer to the main course that lay ahead. It wasn't the three boys from the bowling alley that her technique and hobby became known for; it was the woman up the street from College Park in Lancaster County.

She picked the girl out of a crowd, as most murderers do. She saw her father raping her. And the voices came like they always did. Every question her mind asked, somewhere in a deep dark corner was an answer. Brenda came to her house that night with the thrill of a kill overwhelming her. She had her father's pistol tucked in her low rider jeans. It was the same gun she'd use a year later on a girl who was found floating in two separate barrels. Brenda walked that evening following her own thoughts that often led her into darkness, and to the library. She breathed deep when she stopped in front of 238 Fox Run Road in College Park. Brenda entered the woman's home through the side window and encountered Dawn Ambrose based on the voices in her mind daring her, leading her here.

Dawn didn't say a word as her attacker turned towards her and shot her in the arm. The bullet protruded through her upper arm and into her left cheek. As she fell Brenda fired another round into her already prostrate body. She dragged her into the bedroom leaving a trail of blood behind. Then, Brenda retrieved a knife from the kitchen, and a kettle.

When the young girl's husband came home that night he found the house oddly dark. He entered and saw their dog, whining and moaning. Looking closer he observed the dog's ears were cut off, but the dog itself was still alive. He stopped in the kitchen when he observed the bloodstains, still in shock from his hurt dog he called out his wife's name. Dawn's husband walked back to the hallway following the bloodstains to a parted door leading to the bedroom. His wife lay just inside the door, on her back. Her blouse pulled up over her breasts and her pants down around her ankles. Her knees were splayed open in the position of a sexual assault, although evidence supported no sexual assault transpired. Her torso was slashed open in the design of a wicked smirk below her sternum and her spleen and intestines pulled out.

Brenda stabbed her repeatedly in the lungs, liver and diaphragm. Dawn's husband didn't know that Brenda smeared blood all over her face and hands, licking it off her fingers and that in an oddity was a burden not carried by angel wings. The discarded kettle was tipped over in the bedroom and blood stained. This is what the police believed the killer used for some reason to collect blood, but many people now, know why. The last act that drove Dawn's husband over the edge was that the killer had taken her teeth and sewn her eyes and lips shut with a sewing kit. The Police have not yet connected the killing of Dawn Ambrose to the six teenage victims of Carper Falls, or Victor Colt's death and the investigation although ongoing, has ceased in its leads.

Brenda sits in her college dorm laughing at it all, and yet, she sometimes cries well into the night's grip of loneliness while her roommate holds a pillow over her ears constantly wondering what's wrong with her? Brenda keeps the news articles of her handiwork. In case she ever has a kid of her own, she can show him or her a mother's good work. She pulls the articles out sometimes when her parents fight. The killings are nothing more than a pause in the voices. Seeing the victim's names in the newspaper thrills her to the point of repeating the bloodletting. The way the blood feels between her fingers, like new skin, where under the surface, a young troubled girl has drowned in a sea of regret.

Her interest, other then murder, is cars, especially *Mustangs*. She recently yearned to purchase a used one at a junkyard in Somerset County.

If people read the local papers, they would know the modern trend, at least in Maryland, are the thousands of motorcycles that come every year for Bike Week and the Hot Rod muscle cars that follow. This is what the people of Carper Falls rely on every year to get them through their boredom. In a few days, the tall skinny sophomore of WestPoint College studying history will come to understand the importance of cars. Not that she had a car, or even a driver's license for that matter. Blonde haired blue-eyed Brenda Dejour could barley afford a bag of pretzels while studying for her degree. Her parents dove into their bank accounts to sleep better on the assumption their daughter would get a degree and make something of her life. But what mom and dad didn't know was that she was making something of herself...and others. Her dad still worked at the steel foundry in Pocomoke and has worked there his whole life. Mom up until 1999 had an affair with her boss quite a few times. She took care of his horses on a pond near Assateague and is paid quite amicably for her services.

But Brenda herself, despite the few supposed friends she had, and sometimes wondered if they were real at all didn't understand her purpose anymore. She was bittersweet and 20 years old. An emerged butterfly from a cocoon, obsessed with reading novels on the occult and Dracula. She also loves true stories of death such as the fall of the Roman Empire and Genghis Khan's reign of terror. She was fascinated by Hitler and the other would-be killers of the world's vile past. But Brenda's favorite stories are that of Vlad Tepes or otherwise known, Vlad the Impaler.

As it turned out a history lesson that attached itself to her heart was something she desired. It was something that got her through most of her days. The fascination with vampires was her way of dealing with the reality of killing someone. She never told anyone that before, and didn't know if she could. It sounded funny saying it out loud. It felt peculiar writing it down. Some things can never be said. Brenda thought about it a lot and at night while her feelings stayed true in the darkness of her bedroom. While forgetting she was responsible for at least seven deaths, and hopefully more to come.

The State Police were still looking for what they dubbed "The Violator". That's not to say anyone in Carper Falls was even worried. Most people that live here have home defense, although they generally feel safe that they will never need it. Most folk in Carper Falls enjoy the short hot summers, even though driving on the streets is a burden. Outsiders come from all over, sometimes, to stay forever. Wintertime is filled with the vacant memories of summer, where many enjoy a good book or take on the few local jobs to get them through their car payments and bills till next year.

Most people that live in the rationale of boredom find new endeavors in the local Movie Theatre, or the downtown restaurants that somehow have remained since their births in the fifties. While waiting for the Hot Rod festival in February they yearn for the twinkling of knowledge at the Carper Falls Library. Fire for the mind, and what could possibly fuel thoughts further. Here, we find Brenda Dejour almost every night studying for her Bibliography exam. It was a true test of knowledge. For it was not what was within the books she needed to know, but how she translated the knowledge into her own theories what counted.

Brenda approached the librarian, Francine Bowry and smiled.

"Going home soon?"

"I may stay for a while." Brenda said.

"What's with all the books on vampires?"

"Just interested." Brenda smiled.

"They're spooky."

"Yes." Brenda said. "But someone has to read them am I right?"

Francine shrugged.

"I suppose."

"And besides." Brenda said. "Isn't reading the right thing to do? Isn't knowledge…power?"

Francine gave the College girl an odd look, and observed the clock on the wall and the minutes passing. Francine watched the young woman sit down at the computer researching a few more books.

Brenda couldn't stop thinking about vampires. She couldn't stop thinking about the smell of blood and her mother's wishes for her to become a professor.

Brenda's parent's loved her. Well, that wasn't really true. She knew her mother loved her, and had a relative sense that her father used too. He got so drunk once that he raped her thinking she was Mom, but Brenda did her best to suppress that memory. Ever since Sylvia miscarried the baby the bond between her and her father had been broken.

You came home half-cocked Brenda, it was the night before you slammed into that tree near the old railroad tracks in Carper Falls. Mom was four months pregnant. Her friends, at least the ones she used to have told her she was starting to show remember? And that was great wasn't it? Dad would just look on with that vacant look in his eyes that said no matter whom is born into this world by his seed, nothing demands more respect than he. He'd beat her often. John stopped hitting Sylvia when he heard that door close downstairs.

When you finally came home from riding motorcycles or bowling or sometimes killing cats and dogs. Remember the one time you drove down Hawk Avenue? Mrs. Turner's poodle Elroy barked and barked and got running out of the way when you drove towards him. But you turned around didn't you? You turned around and chased Elroy down till there was no Elroy left, and spent the remainder of the night digging that dog's guts and hair out of your tires with a broken stick.

Remember what you thought of when you ran that dog over? You saw your Dad lying there, Mr. Wonderful himself. He was screaming at you like he screams at Mom. He was screaming for you to drop your pants. His breathe smelling of booze and cigarettes. It was that night that ended it though, that final night when John went mad, and screamed at Mom over what she made for dinner. He kicked her in the stomach and-

Brenda snapped out of it. She was in the library still, the novel beside her called VIOLATOR. She was thinking of regression and disappointment. All these people she was killing she never realized till that moment maybe her parents were the ones better off dead.

Maybe we all are...

III

There was no logical reason for Brenda Dejour to commit the atrocities she believed must be done. There was no reason for going into another girl's home when the fall had been invited into December as if by a witch's cracked hand. The December of that year was still recovering from a maddened October where the dulcetness of murder changed the peaceful off-season of the region forever. This town would never return from the grave of reckoning. This town was as murdered as all that lie in the local funeral homes awaiting burial. Awaiting the silent rooms of autopsy skill to revel in the sounds of flesh being freed from bone and soundness from minds.

Timber McDonald made fun of Brenda Dejour in school. She once put gum in her hair and tripped her in the hallway. That was many years ago, but sometimes people can keep a grudge. Timber was filling up a washbasin with sudsy water. She was tying her long auburn hair into a ponytail and wondering about college. Despite her wishes for more out of life, Timber Mcdonald was a gorgeous girl but poor. She knew in this life you can't have everything, and maybe her looks would carry her on for a while. That was however, dangerous thinking.

Brenda sat in front of the computer lost in the past week, and what she done to Timber Mcdonald who was her most recent victim. The Carper Library was screaming quiet. Not even the sounds of her own breathing could be heard. I t was a perfect place to study and a perfect place to recollect.

You killed her the voices said.

Her eyes blinked fast, as if something perhaps violated them.

You cut her up into pieces because she was prettier than you. Brenda heard the voice but looked onward focusing on the computer screen. Her eyes were as clear as a newborn's gaze as the computer screen seemed to open to the past week. As if she could see her life unfold. The novel she was reading remained closed for now.

Timber Mcdonald was murdered a few days ago on Saturday December 28th 1999. Her body was found on the front porch of her parent's house. Both her parents were at work. Her father was the first to arrive and the first to lose his mind.   Whoever committed such horrible crimes had been somehow messy about his or her practice. It was found under the police's assessment, a definite amateur, but a vicious one all the same. Timber was found literally all over the porch.

Her attacker committed so much brutality, it was hard for the coroner to assess what happened first, but one thing was certain. Her attacker walked up from behind and made one stab to the back of the neck. It came from a pair of large scissors. The second was to the spine that severed Timber's vertebra in two. There were several stabs that followed, and they were mainly into Timber's face. The coroner assessed that the killer focused on the face in this murder, but he was uncertain as to why.

The victim's tongue was sliced off with the scissors, and so were her hands. The attacker cut off Timber's nose and made her swallow it before she died. Her killer imagined what it was like to swallow one's own nose while laughter rang out on the porch. Timber was stabbed many times long after death. Timber was wrapped in a wet blanket pulled from the washbasin. Her father found her frozen naked eyes splayed open and unmoving that afternoon. Most of Timber's blood had soaked through the blanket and contaminated the porch.

The killer left no clues behind as before. This was no surprise to the State Police. Like many madmen in history, murderers have an ingenious artistic quality about them that helps them to remain clam and focused when executing well thought out plans for murder. It's this calmness that makes them feel they can never get captured. When they loose this calmness this confidence, that's when we should be afraid. It is then that the lights should stay on.

So it begins at the State Police Barracks in Berlin Maryland. An investigation ensued into the capture of the purported killer of Timber Mcdonald.   A connection to the other six murders in the past few months. All teenagers and all with blue-collar-worker parents like most folk in Carper Falls. Now, as winter comes full swing into the end of December, it's friendliest month, Timber lay in the ground frozen.

Entombed in a lost innocence that is like an undying thirst, which can never be sated.

The person responsible for killing her was not a first timer, but felt as though she was every time. She wanted to try it. Like climbing in a brand new car and smelling that new car smell. Feeling every crevice, every inch of the gearshift and steering wheel. Even the most novices of law enforcement officials could tell the killer was enjoying his work.

Brenda Dejour once delivered newspapers on Sunday morning to every house on Shore Lane. She remembered the seashell-lined driveways. Where you can hear the crash of the surf on the privately owned beaches behind them, making it especially appealing at night. She counted in her mind of all the people she murdered, and all those to come. As she sat alone in the library studying for her Bibliography exam on vampires, never did she believe that one-day this diabolical murderer no one would suspect would perhaps really meet one.

And then…the real terror would commence.

Her mother, Sylvia Dejour and God bless her soul, has done so much to rectify her situations, but alas, failed miserably. She drove home in her coveralls. Her dark blonde hair tied in a bun that was beginning to show signs of age. Strands of gray hair ran through it. When she squinted she could see the settling of crows feet around her brown eyes. None of this much bothered her anymore. Her husband, who had taken the light in beating her for the past four years, has slipped further into dementia.

The real horror of this story was not what her husband did to her. But what she did not know, that her daughter was a prolific murderer and had developed problems most psychiatrists would attribute to her upbringing. When she married John all those years ago, the skies were blue with other people's envy for their happiness. Now, the storms had fogged her mind. She drove from working with the horses the night her only daughter studied at the local library thinking of what to expect when she got home. Would Jonathan be waiting for her? Wondering why dinner wasn't cooked? As she stood on her own two feet watching him barely able to stand on his, wondering what the new neighbors moving in across the street would think about all the screaming? A mother and a father with a young teenage girl fresh out of high school who she had yet to meet.

She saw the mother and daughter, and just a glimpse of the man driving the U-Haul truck, but that was all.

Her Pontiac rolled into Southern Lakes as inside an older black man still trying to recapture his youth sat looking onward. Freddie Hurst was in his mid-fifties. His gray hair laid back as well as it could with streaks of white made him look more like a male version of the bride of Frankenstein. Sylvia entered the store, looking inside her purse for her credit card.

"Hello missus." Freddie winked. "Hell of a day isn't it?"

"It will be if I can't find any money to pay you."

Outside, on the other side of her car two pumps over, a muscle car rolled to a stop. Both Sylvia and Freddie looked on with a newfound curiosity.

"That's different."

"Yeah." Freddie said. "He was here yesterday too, strange fella. Don't have much in the way of conversation either. My guess is he's from New York or one of those big snobby cities."

"Tags are local." Sylvia noted.

"Are they?" Freddie looked on. "I haven't noticed."

Sylvia handed Freddie her credit card, then walked to the glass covering the front of the store. Watching the Shelby Cobra, she observed its rear end raised and raked.

"How much?" Freddie asked swiping her card.

"Twenty's fine." She said. "Have you ever heard anything else on that maniac hiding in this town?"

"No more than you I reckon." Freddie handed Sylvia her card. "Makes me sick to the stomach knowing there's a sick bastard out there killing young boys and girls."

"Local?" Sylvia asked.

"Come again?"

"You think he's local? The guy killing those teenagers"

25

"I doubt it." Freddie said, placing a potato chip in his mouth. "This town's small enough so just about everyone knows each other. I think this psycho is definitely from out of town, probably out of State. Probably staying up the road at the Holiday Inn or Comfort's Well. If I was the cops, that's where I'd start my manhunt."

Sylvia watched the man exit from the Mustang wearing a coat as dark as his car. The leather jacket was sleek as the man wearing it. His sunglasses were dark and flooded Sylvia's mind with the thoughts of funeral homes. A chill was born. And she felt it in her neck.

"That guy there must have some money. Past few days all he's been putting in that baby is hi-test. That shit's $2.99 a gallon."

"Really?"

"Yeah well, gas isn't getting cheaper." Freddie ended.

"No it sure isn't" Sylvia smiled; she walked to the door and said her goodbyes to the friendly half owner of the gas station.

Outside, the man who owned the Mustang placed the nozzle back on the pump and twisted the cap back onto the car. Sylvia carefully watched the tall man walk aimlessly to the driver's side door and climb in. The car started and it made her jump. It was loud and mean. The driver pressed the accelerator quickly, and the sound that emitted was like that of a murderous pack of dogs. The car rolled out of the lot then tore down Sun Valley Boulevard breaking into the night.

Sylvia finished filling her car, when she suddenly thought about going home. The closer she approached the more the butterflies of absolution fluttered in her stomach. Soon she would see her husband pull into the driveway, and there was no guarantee he would be in a good mood. She drove out of the gas station lot and felt the tears heavy in her eyes with the confusion of it bright and loud. Sometimes she was amazed the Pontiac went home at all. On several occasions she believed in just running away. Once, she even packed what bags would fit in the back of her car, but Brenda brought her back from leaving. Brenda's first year in college was when it all began. The kick to the stomach and presto, Brenda's sister came out in a puddle of horror.

Sylvia thought,

He'll be waiting for you like he always waits for you; a wad of snuff buried under his lip, and when he spits a wad of black horror

*comes along for the ride splashing on the cobblestone walkway. His
engineer boots click, heavy and dusty. Duct tape wrapped around the
toe of the right boot. He'll bitch about how he never has the money to
buy new boots because he spends it all on college for his useless
daughter. Do you think he has ever touched her the way he touches
you? Do you ever suspect he leaves the bed at night and watches her
sleep in the next room awaiting the switch to take place? Has he ever
touched her like a vampire touches an undying lover in the dark?*

*Men like that don't see a line to cross they just keep walking,
new boots or not. They keep walking towards their goal and
destination. You've learned to live with how he treats you Sylvia, how
he sometimes forces you to do things you cry about in the dark hours
later, when you hear his truck leave for work. He tortures you with
matches, with candles. He shoves things inside you that hurt and don't
fit, but you don't turn around to see what they are you don't dare. But
the great thing Sylvia, is that when he does finally go to far, when he
finally reaches for the bedroom mirror and smashes it over your face
letting the shards tear out your eyes you'll know your daughter is still
in the next bedroom awaiting the sounds of his boots, now won't that be
grand?*

Sylvia wipes the tears away as her Pontiac rolls into the
driveway. John wasn't home yet, and neither was her daughter.

Closing the door to the car and standing back to feel the sun on
her face, she sighed. Sylvia glanced at the U-Haul van across the street
as the day fell victim to the night. A great and fantastic horizon
appeared in the west. The clouds perched among the purple evening
miscarrying the day into darkness. Sylvia's involvements in the
matters concerning her abusive husband were momentarily forgotten.
The woman across the street waived to her with glee, and Sylvia looked
down at the concrete driveway. She wasn't sure if she wanted the new
neighbor's attention or not. In her life she has made many friends, but
none of them like John, and frankly, who could blame them?

Women learn to loose much of their outgoing spirit, especially
when heavy ringed fists of foundry workers are bashing their heads in.
Where did she go wrong?

"Hello there." the new neighbor finished waving. She was a dark beauty. Even across the street Sylvia could acknowledge the woman's looks. A pleasant curvy figure Sylvia once adorned herself. Outside on the porch a young girl reminiscent of the woman holding out her hand for Sylvia to shake busily carried boxes.

"Hel...lo" Sylvia said. A timid smile was born across her face. The dark woman walked across the quiet road with her hand out wanting to meet. She was olive skinned with full lips like the kind you see on the cover of model magazines. Sylvia observed how careful the handshake was; a well-manicured hand shook her own.

"Nice to meet you finally."

"Yes."

Sylvia smiled fluttering her eyes. She wasn't used to talking much anymore. She wasn't used to the comfort of canter.

"Holly Raven" the woman said. " I don't know your first name Mrs. Dejour."

"It's Sylvia." She smiled again.

"Sylvia Dejour. Dejour...hmm...isn't that French?" Holly asked.

Sylvia noted quizzically.

"It is...not many people know that."

"They probably do." Holly noted. "They just don't take the time to mention it. I actually feel a bit embarrassed that I have."

"Don't be." Sylvia said. "I'm glad someone noticed."

Holly watched as Sylvia pulled a cigarette free from a holder in her purse, her left hand shaking. A bandage was around her left pinky.

"Broken?" Holly said.

"Excuse me?' Sylvia said.

"Your finger, is it broken? I once broke my finger. Slammed it in my husband's car door. That damn Mustang is fierce."

"Oh." Sylvia laughed. "No, no it's not broke...I...I mashed it with a hammer on the horse farm I work at. I help train horses."

"Really?" Holly asked excited. "My husband and I love horses!"

"Do you have a light?" Sylvia asked, noticing Holly going for a pack of cigarettes in her pocket.

"I sure do."

"I'm sorry, I seem to misplaced mine."

"Don't be sorry." Holly said.

Her dark eyes were submissive, but that was perhaps caused by the sunset.

"Sorry is for sinners."

"Yeah well," Sylvia laughed. "I never heard that before."

"I've never said it before." Holly smiled.

"Well then, where are you folks from?" Sylvia asked.

"Las Vegas."

"Vegas?"

"Nevada."

"I know where Vegas is, when John and I…John's my husband. We went there for our honeymoon. That seems like a distant memory now."

"My husband is a lawyer, well, was a lawyer. He's retired from that now. We own a candle making business."

Both women smoked and shared a moment of pause. Sylvia immediately liked the woman. She wasn't disdainful or bratty. She wasn't one of those rich snobs that closed the curtains to other people's troubles. She didn't seem like she belonged in Vegas however.

Holly blew smoke.

"My husband should be home soon, you should meet him."

"Perhaps I will." Sylvia smiled. "My husband works pretty long hours down at the steel foundry in Pocomoke. You won't see him much unless there is a party or beer around."

Holly laughed.

"Well, maybe we can all get together sometime."

Sylvia noted. She was careful to keep the right side of her face away from the dying sunlight. That side is where John liked to hit. Although last month's bruises had disappeared, there was still a trace of abuse. Black and blue has turned light yellow above her eyebrow, and telling the little friends she still had in this world that she bumped it on the refrigerator door has worn out it's welcome.

"I'd like that." Holly said.

Her eyes were as blue as a porcelain dolls. To the right of both women, a young girl with hair like Holly Raven was standing with a smile on her face. It was an inviting smile at that. She was wearing a t-shirt with the insignia Raven LTD. Evidently, they owned a family business that was lucrative if not prospect able.

"This is Winter, my daughter." Holly said.

"Hello." Her hand was soft and supple. "What a different name, it's bold."

"That's what I said." Holly said. "Her father found it befitting considering she was born in the winter."

"I see."

Sylvia thought the Ravens were a nice family. Perhaps they didn't deserve to move into a town with what has been going on. They didn't deserve to live across the street from such filth as her own husband who enjoyed beating his wife.

"Well I have to go inside and start dinner for my family who should be home any minute. It was nice to meet you both."

"Likewise." Holly Raven smiled, walking back across the street with her fifteen-year-old daughter.

Sylvia wondered if Holly knew about the murders or the fact that there was something wrong with the conversation at all. Sylvia wasn't used to living a lie. How long has it been since she has held onto tears while staring at the exam room ceiling looking for an excuse, only to let those same tears fall away to the loneliness of a barren floor. While everyone really knew what was going on, but was afraid to say anything. And if she knew what her daughter had done, and what she planned on doing again, she probably would lose what was left of her sound mind?

Abuse is a disease and it affects the whole family. There is no way around that fact except to dive right in it.

Jonathan Dejour came home an hour later that evening, drunker than usual. He crossed the front door with a jingle of keys in his jeans and a set in his hands. At the dinner table, their daughter Brenda sat finishing her chicken and dumplings, and looked onward at her father who smelled of sweat, soot and booze. Silence was heard for the first several minutes, before he actually fell down into the seat in front of his daughter. John's greasy brown hair was in wads of distress. His eyes were like two lanterns swaying in tin darkness. They were tired, and red from loss of sleep and appetite. And also from the booze and cocaine he recently required a taste for.

Holding out his hand in a closed fist, John opened his palm letting a nest of car keys on a rabbit's foot ring fall on the wooden table. Brenda stopped chewing what was left of her chicken.

"What's that?" she asked.

"What does it look like?"

"Looks like car keys." Brenda said.

"College is sure making you smarter." John said. "Why don't you go look out that window?"

Sylvia looked on, her face sullen with a mixture of disgust, and then outright surprised shock. Jonathan watched as his daughter walked to the front bay window. There in the yard was a car, but not just any car, a 1999 Ford Mustang, brand new in fact.

"Holy shit!" Brenda yelled. "Dad!"

"Yes?"

"That's for me?"

"You're goddamn straight it's for you. It's not for me. I don't like Mustangs. They're death traps in my opinion."

"But it's brand new! How could you afford a-

"Don't ever look gift horses in the mouth Brenda." John said, wiping his face.

In fact, he needed a drink.

"You're gonna need a car to get back and forth from college. Riding the bus is dangerous at night, especially with what's been going on. Besides, a drunk driver wrecked it a few months ago when it first came out on the show room floor. My friends spent the past few months restoring the engine and the whole front end. It's black as the ace of spades, but if you look at it just right in the sunlight, you'll see the paint job doesn't quite match."

"Dad...it's perfect."

You son of a bitch. Sylvia thought. *You bought that with our money. With the money I had saved for the new baby before you killed it! And there you sit making it seem like you worked so hard for it! Motherfucker!*

"You have your permit and all, so I'll take ya out this weekend and practice. All I could find was an automatic."

"Thank you dad."

Jonathan stood in the kitchen light, proud as ever.

"After dinner I'll go outside with ya and look her over. Son of a bitch is fast, so you have to be careful."

"I will pop." Brenda laughed in joy.

But Brenda's father never went outside that night as the beginning snowflakes fell to a flurry. He fell asleep drunk in the kitchen chair, making Sylvia wonder how he ever drove the car home at all. He lay asleep slumped back with his neck out and wide, eyes closed arms down to the side.

I should go up there and cut his goddamn throat. Sylvia thought.

Brenda went outside, dressed in a sweater and jeans. There in the darkness sat a brand new Mustang, brought back from death of course. It reminded him of vampires all to suddenly, and that she had first thought if Dracula were alive today, he would drive one.

But Brenda believed he would in fact drive this one. And that made her all the more excited to turn the key in the ignition. It reminded her of what Bram Stoker wrote in Dracula.

"The dead drive fast."

I bet they do. Brenda thought. Walking up to her new ride she jingled the keys in her pocket and rubbed her thumb over the soft, white rabbit's foot in there. When she pulled the keys out Brenda observed her mother watching from the window. Sylvia was happy for her, but all the more hateful for her husband.

Rabbits. Brenda thought. *I used to eat them didn't I? I used to drink their blood; this foot is a sign, that I've been doing the right thing. This car is a sign.*

She couldn't wait to get in and drive it. She could drive all night long, which would make her happy right about now. That would make her forget the voices of what made her do the bad thing. The bad things may be pushed aside, but they always need done, or mom could get hurt. And we don't want mom to get hurt.

Do we?

Brenda walked along the Mustang eyeing it deeply with a newfound resolution for her tastes. Now her life would change, and she believed for the better. She had named the car in her mind and would tell anyone who asked what the car was named. So she pondered one while rubbing the rabbit's foot in her pocket. The car was her new sweetheart.

"Enola." Brenda said.

Enola will be your name my sweet ride.

The police had been on the look out for a white male in his early thirties relying on the typical serial killer profiles used by the FBI. Because she was far from that profile, Brenda believed she would never be caught. If the books she was reading were correct, she would be getting away with it for many years to come. She just needed to be more careful and keep praying and the police would never know.

Someone else would. Someone always does.

Brenda Dejour went to bed early that evening, while downstairs, her mother watched television. Hearing her husband moan and shift in his sleep made her eyes swerve, worried and resilient to a newfound perplexed fear within. John lifted his head awake to the local news reporter, switching from the weather to recent disturbing news on the police's efforts in finding more leads on the Violator. A madman that preferred young children perhaps lived in Carper Falls.

"What are you watching woman?" John asked, rolling his drunken hazel eyes towards Sylvia.

"The news." she said in a whisper.

"Can you turn it up louder? I think God can't hear it. Maybe the neighbors across the street want to know."

"Speaking of neighbors." Sylvia began. "I met them today. Everyone but Mr. Raven. They seem like nice people."

"What do they do for money?" John asked.

"They have a candle making business."

"What?" John asked, trying to stand, he almost keeled over laughing.

"You're shitting me!"

"No, I'm serious."

"Sounds like a bunch of worthless fucks to me."

Sylvia closed her eyes, knowing what was coming; this would begin like all other nights.

"John, you really ought to go easy on the booze."

"Don't you tell me what to do Silly Sylvia, I can handle my booze."

"No you can't either John." Sylvia said. "I don't know how much more of this I can take. You bought our daughter a Mustang for Christ Sakes! Do you know what the insurance is going to cost?"

John stood quiet; the demons inside him wide awake from the alcohol.

"You know I don't get you Silly Sylvia, every time I try to do good, it's never good enough. You bitched cuz you didn't want that rat fuck daughter of ours taking the bus at night because you're such an overprotective cunt. So what do I do? I buy the girl a God damn car and this is how you thank me?"

"But John I-"

His hand moved quickly across her face. The slap was fierce and the sting of it flew into Sylvia's eyes.

"DON"T YOU TALK UP TO ME!" John screamed.

He suddenly leaned down beside his battered wife. Sylvia remained quiet; little hurt sobs escaping in and out of her in manifestations.

"I'm sorry John I-"

"You're always sorry." John exclaimed. "But I bet not nearly as sorry as your mother for having you are you Silly?"

John reached under the desk beside the couch. He retrieved a hidden bottle of Glenlivet. Twisting off the cap he drank deeply.

"Always fucking SORRY!" John screamed.

He stood tall and enraged. He turned and stomped his feet up the stairs to the bedroom. Downstairs, Sylvia Dejour remained in the middle of the couch trying to calm down. Already she was looking for another excuse to tell her boss. She was already wondering what the bruises would look like this time. A trickle of blood leaked from her nose and she wiped it away with the side of her hand. She looked up from the blindness of her blonde hair hanging in her eyes seeing the clock on the wall. It was past 9 in the evening and still snowing.

Sylvia leaned back against the couch, her cheek throbbing. A little cut had grown on her face from her husband's ring, and the contusion underneath was already swelling. As she focused on this, trying to find the courage to look at herself in the bathroom mirror she heard a sound outside. A rumbling like that of a Harley Davidson Motorcycle filled her ears. Carefully but quickly, she turned towards the window behind the couch and lifted the curtain back. She saw the headlights of a monstrous car from the sixties. Those times were her favorite.

Suddenly, she realized it was the car she seen at Southern Lakes earlier that day. Freddie Hurst proclaimed the driver only used Hi-test fuel. The vehicle stopped in the street and turned into the driveway of the family she had met earlier that evening, the Ravens. The taillights of the car wrought ghostly light upon the fresh snow covered ground. The driver gunned the engine before turning off the ignition and it scared Sylvia.

Sylvia let the curtain fall back as the door to the car opened. All she had observed was a pair of black dress shoes fall out attached to dress pant-covered legs. Sylvia waited for the sounds of the door being shut: she listened to the snowfall. They say you can't hear it, but Sylvia tried too. Finally she fell asleep on the sofa to the dreams of her past, so sweet they couldn't possibly be real.

IV.

Brenda Dejour longed for her driver's license. It would make everything easier. At two in the morning she lay tossing and turning in her bedroom. Brenda couldn't sleep. She was behind the wheel in the Mustang in her dreams, driving to Las Vegas. At least in her mind that's where she wanted to be. That's where she believed all vampires today would live, not in Maryland, but in Las Vegas, where all lost angels are found. Where there would be a better sense of things to come and go.

Vampires. The word danced in Brenda's head.

Dressing in the dark, Brenda heard the noises of trees blowing outside. She discovered her sleepless night was without merit. Grabbing her car keys, she thought of testing her new ride, but that would be careless. She would lose all her privileges before she ever had them. So instead she threw the car keys back on the desk and grabbed the pistol between her mattresses. Climbing out of the second story window where the trees hid her existence was no longer as hard as it once was. Brenda jumped from the lower overhang of the bottom window. Hopefully in the next life she would learn how to fly. After all bats can fly can't they? She was no more different from them. She simply hasn't evolved as of yet.

A long walk is just what she needed. She never intended to commit murder on this dark morning. Brenda was overly thrilled. She had a new ride. The Mustang awaited her company. Until her freedom to drive alone was allowed, her boredom needed sated. It was the rabbit's foot her father gave her that more than made up for her thirst. The stunning part of this journey was all the choices she has been making. The rabbit's foot was a sign. It would tell her which house was next.

It was the morning of January 4th 2000. The dark of night was still evolving into morning. Brenda was right about the questions in her mind as usual. The world didn't end as everyone thought it would. This was a new millennium where opportunities existed and often

36

knocked on the front door. Along the beaten sidewalks of Carper Falls, Maryland people slept during the New Year's first snowfall as it quickly turned into a drizzling cold rain. They slept oblivious to the fact that a psychotic woman walked among them. Which innocent mind would end forever? Who would fall victim to this diabolical and ruthless killer, driven by an undying thirst for more of it?

The Violator was here to stay. Even as Brenda walked along the wooded lands of Ocean Street where the buildings and Food Lions disappeared into a scenic wonderland of trees and trailer parks far away from the inlets and sandy beaches, did she believe she was alone. The voice in her mind kept her company. She didn't know who it was. All she knew was that she had heard it most of her life. The voice of a keen spirit locked within. Perhaps it was her father's voice.

As the sun peeked through the dark, Devana Mirrow, 38, was in her house with her twenty month old baby, one mile from Frederica Maryland. A close suburb of Carper Falls, which was perfect walking distance from the main streets and could be seen very easily at night. Devana was never married, the father of the baby named Jack who she called " Little Jack" ran off with a whore from Ephrata Pennsylvania many moons ago. Her new friend Mark Daniels had taken the place of the father. Although Mark was a little old for Devana, who still held her beautiful youth, Devana grew to love her new boyfriend. She was in her late forties, but every bit as gorgeous as she had been 20 years ago. Brenda watched the two lovers kiss inside their well lit home as she stood beneath weeping willow trees in the rain. There, the voices came to life like a birth of some dark new element. There, the jealousy of a love never known sparked something under the roof of her skull illuminating a newfound madness.

Four hours into daylight an AVON sales woman called 911 when she observed the front door to the house ajar. A stray dog was standing inside licking blood off the floor. The AVON woman told police that she believed someone was killed inside the house.

Police arrived shortly thereafter first finding Mark Daniels in a pool of blood. The deputy who checked him found a gunshot wound on his temple. The Deputy followed a trail of blood to the bathroom where he found bloody water in a half-filled bathtub. Then, the deputy found Devana lying naked on the bed, her legs open. She had a gunshot wound to the head. Her brains were still sticking to the picture of her family hanging on the wall. Her abdomen was sliced open with the intestines pulled out. Two carving knives were lanced through each eye. It appeared she had been taking a bath when she heard the gunshot. Although caught by surprise, evidence shows that she must have fought.

Her hands were covered in deep lacerations. The killer dragged her to the bed. The killer stabbed Devana in her uterus twelve times, and made several slices across her face and neck. Bloody ringlets on the carpet suggested that the killer had once again used a container to collect blood, perhaps to drink it. The psychopath stabbed several of her internal organs that the coroner later noted would facilitate getting to the blood in the abdomen. Inside Devana's rectum were bullets, where her attacker finished her off with several shots way up inside her.

On the other side of the bed, Police officers discovered the body of a boy who had been sleeping over. He was shot twice in the head at close range. The next thing they found shocked investigators so much they had to leave the crime scene. No one was prepared for the bullet hole found in the pillow in the crib of Little Jack. There was a lot of blood. The baby was found dead in the bathroom. The Violator mutilated the baby's body, opening the head and spilling pieces of the brain into the tub. Several organs in the infant were partially eaten.

This time, the killer left a small note, one that will haunt Carper Falls forever. Across the bathroom mirror in the baby's blood were the words, ENOLA.

The police left that long afternoon, curious of yet another mystery. Did this killer believe the he or she was a vampire?

Deputies, State Police, and FBI began to work together on unraveling the mystery of this ruthless killer. The deputy that was called to the scene that frightful morning was Liam Griffin. Some of the locals call him " Duke," for short. What he found at the scene was enough to make him quit the force forever.

In a brief but apparent act of curiosity, the townspeople bought all the newspapers that evening when the headlines displayed yet another act of grisly murder. The death toll was now very high. 11 people have died by the hands of what Police believed was the same killer. All the Carper Falls community could do to protect themselves was to follow the advice of the local. "Lock your doors and watch your children there is a violent person among us all."

Sylvia Dejour watched the news carefully, and so did all her neighbors. Sylvia was retarded to the fact that the killer lived within her own home. Right now she was upstairs in the quiet solitude of her room watching baby brains dry on her pants. She thought about driving the Mustang. However she waiting for driving practice this weekend would benefit her more. More practice meant perfection towards acquiring a license.

Brenda changed clothing that night before she left with her father. They went into town doing weekly things. The lottery tickets and wishes that remained locked within comprised their casual conversations. Conversations about the Violator remained distant. Brenda would either buy coffee from the local Star Bucks, or an issue of Nightmare Magazine for the few dollars she had. Brenda was obsessed with reading almost as much as she was obsessed with killing. The only difference between the two was that she could close the book on reading.

The SUN POST was the newspaper Jonathan Dejour bought for fifty cents and often bitched about that the price of gas wasn't the only thing climbing sky high. He stood reading along the sidewalk that evening ready to go home and have a few more drinks. His daughter walked out of the convenience store. Her head quickly turned to the right. A massive black muscle car, all but the front windows tinted, pulled into the parking space, as the sun set into the West once again. Brenda Dejour stood with a bottle of Gatorade in her hand with the cold wind blowing her long blonde hair all around her face. Her eyes blinked twice in disbelief. She heard her dad call for her, but Brenda's mind was fixated on what she was observing.

Perhaps you should bring along a steed for this adventure, a horse of sorts, perhaps a…Mustang.

It was a 1970 Shelby Cobra Mustang, shining brightly in the dying sun.

"Brenda!" Her father yelled again, but Brenda walked two steps closer towards the car. The beautiful machine made her want to go home and drive hers even more. *That was a grand car, but this! This was the real Nola baby.*

"Come on Brenda, I want to go home and eat more of your mom's lousy cooking."

"Just a second dad." Brenda said.

That's when John Dejour observed the muscle car as well, black as darkness and mean looking as all hell had to offer. The tires were new with chrome Krager mag wheels. The rear end was raised high like a cheerleader's mini skirt giving the vehicle a wild raked look. The car door opened, and out stepped a man as if he was born from it. A tall man slightly pale, with the eyes of a fallen angel, dark, and mysterious. His Ray Bans sunglasses were hanging from his leather jacket pocket. They were as dark as his car and every bit as shiny. His hair was black and nicely groomed against his skull, short and cut professional pushed forward into a widow's peak. Many rings adorned both hands, and his walk was a gait of seriousness. The owner of the Mustang picked up a copy of the newspaper and stood silently reading, before Brenda and her father watched him pay the clerk and walk away.

"Now that's a nice looking horse my girl." John said, slapping his daughter on the shoulder that stood in a gaze. "Come on damnit, I'm hungry."

You may be hungry Father, Brenda thought, *but I'm making headlines. And if you ever rape me again, father oh father, I will keep your penus in the glove box of that new ride waiting for me.*

Brenda didn't understand that last thought. Nor did she know if it was deserved.

The Mustang thundered to life and rolled out of town just as fast as it came in. On the license plate, Brenda observed words other than numbers. One of those custom tags you could have made at the DMV.

CNDLMKR

"That's an odd license plate tag."

John's daughter didn't respond.

"Probably another weirdo, there's lot's of them moving here to Maryland."

John's Ford Pick-up drove back to the Valley. There, Main Street shined with the end of sunlight. Here, the Dejour's would eat one last meal before Brenda went back to College till the weekend. Then she would drive her car, preparing for the test to get that license. She yearned for it. She has never wanted anything more. Seeing her car parked in the driveway waiting to be driven was a terrible feeling and a great one all at the same time. It was like being with a naked man for hours and not being able to touch him (although Brenda didn't like men that way anymore, her tastes, lay elsewhere).

At dinner, Sylvia Dejour fixed salad and steak, carefully loading her daughter's dish with more than she could possibly eat. She smiled warmly and passed the salad bowl to her husband.

"What is this shit?"

"*Dad.*" Brenda said with contempt.

"Dad hell, what am I a God damn rabbit?"

"Sorry." Sylvia said with tears in her eyes.

"Thanks mom. You did good." Brenda said.

"Yeah mom." John sarcastically said looking disgusted at his plate.

"Thanks."

The three of them ate heartily, and at first, Sylvia sat quiet.

"I have to go overnight tomorrow. We're adding iron to a new cruiser ship that's come into the docks. I volunteered of course, that's good green for my pockets."

"When do you have to leave?" Sylvia asked.

"Tomorrow morning. I'll be gone all night, probably most of the next day too. You can cook your own food; so don't expect me home for dinner. Oh by the way, the cable is due, you can pay it out of your own money."

"But I gave my check to you honey."

41

"I don't give a shit." John snapped. " I guess you'll be watching snow on television too then, or you can watch it outside. All I know is if I come back and there's no television, me and you are gonna have a talk Silly Sylvia."

"I don't like it when you call me that."

"I'm sorry Silly." John mocked.

"And I don't have any money left in the bank John. You spent it all on Brenda's ca-

"What the FUCK did I tell you yesterday Sylvia? You just don't let up do you? That's why we both have jobs don't we? Brenda here is in college and she needs a ride, right? I'm being the good father and providing for my family so don't call me down off of my horse to tell me otherwise. You got that sill...sill...silly...Sylvia?"

Sylvia looked away. Tears filled her eyes.

"Yeah I got it."

"Pop, maybe you should go easy on mom."

"And maybe Brenda, you would like me to take those keys back. I'm sure I could sell your ride to any of the young bucks at work."

"I'm just say-

"Brenda." Sylvia said. "Just stop. Don't get in-between."

"That's right Brenda." John said chewing on her steak. "Don't go where you can't come back."

A knock fell on the door, gentile and inviting.

"Brenda would you get that?" Sylvia asked.

"Sure Mom."

Brenda walked forward, a sudden terrible feeling hit her square in the gut. *Was it the cops? Would they be the ones knocking at the door? Did they somehow know it was her who was slaughtering the children of Carper Falls?*

"Who is it?" Brenda said with her hand on the knob.

"For Christ sakes! Open the door!" John yelled.

The door opened before the young girl behind it could answer. There she was, as gorgeous as her own mother with dark hair.

"Hello." Winter Raven smiled. "Is Mrs. Dejour here?"

"Winter?" Sylvia smiled from the table. "How are you?"

"I'm fine." Winter smiled.

"Please, won't you come in?"

Winter stepped forward wearing a fake fur coat. Her hair was tied back in a long ponytail. Bubble gum colored lipstick stained her lips. Above her eyes she wore slight blue mascara, the color of dangerous nights.

Winter glanced mysteriously at Brenda.

"I don't mean to intrude but mom sen-"

"Oh dear, you're not intruding, not at all." Sylvia smiled.

"Another country heard from." John mumbled.

"I don't believe you met my daughter Brenda. This is Winter Raven. Winter, my daughter Brenda, and this is my husband John."

"Hello." Brenda said timidly.

"Hi."

"You're the new neighbors across the street right?" John asked chewing into his steak.

"Yes sir. I came over to ask, well, my mother sent me over to ask if you would all like to join us for dinner tomorrow night around six?"

"Sure." Sylvia said. "We-

"Nope." John interrupted. "Sorry little girl, but we can't"

"John you're going to be working and Brenda's going back to school, what am I supposed to do, be by myself all night?"

"Yep." John noted.

"Well." Winter started to talk, then became flush with embarrassment from John Dejour's tone. "Sorry to bother you, just thought I'd ask."

"My mom and Dad sent this over for you guys, just a house warming gift."

Winter held the box out to Brenda.

"Aren't we the ones supposed to give the gift?" Brenda asked with a smile.

"It was nice to meet you." Winter responded.

"You too." Brenda smiled.

Her cheeks were freckled and when she smiled a small chubbiness came from them, dimples were made.

"Seeya around." said John.

The girl waved, then walked onward into the darkening sky. Sylvia waited until the door was closed.

"That was so fucking rude!"

John stopped eating. He was surprised by his wife's tone.

"Woman." John said with his right fist clenched. "If you open your mouth to me that way again, I'll shut it forever."

"I wonder what's in the box?" Brenda asked, trying to break up the argument.

Sylvia began to cry. She quickly she wiped the tears away so John couldn't see. She didn't want to show him any more of her tears. They had cost her much of her life and were too important to give away anymore.

"Well open it, then we'll all know right?" John said rolling his eyes. "Maybe it's a bottle of Scotch. They want to be so God damn nice, send that over."

Brenda flipped open the lid; her eyes grew with a perplexed look, and then widened as she pulled a massive wax sculpture of a rose from the box. The rose was a candle, and around the rose were wax figurines of more miniature flowers.

"That's beautiful."

"You gotta be shitting me." John said to his wife. "A candle?" He got up laughing. "A god damn candle?"

"John."

"Faggot shit!" He said, and sat on the couch.

Brenda and her mother looked at the candle which, judging by the way that the wax was crafted, must have taken quite awhile to make. The wax roses romanced each other in it's own display, interweaving with a skilled craftsman's touch. Along the green leaves were words scrolled together.

OUT WITH THE OLD IN WITH THE NEW

"That's so lovely." Sylvia said, admiring the candle.

Suddenly John stood in the middle of the living room, smiled, and hurried forth grabbing the wax candle.

"NO!" Sylvia screamed as John hurled it against the back living room wall.

The candle exploded into pieces.

"YOU SON OF A BITCH!" Sylvia screamed.

She began to sob so deeply, her chest heaved with misery and rage. Brenda stood placing her hands on her ears, and stormed upstairs. She needed her Rabbits foot. She needed it more now than ever.

"Awe come on! Hon!" John laughed. "I don't like any of that shit in my house, you know that?

"Why?"

"Why what?" John snapped.

"Why are you so mean?" Sylvia cried. "So HEARTLESS!"

"You made me what I am." John pointed at the blonde woman before him.

His ruddy eyes filling with rage pierced her soul. Soon, his fists would close.

"You made me what I am you fucking cunt." John took a step towards his terrified wife. "And I'll be calling tomorrow to see if you're eating here, or if you're over there with those two fucks!"

Sylvia placed her hands over hands her eyes and cried into them. The darkness was all but comforting.

"Aren't you gonna say you're sorry? Hmmm? You're always sorry you bitch. "

John walked into the living room and fell asleep on the couch. His wife picked up the pieces of the candle, sobbing all the while.

That son of a bitch. When is it going to end? When is it going to stop? Why haven't I called the cops? What is my boss going to say when I go into work tomorrow and he sees the bruises on my face? I can't go out anymore. I can't let anyone see me. It's a good thing I'm not going to the Raven's because they wouldn't say anything, but their eyes would ask. I would feel them digging through my heart to see why I cry. I can't keep this up much longer. What happened to my husband? Where did he go? Ever since I miscarried my life has been over. I can't clean the horses tomorrow. I can barely walk since he kept me up all night. I hate the things he's done to me. Where has he learned them? Where do men learn to beat their wives?

The candle pieces were placed into a Rubbermaid container and while John slept, she placed them in the bread closet. Never has she felt more hurt. Never has she wanted to kill her husband. Brenda watched the television in her room rubbing the rabbit's foot on the key chain seeing the faces of those that have been butchered by the Violator. How with each escapade murder taste's so much sweeter. Beside her on the bed was an array of books. Mostly, vampire related. Some were of literature involving eighteenth century torture. Others were books on the Roman Empire.

She listened for the scream of her parent's fighting; when none came she believed that was a good thing.

What of the girl that came over? Her thoughts betrayed her on that. The girl named Winter Raven. She was prettier than Brenda, and Brenda knew it. Surely, once she got NOLA out on the road, she could take her new neighbor friend for a ride. Winter would be all right in the passenger seat as long as Nola didn't mind.

Brenda didn't think Nola would care.

But that was now...

V.

Jonathan Dejour left for work the next morning for the last time. Brenda caught a ride with her mother to the bus stop. There, Brenda said her goodbyes to Sylvia. A breath of relief exhaled as she watched her only daughter walk to the rear of the bus. Tonight she would have an evening without her abusive husband. The dragon has left the cave to allow those still alive to breathe. Being a victim of spousal abuse Sylvia understood that relief is only an illusion, a pause before torture. Jonathan was a man Sylvia no longer knew. Her eyes said it all, and sometimes spilled what was left of their hope down her blouse.

She wondered what changes a man over time into a vicious beast like John? The wedding pictures at home resting on the dresser drawer depicted a different person that's for sure. John's hair in the picture was once black, shining with youth and straight. Not like now, where his locks are twisted with sweat and dirt. Father time has riddled him with age, helped along by the benefits of an alcohol problem. What changes a man like Jonathan Dejour into the wife-beating monster he is?

Sylvia sat in her Pontiac as the bus roared away bouncing on diesel fuel fumes. She paused for a moment looking across the river bridge canal. A seagull swooped down and perched onto a light post. It stared at her as if feeling her.

I could kill him. She thought. *I could kill him, and Brenda would never know, she would suspect maybe, but she would never know.*

At that moment, the seagull left for the skies, joining others as they circled the boardwalk adjacent from the bus terminal. Sylvia drove her Pontiac away from the bus station, and onto lost roads where perhaps her new world would be found. She switched on the radio, as Bruce Springsteen ended one of his songs abruptly. 93.5 broke into an announcement, as a reporter started with:

This just in:

Several police officials have been investigating yet another bizarre rash killing near the Valley, which is five miles from Maryland's Eastern Shoreline and the boardwalk of Ocean City. Although Police suspect it is the work of the serial killer The F.B.I. has labeled The Violator, a few skeptics are not so sure. Devana Mirrow and her family, who were believed to be the latest victims, may not be. Two men, as yet unidentified, were found lying on the beach yesterday. The coroner believes they may have been lying there for the past week. Beside them, Police found a Mercedes Benz. The two men were murdered at nighttime, but it isn't clear as to when. One victim's tongue was torn from his mouth and puncture wounds were found on his neck. A local sanitation worker, working at dredging the beaches for the summer community, found the other victim. The body was found decapitated, lying on his back under the boardwalk. The victim's head was impaled on a piece of beach wood. Puncture wounds were also found on this victim's neck, and on his face.

Sylvia flipped the radio to a national station. The purported killings shouldn't be found there, but they were. As the Pontiac made it to Route 50 in Carper Falls, the streets were busy with traffic and people, something very unusual for this time of the year.

Suddenly, Sylvia was afraid. For the first time since John had began beating her, she was afraid. Sylvia for once had time to think about what has been going on in the town she grew up in, rather than her husband's fist. The abuse at home ends sooner or later.

However, sharks stay in the water, and close by if there is food. Her husband was supposedly away working (not that she gave a damn what John was doing). All she cared about anymore was her daughter Brenda. The silence that occupied her mind as she turned the radio off allowed her to focus on what her surroundings. There was a mad man out there that the police couldn't catch. Her husband expected her to stay alone in the house all night?

I'll drive by the Raven's see if the offer's still on.

But you can't. Remember what John said? If he knows you went over there he'll-

What? That was the question Sylvia needed answered. *What could he do that wasn't already done? Kill her? At this point that would be a blessing. I'm going to enjoy myself for once and not worry about the outcome. Out with the old, in with the new.*

Her car rolled to the traffic light.

And fuck what John says. As far as I'm concerned the marriage ended four years ago...the night he raped me in front of our daughter.

Sylvia drove on into the new day as the darkness was temporarily behind her. A storm was brewing in the West. In a few days, it would be snowing in an unforgiving way. It would be here on Monday and according to the weatherman dump more than seven inches on Carper Falls.

Sylvia pulled her Pontiac over to the side of the road. She stared at her house for a moment before opening the door and stepping into the fresh cold air. It slammed her with a crisp realization that perhaps Holly Raven wasn't home. Perhaps her husband would answer the door. The man she had yet to meet the dark man with the old Mustang Cobra. That mean and fast car, black as forgotten nightmares.

What would she say to him? She didn't get to say too much at the gas station Southern Gale owned. Sylvia walked towards her answer as the wind picked up from the north. She observed the overly white house with the scarlet red door. The siding on the house was very white, like all the houses on this street. They were all stick built ranchers and condos. And they all looked the same, even the doors. Except, Sylvia observed the candles burning in the enclosed glass bulbs hanging upon the eave of wood near the welcome mat.

They make candles.

Sylvia almost slipped on the ice as she ascended the first three steps onto the small wooden porch. She opened the screen door to rap her closed fist softly. She thought of John calling like he said he would. She thought of the phone ringing and then thought of the calamity known as John Dejour racing home to do the nastiest things to her.

No matter who was watching. He'd flip a dining room table chair over and then-

Oh and *then...*

Would Sylvia really be this ballsy when he indeed came home from his trip? Or when his calls were found unanswered?

49

The door opened at the same time her fist knocked. Holly stood before her. She was clad in a long flowing dress of silk, red and shiny as newborn blood. Chinese lettering in gold ran across the bridge of her shoulders. Her dark hair tied in a bun.

"Sylvia?" Holly asked.

"Hello."

"Hello to you too." Holly Raven smiled.

"Would you like to come in?"

"No." Sylvia said, "I have to be off to work soon. I just wanted to stop by and apologize. Actually, I was hoping Winter was around. Is she here?"

"No actually." Holly grinned. "She went back to school today. Won't be home till around three. Her father took her this morning. What's the matter?"

"Nothing." Sylvia said.

She looked away towards the empty street.

"It's just..." Sylvia hesitated, and looked on with cold, tired and winter-dried eyes. "It's just that I didn't get the chance to tell your daughter I wanted to come tonight...for dinner. My husband's not going to be home, or my daughter for that matter. I didn't really want to spend the evening alone. John is working an all-nighter. Is the offer still on?"

"You know it is." Holly said. "Friends are hard to come by my dear."

"Yes I know."

Holly noted with a laugh.

"Sorry, I prattle off sometimes, and say the wrong things. We're having steak I believe and some other things. We'll open a bottle of wine, trust me, Sylvia Dejour, the wine here is excellent."

"If it's not to much trouble and all."

"Don't be silly!" Holly cackled. "We'd love to have you!"

"Thank you very much." Sylvia said.

"You're welcome very much." Said Holly. "I believe it's gonna snow a mess on Maryland."

Sylvia looked at the skies above, gray and overcast.

"I believe you're right."

"It never snowed in Las Vegas you know."

"Really?" Sylvia said.

"Really, although once, according to my sister who died a few months ago, she remembered it snowing."

"Oh I'm sorry to her that Hol-"

"Nonsense." Sylvia said. "People die you know. It's the answer to the ultimate question."

"What question?"

Holly turned towards her friend.

"What's the only way out when you have no where else to go?"

Sylvia hesitated. A chill ran the length of her spine, not any of it was from the cold air.

"I have to be going then." Sylvia said.

"Say hello to that daughter of yours for me. Winter and her are going to be great friends I believe."

"Will do." Sylvia smiled, backing away from the door.

"By the way, thanks for the candle, it's absolutely stunning."

"I'm glad you like it. Robert and I spent some time crafting it for you."

"No doubt." Sylvia lit a cigarette. "You didn't have to do that."

"I know." Holly said. "But we Ravens take care of our neighbors, we always help those that need it."

Sylvia became choked at that comment.

"Oh and Sylvia?" Holly said.

"Yes?"

"Do be careful out there, I hear the police are everywhere looking for this guy. But I don't know if they will ever find him."

"I will." Sylvia said, giving a wave and walking back to her Pontiac Grand Am.

She had already admired her next-door neighbors for who they were. And it's been a long time since she has been able to have friends. She wondered if Holly could see her bruises. If she could figure things out on her own. According to her comments earlier, that assessment was ascertained. In truth, they have been there so long that Sylvia Dejour really couldn't remember living without them.

Eric Enck

Harrison Turner was an exhausted middle-aged Sheriff, with less hair than he once had, and with fewer years on the force than he liked to admit. He had been the one who entered the home of Devena Mirrow after Liam Griffin a/k/a Duke. Duke could barely call it in. When he went into the home, he tried to bring his police training with him. Turner never believed he would have to see anything like what he witnessed that morning. He didn't like recollecting on crime scenes. Being thirty-two years old with three kids and one on the way all of a sudden he had a quick flash of doubt about his job.

He snapped back to the reality of his job and pushed the envelope with the crime scene photos aside. He was happy the FBI had taken matters over. Harrison didn't have the police force necessary or the right facilities to handle such atrocities. That's what really disturbed the balding Sheriff. His heart began beating an unknown fear.

Carper Falls had never been subjected to such a rash of bizarre killings like this. Not even Baltimore had bore witness to what had been transpiring as of late. There was no motive other than the killer seemed to pray on youth, and each crime scene had been different as well. The latest of which, the two men found murdered on the beach had the FBI by the balls. They didn't think it was the same killer. Sheriff Turner had his fair share of education on psychos but shivered at having to put that knowledge to the test.

Where does that urge come from? Harrison thought as he opened his unmarked patrol car door. A cold wind blew across his police jacket inside where the zipper did not go all the way up.

Where does the urge to kill a child come from? To kill anyone for that matter? Why is so powerful?

Turning the ignition, the police cruiser exited the underground terrace-parking garage and found its way onto route 50. Turner sat in thought mulling over facts and opinions. He wondered why does a person lose control? The Police were looking for a white Caucasian male roughly in his lower thirties. And he had to be relatively strong to have done the things he has done. Harrison wondered if it was really genetic, or traumatic? Did a person do the things like what the Violator had done because of stress or abuse? Because of cultural conditioning?

Does a serial killer have control over their twisted desires? Is the desire for blood and mayhem somehow locked in one's soul? And if so, where do you find the lock for the cage? Harrison knew age and inappropriate sexual thoughts were not all that uncommon and often led to the unlocking of floodgates of pain and torture. Men, women, priests, all people sinned. It was apart of life. What the Sheriff wanted to know was what kept the mad man from keeping his monsters within locked away?

Turner believed that the madman in Carper Falls had no excuse for what he did. He just believed the victims chosen deserved to die in the psycho's eyes. Not only that, but evidence showed the madman got some sort of nourishment or sense of sustaining from the killings. After all, what normal person would drink the blood of others? Someone pretending to be a vampire? That's why the press had been ordered to keep the word *vampire* out of the papers, in case the killer himself was reading. The FBI called him Violator, but not Vampire. They believed the killer wanted to be known as a vampire. The Feds thought it would be a bad idea to give the killer what he desired. By not giving the suspect what he wanted, hopefully it would eventually piss him off enough to foul up in his hidings. The authorities speculated like always, this guy would be caught. Without a shred of doubt, he would be caught before Spring's first thaw.

Serial killers, like the supposed Violator, are not insane. Not at least in the eyes of the knowledgeable, but just plain evil. Often, killers are very brilliant and rational. There is a fine line between ingenuity and insanity. Most of us cross it every so often. Serial killers are usually emotionally scarred. The turmoil of early life deprives them of the knob to turn off the faucet of rage, resulting in them committing heinous acts.

Many madmen have attempted to become police officers. One common trait of a serial is a fascination with police action and reaction. Harrison wondered if their local killer had once submitted an application to his own office. Harrison didn't know that the killer they were looking for had a homicidal rage within because of one thing and one thing only. It wasn't an obsession with vampires or police. The rage was projected onto the youth, the girls and boys that had been found brutally murdered, because they represented all the inadequacies the killer had in the eyes of an abusive father.

We think we can spot the bad men and women in this world. Those that have the psychotic seed within society in the minds of most should show some flowering from the fruits of their labors. A maniac with uncontrollable urges to desiccate and destroy will be easy to point out, but we would be wrong by that assessment. Never judge a book by its cover. No matter how many stereotypes we avoid. The unshaven man with grisly long hair who talks to himself or the old man with more wrinkles than the bark of an old tree in Ocean City who likes to feed the seagulls and yells at passers by. The quiet young man working at Starbucks or the Post Office who loves making eye contact with little girls. In truth we never know who among us will loose to the desire to hurt and inflict terror on those around them.

It would both shock and fascinate Harrison to hear Brenda's tale. The cute young blonde who so badly wanted a sister growing up. The girl that developed nightmares from her father's excursions into her bedroom. The same young woman who slept many nights with her eyes open watching the bedroom door, wondering when it would open after hearing those heavy boot heels. The same girl who woke from nightmares of the terrible man who worn those boots just to have him began a waking terror session. The girls whose nostrils would be flooded with the smell of bad food and spent as he would stand there watching her. He'd climb in bed with her and pull her down into the quicksand, where the undertow ran with sweat and angry words. He would wrap one good hand around her throat so no words of mercy or hate could be heard. She would lay there in agony watching the shifting eyes of the wall clock as the moving tail ticked away the endless seconds. His hard knees would spread her legs and he would tell her so softly to shut up, don't say a word, or the Devil would kill her in her sleep. Brenda Dejour often believed, the Devil, if the devil was real, hid under her bed, and was always there when Daddy came home from work, drunk and enraged.

Brenda's father took care of the possibility of her ever having a sister. One swift kick to Sylvia's womb and bye-bye love. Her mother had miscarried. Brenda Dejour wasn't born bad as one could believe, if they knew of her affinity for blood lust. She wasn't precociously demented. Brenda was molded into the woman she was by her father. The exchange of bodily fluids from her father nourished her own seeds of evil. Now the voices were there giving her instructions as to how to kill. They gave her the companionship she had missed growing up.

Harrison Turner believed sometimes, people just snapped the way a branch weighed down by too much snow snaps in the breath of winter. The way an old board bowed in the middle can sometimes snap if you walk across it. People are sensitive, and able to adapt to a degree of abuse, but something must make up for it in the end. Something has got to give. The intrusive belligerency of evil is sometimes there within us all. It's up to us, to drown in the undertow of sanity. Otherwise we can loose our humanity to the demons that prey on men's souls.

In with the old, out with the new…

VI.

The factory stood desecrated by the inner city folk. The city kids had been the most creative. Spray paint and sidewalk chalk had turned this canvas into mirrors of the spirit of youthful rebellion.

Graffiti illustrated the walls reflecting a strong distaste for authority and an expression of freedom. Kids will be kids. This old shoe factory is where some of them used to go as opposed to school. It's where older males often went to exhibit their first openings into a lecherous desire with a teenage girl. But certain times during the year, especially when the summer wanes to the love of fall, the desecrated factory was used for young adult parties. Beer and drugs are the casual forte of telling wild stories into the summer breeze. Now, it's winter. Now, it's a desolate place. Near the third floor is an office area that has been turned into a chemical lab.

Boxes upon boxes of wax chips and wicks lay stacked on each other. The main office area has been cleared of mice and debris. A nice oval cherry wood desk sits under the tall and bright office light. Behind the expensive desk, is a crystal wine goblet, resting upon a table. Next to the table are files, papers, pens and a phone. A fax machine, photocopier and the latest computer you could buy.

In the black leather office chair sat a tall man. Dark hair bridged his temple, short and furrowed to a widow's peak. His face was drawn together with a pleasant seriousness as it befell the room. His eyes were a dull gray, the color of skies in December mornings or the color of slate in the rain. His leather jacket lay draped over the chair behind him. It was a jacket that didn't scream lawyer. But that was okay, this man wasn't a lawyer, at least not anymore. He was a man of domicile knowledge, a Rhodes scholar.

Robert Raven liked the night.

The shipping companies that delivered and expedited crates were finishing with Robert's shipment that last evening. The Raven's candle making business was becoming an internet sensation. It was a sensation in the UK. Candles by Night had a good marketing campaign. Robert Lee Raven owned subsidiaries all over the world. It was the reason he could afford and restore the massive black muscle car that waited outside of the deserted factory.

His last shop was much smaller, located in Vegas. It didn't take long to acquire many clients. People found the artwork in Robert's candle designs to be unprecedented. Robert was a pleasant man. He had lived a long and glorified life abroad. France, Paris, London, and Italy were all his. Finally, after all the years, Las Vegas is where he found home. For the past twenty years, he had helped people and one of them he has married. Holly Frost, had a child with another man who disappeared shortly after Robert and Holly met. The man never cared to come see Holly's daughter and Robert raised her as his own.

"Mr. Raven." Bob Veroy spoke out in thought.

Robert turned towards the truck driver. The man was standing atop of the wooden stairs, peering in on the owner the candle company. Robert had workers all over the company. He looked back down at his receipts as his fingers went dancing across the calculator. The small oval glasses rested on the bridge of his nose.

"Sir, we have your boxes ready for shipment."

"Well done." Robert said.

"Is there anything else you need sir?"

"No Bob that will be all."

Robert Raven busily finished his paperwork as a crow flew to a stop perching itself on the windowsill of the office. Bob Veroy looked on with his toothpick rolling in his mouth.

"Well would you look at that." Bob said. "What an ugly fucking thing that is."

Robert looked at the trucker then the crow over the bridge of his glasses.

"You have to admire nature Mr. Veroy. Perhaps that crow is a messenger."

Bob sucked on the end of the toothpick, and then moved his hand towards the crow. The bird stared unblinking with its shiny eyes.

"I've never seen one that close." Bob said.

"Then you should consider this a life changing event, perhaps Mr. Veroy…you should even make a wish."

"The hell with that." Bob said. "My wishes never come true."

Robert Raven leaned back in his chair, and closed his laptop. He took the glasses from his face and gently chewed on the frame's earpiece, like an old librarian focusing on a text.

"Ugly things, do you want me to get him out of here? You got a broom so I can shush the damn th-"

"No Bob." Robert said and then smiled. "To tell you the truth, I kind of like the little guy. He reminds me of my Mustang. Black as night, you know what I mean? There is no darker color than night Bob, and there is no holiday without a funeral."

"You should write a book Mr. Raven." Bob said. "Hey that's odd"

"What's that?" Robert inquired.

"Your last name, it means bird of prey. The crow is a Raven to some, what are the odds to that? That's gotta mean something don't it?"

"It's a paradox Mr. Veroy." Robert said.

Bob Veroy pulled the toothpick from his lips and replaced it with a half-spent stogie. One of those cigars you can buy at cheap gas stations and liquor stores. Bob chewed on the end of it.

"Well then sir, the boys and I are off. Rest assured, your shipment is as safe as pillows. We'll be arriving in Pennsylvania tomorrow, if you'll just sign here."

Robert looked at the clipboard, placed his glasses upon his face, then took a black pen from the desk and signed the documents. Bob Veroy always liked the way Robert signed his forms. Always with a different name then the one he used before. He never saw that before. Out of all the chains of suppliers he worked for, Robert Raven signed his documents different then his name. But that wasn't really true either, considering it wasn't really a name he signed it with. It was a letter, one single letter. Robert told the closest people in his life that his signature is never done as Robert Raven. It will always be a letter. That's how you will know its Robert. That's how you know the check he writes for you is from him and worth cashing.

When he signs his name with only one letter, and that letter is "D".

"Have a good trip Mr. Veroy" Robert said. "Be careful out there, there is a lot of maniacs running abroad."

"Oh believe you me sir, I know all of them." Bob Veroy said, tipping his hat.

Robert smiled.

Robert Raven filed his paperwork away, as the crow resting upon the perch of the windowsill made a slight squall. Perhaps it was a scream of freedom, or maybe it yearned for a lost dream. Robert stood and stretched his tired bones into submission. He felt rather good. He took his leather jacket and car keys. He past by the office where the walls were covered with newspaper clippings held by thumbtacks. He glanced at one in particular. He had cut out and circled in red magic marker. The article depicted the word VIOLATOR, and went on to talk about the murders being committed in Carper Falls.

Robert walked out of his office to the top of the rickety stairs built by amateur carpenters, fly by niters who came and went during the long hot summers in Maryland. Robert looked back and the crow called to him. Robert smiled back at the crow and it screamed again.

He turned back towards the descending steps. Each footfall threw dust into a fog of sawdust. The shadows among the swinging light bulbs made a concourse of phantasmagoria as they danced with Robert's. There along the lower extremities of the factory brick walls were more newspaper clippings tacked to cork boards, describing the routes in and out of Carper Falls.

In truth, Robert didn't much care for the new town. Carper Falls was the last place he wanted to live, but the rent was cheap and that in itself was a blessing. The quiet the houses and serene neighborhoods were more than enough for his wife. His daughter, Winter, didn't mind. She would blend in anywhere. Robert wanted New York more than any place. He had enemies there, but everyone has someone who is left behind in the darkness of the past. No, Carper Falls was a better place to start over. Out with the old, in with the new.

The true endeavor was the family business. He had made the most magnificent candles as a hobby while being a prosecutor in Venice. There he had learned the ways of literature, law and mastered over a dozen languages. New York reminded Robert of a cattle drive, so many people, and so little time. Time however was only significance to mortals.

Venturing along the long hollow hallway of the deserted factory drew out to a door at the end of the brick hall. He slid his leather jacket on, one sleeve at a time. The smell of mildew triggered a distant memory. His face was olive skinned and heavy with five o'clock shadow. His eyes grew beady and deep within his face as he pulled the light chain leading to the single light bulb above. Robert reached out to the brass knob and turned it to open the door to the small room once used as a drafting room for inventors. Two rats scurried away from the man who entered. Robert came into the dark room and switched the light on. A humming sound of dim blue fluorescents cast illumination across the windowless room like magic. Robert was smiling, and his smile spread across the terror the older man in the room was feeling. The older man with duct tape over his mouth and blood dribbling from his nose moved his face towards Robert, as Robert hesitated in front of him.

"Mr. Watts, hello again." Robert said.

Mr. Watts mumbled something. Robert reached forward with his long fingers and ripped the bloody duct tape free from Watt's face. The man hanging on the wall screamed, and then breathed heavy. The right side of Watt's face was pushed inward and outward at the same time. Part of his skull and eye socket had been crushed. His right ear was gone, nothing but a gaping hole. Watt's right eye was hanging partially out on his cheek, blood drizzling from it, and yet Robert respected the man. He was still alive after all he's been through. He was still alive and well respected.

With swollen lips and slurred speech, Watts tried to speak.

"What, are…you.gon."

"It's funny Mr. Watts." Robert said, as he pulled a cigar from his jacket pocket.

It wasn't one of those cheap ones like Bob the trucker smoked. Just like his sunglasses weren't of the kind Southern Gale sold in his gas station. It's as if the wealth of life and finer things followed Robert all the way from Vegas. He raised the cigar up towards his view and with his other hand reached for a cigar cutter in his jacket pocket. It was a small device with a blade in the center, and operated similar to a guillotine. The idea was to place the cigar in the center of the blades and squeeze the small end shaped like a trigger, and off would come the closed cigar end, so it could be smoked.

"Would you like a cigar Mr. Watts?"

"Let me go…you can have the car." Watts begged.

His eye was killing him, every time he moved his head, the exposed nerves and loose veins dangled on his cheek. Robert stepped closer. He cut the cigar, placed the cutter back in his pocket, and then placed the cigar in his mouth. He felt his jacket for a light, frowned at the fact he didn't have one, then smiled with the cigar at the fact Watt's did.

He reached forward, seen the pack of cigarettes hanging from Watt's shirt pocket which were smashed to oblivion from the car backing over them while still in Watt's pocket. He observed the matches twisted like broken fingers, a few of them still with their heads in tact. He plucked them free from Watt's bloody pocket, and struck flame. Watt's watched in horror as Robert Raven puffed away on the smoke, enjoying the moment. The woody smell of the robust cigar smoke filled the small room. Blood pooled slowly from Watt's hole where an ear used to be. The tire of Watt's car spun so fast, the ear was burned off.

"I'm going to let you free Mr. Watts." Robert said around the cigar.

"You know why I'm going to let you free?"

Watt's didn't respond, but his eyes were screaming.

"I'm going to set you free because I know, you were sorry for what you did. You sent those two guys down here to make me pay up, but a deal is a deal Mr. Watts isn't it?"

"Yes." Watts gagged.

Robert smiled; his eyes were bright with lucidity.

"This really is…a delicate and enjoyable smoke Mr. Watts, it's a shame your jaw is broken. I'd offer you one."

Robert blew smoke in Watt's face. And continued to smile. He reached over to the wall and pulled the chain holding Watt's against it.

Watt's fell to the floor in a heap. A scream followed him down. The chains fell on top of Watts like metal rain.

Robert stooped over Watt's face. He pulled the cigar free and slowly lowered it towards Watt's eye dangling out of its socket like an exploded tadpole. The cherry on the cigar emanated a terrible heat. Robert lowered the cigar down towards Watt's eye.

"I could burn it off you know."

"No...please, please dear God"

"I could burn that eye right off of your face, and then I'll eat the other one, what would you say to that Mr. Watts? What would a good for nothing car salesman who beats his wife say to that?"

"Robert. I."

"Don't talk please. You just listen."

And Watts did.

"I'm going to kill you. We both know this. If you haven't figured that out by now, shame on you. I didn't back over you with your own Mercedes because it was a mistake. And I didn't kill your two buddies and take them down to Ocean City beach because it was a mistake either. Do you know what their blood tastes like Watts? It tastes like a leech's. As I probably imagine yours tastes the same. Do you know what a leech is Mr. Watts? It's a worm that sucks blood off of other animals, off of other humans. Much like you and your boys suck off of other people's bank accounts and lives."

"That's...not tru"

" No Watts." Robert said. "It *is* true."

"You people act like... vampires." Robert said with a smile.

He stood from Watts who lay badly injured. He walked over to the corner and pulled an empty crate from the wall. With both hands he pushed the long crate across the floor, dragging old dust along for the ride.

He returned to Watts, grabbed him by his legs, and pulled him towards the box. He gently lifted the old man into the box and Watts fell in like a fish.

"NO!" Watts suddenly became lively through his pain. "NO! NO NO!"

"Relax Mr. Watts." Robert said.

He pulled a large bucket up to the side of the open crate. In the bucket was over a dozen long railroad tie nails. Each iron nail was over nine inches. Mr. Watts didn't scream not even when Robert showed him the framing hammer.

"In the old days, Jesus was nailed to a cross, I had the pleasure of knowing what this was like. You wouldn't believe it if I told you, that I saw Jesus. I was there when the Romans drove that last nail in. I heard the bones in his hands crack.

Not many people ever get to know what that's like Mr. Watts, and if this is any comfort to you, I can assure you, heaven *does* exist"

Robert slid the lid onto the crate, just as Watts began to scream.

"And so does hell" Robert whispered.

He dropped the lit cigar, and crushed it with his boot heel. He pulled the first nail out of the bucket, and placed the point on the side of the crate. He held the hammerhead onto the top of the nail and paused.

"Before I drive this nail into your ribs Watts, I want you to remember something. That for every nail that goes into your flesh and bone, is for every mile you journeyed to find me. It's for that last sunset you probably didn't even admire on your way down here. People take such things for granted, just like they take their fears for granted. But I'm probably safe in assuming your scared now aren't you? I'm probably safe in saying you're sorry too."

"I *AM* SORRY!" Watts screamed from the crate.

Robert lowered his face towards the crate, as his eyes grew dark with gloss, black as police shoes.

"I forgive you."

The hammer fell; the nail was pounded into the box, and into Watt's left rib. He felt it rip the flesh in a cold hard pierce. He felt it sneak into his rib, slide off of it, and tear through the meat between bone. Watts screamed in terror and pain, and paused as another nail came in through the other side. It was the pause that Robert cherished, each scream, Robert has heard before. It was the pausing between screaming that Robert smiled at.

It took one hour for Robert to drive over forty nails into the crate marked FRAGILE as blood began to pool from underneath.

It took two hours for Mr. Watts to see if Heaven was real.

Robert shut the door behind him and advanced towards the long hallway finding the exit door to the outside world. His black mustang sat perched under the moonlight, which reflected its madness off of the black car like an idealistic beacon of doom. The black muscle car was as dark as Robert's eyes. The Mustang roared down the long narrow road into the country fields of Carper Falls. He was nine miles from the sandy beaches, and close to twenty from his new home when the cell phone in his coat pocket vibrated close to his heart.

"Hello?" Robert said.

"Hello honey." the seductive voice said from the other side.

"How is my sweet darling his evening?"

"Fine as always."

"You're locking the door like I've told you right? That madman is still on the run. Makes me want to leave Maryland to be truthful."

"I lock it always." Holly noted. "Bob, I wanted to let you know we're having a guest for dinner. She should be here any minute.

"The woman across the street?"

"Yes." Holly said with excitement. "Is that okay?"

"Of course" said Robert. "I'm glad you found a friend, I've been wanting to meet her."

"I haven't met her husband yet, but I think there is a few problems there."

"Remember Holly." Robert started. "Don't get involved if there is. Remember what happened the last time. It's why we're married and why we moved."

"I won't baby." Holly said. "I promise."

"So what else is on your mind?" Robert asked.

"Well, I think you should enter the Hot Rod competition this weekend, your car is a show car."

"I might do that." Robert said, looking on puzzled.

"It would be good for both of us to get out and meet people." Holly said.

"Speaking of which, Mr. Watts won't be calling anymore."

"Who?" Holly asked.

"The car salesman that sold us the SUV in Pennsylvania, the one who left threats on our answering machine?"

"Oh him." Holly said with grimness in her tone.

"The one who threatened our daughter."

"Yes, Robert, I remember."

Robert paused, and then spoke.

"I've taken care of things honey."

"You have?" Holly asked.

"Yes." Robert said. "We have come to an arrangement. He won't be bothering us anymore"

"He understands you?" Holly asked.

"Holly." Robert said. "When it comes to Mr. Watts understanding me, he *nailed* it."

"That's good baby. Listen, the steaks will soon be done. I'll see you when you get here."

"Yes you will." Robert said, and closed the flip phone.

He thought of the arrangement he had spoken of with Mr. Watts. How he had traveled from Vegas in the U haul, as his wife followed in the Mustang. They entered the State of Pennsylvania before things...

Before things went a little awkward. Robert Raven stopped in a little town called Ephrata, stuck in the center of Lancaster Pennsylvania. The town offered nothing more than suburban socialites with a taste for wine much like Robert had a taste for. It was there that the Mustang overheated. He found a used car dealership towards the limits of the town, and even though they were closed, the door to the place was open. Robert went in, without any types of weapons (after all, why would he need his sawed off shotgun at a car dealership?). It wasn't like the time he drove down Enckton Avenue in Vegas when he was drunk on Holly's Father's blood. It was the night he took her as his own, saved her from that abusive son of a bitch. Holly's father used to beat her and rape her sister Mary. What's worse, Holly's brother Casper used to help. They weren't ready for Robert though. No ones' ever ready for Robert.

So yes, Robert took Holly's own father out back one night while he was good and drunk, toasted beyond burnt, and slit Olsen Frost's throat from ear to ear with a piece of green bottle glass. He propped Olsen up by an old tree and collected his blood in an old beer bottle. He drank Holly's father dry, for whatever reason, Robert Raven drank blood, like Brenda Dejour drank blood He tossed the St Pauli girl bottle deep into the woods, and drove around town in the old mustang drunk off of Olsen's blood. He sideswiped over twelve cars on the way down Enckton Street and kept going.

Robert Raven wasn't the type to stop. After all, why stop now when you got a good thing going? One old lady had a heart attack seeing the Mustang coming. And if anyone knew Robert long enough, they'd have one to, if they saw his driving. Getting in the car with anyone when they're drunk is a death wish. Getting in the car with Robert when he's sober is suicide in its most wondrous glamour. It was good no one saw it coming. And it's amazing when people and things live beyond years, beyond other people's tales. Robert has been at one time or another part of everyone's story.

Robert Raven has seen the fall of the Roman Empire. The hangings in Jerusalem. The end of Jesus, and the rise of the Anti-Christ. Robert has seen the statue of Mary Magdalena bleed from her eyes when he reached the ripe age of, well, he doesn't know. He's lived so long, birthdays didn't mean much anymore. The darkness is different for a mortal than it is to an immortal. But even still, through all the years Robert had lived, not in any of them has he learned to drive a car correctly.

Which is perhaps living proof time does not wait for anyone.

And also living proof the DMV is relaxed to everyone's wishes.

But the car dealer ship where he met Tadius Watts was like many he's seen before. The Mustang billowing steam from outside made Robert hurry. That car was important to him, and not in the normal human way cars are considered important. The car was Robert's extension. The car...was ...

Haunted.

Tadius Watts and Robert talked for the next few hours as Holly and Winter slept in the U HAUL. And Watts made a deal that evening little did he know it was sealed in blood. He sold the Raven's an SUV, a Cadillac Escalade to be exact, and way under invoice for that matter. Total costs with taxes and such were crucially low. Robert paid for them up front. He told Watts he'd pay for the remainder of the vehicle after he drove it for a few days, which was the deal. Watts agreed and took the money for. In the meantime, the Escalade started falling apart, right after Robert's Mustang was fixed. Robert told Watts he wouldn't give another dime until the SUV was fixed. Watts disagreed and advised Robert if he didn't pay up he'll in turn get a visit from him.

That the world is not big enough for birds like the Raven's to hide in. Watt's finally advised that Robert's daughter should watch her back. A few nights ago, while Robert had been packing to leave his office, the crow swooped down onto his windowsill. In the midst of night, Robert observed the luxurious Mercedes Benz pull into the deserted factory lot. Tadius Watts stayed in the car while his two henchmen, who were later found dead on the beach, exited the vehicle. Robert Raven came outside to humor them, and perhaps while Watts bled to death he remembered what Robert said. Or perhaps when Robert beat Watts for over an hour before backing Watt's own car over his face popping his eye from his head like a fresh grape in an angry child's hand he remembered.

The only thing Robert said to Watt's men was, "I don't need to watch my back, when I got these."

Watt's didn't see what the henchmen had the pleasure in seeing. But it was something in Robert's smile. It was something in Robert's lurid grin that invited their death. He was talking about his teeth, and somehow Watt's knew that when that final nail was driven through his good eye that Robert was talking about…his teeth.

When Robert Raven pulled into the driveway of his new home, he observed the police cruiser containing Harrison Turner slowly driving down Main Street. Local law enforcement was still looking for signs of a suspect involved in the Maryland murders, the guy the newspapers dubbed, "The Violator." The papers were calling these killings the most bizarre serial murders ever. Robert however wasn't prone to be impressed or moved by tales told by others, no matter how morbid or perverse they seemed. Even if the atrocities had been conducted before his very eyes he would not be move. In his own right after all, Robert Raven was a legend amongst humans. There was no doubting that.

VII.

Inside the home of the Ravens, Sylvia Dejour stood leaning against the wall, enjoying the glass of wine Holly had poured for her. They had been talking for the past half-hour in the kitchen, mostly about their kids, but every so often the grisly murders came up as well.

The door opened and a tall man wearing a black leather jacket and a serious face yet intimidating face entered. It was a face that perhaps all women could love but only the devil could know.

"Hey there darling." Holly said as her husband hung his jacket on the rack by the wall.

Winter remained on the couch by the fireplace. Her mind stuck between the pages of the horror novel she was reading. Robert walked forward holding out his hand to the guest.

He's gorgeous Sylvia thought.

"Good evening Mrs. Dejour." Robert said.

His tight chiseled face formed dimples around the mouth.

"I hear you like the candle we sent you."

"Oh I do." Sylvia said. "It's so pretty, I told your wife you guys shouldn't have done that."

Sylvia felt Robert's hand. It was strong and tight, yet oddly cool even for the wintertime weather.

His eyes. Sylvia thought. *I've never in all my life seen a man with eyes like that.*

"Yes well, we Ravens take care of our neighbors." Robert said. "Please, sit down."

Robert made a gesture with his hand. He grabbed a crystal goblet similar to the one he kept in his factory. He poured his guest another glass of wine. The liquor it poured into the glass with a thin liquid rush smoother than silk lining a coffin. Sylvia observed Robert Raven's hands. They were long and strong looking. Many rings adorned his fingers. One of them had a white stone with a scorpion under the crest. Another, a deep red ruby jewel encased in a sterling silver dragon's mouth. Robert poured a glass full of wine for his wife and one for his own pallet.

"So how do you like living in Maryland's oldest town?" Robert asked. "I mean, besides the latest occurrences of course."

"I'm sure there are worse places to be Mr. Raven."

"You're right about that." Robert said, thinking of a specific closed crate in the back of the deserted warehouse where he stocked the world's most beautiful candles.

"Still, I have much to learn about Carper Falls."

"I'm sure in time Mr. Raven, you will."

"You can call me, Robert, Sylvia. I believe we're friends here."

Sylvia blushed.

"You know Sylvia, the people here are different."

Sylvia leaned back from the table.

"How do you mean?"

"Well, it just seems like they don't warm up to you, not right away. I imagine like anything else they have to just get used to you."

"I suppose you're right." Sylvia said.

"What's this?" Robert asked, making a gesture across the side of Sylvia's heavily made-up face

"What?"

"Did you fall?" Robert asked.

Sylvia acted surprised.

"Oh that?" Sylvia laughed. "Yes I got kicked by one of the horses on Mr. Brown's farm. I tend to the horses on Assateague Island until the summers hit. I love to watch them walk across the marshes."

"I like horses myself." Robert acknowledged. "Especially Mustangs."

Sylvia grinned,

How can he see the bruises? It must be worse than I thought

"I'd like to propose a toast." Robert said while holding up his glass. "To old friends."

He looked at Sylvia.

"And new ones."

All three glasses chimed. Robert took a seat at the end of the marble dining table. Sylvia was staring at his dark silk shirt. The top buttons opened to a manly chest before her. Strands of dark hair lay to and from, just enough so she could get her fingers through.

What am I thinking? She thought.

"Dinner's almost ready." Holly said. "So Sylvia, tell us more about your daughter."

"Yes." Robert added. "I often see her outside just standing there reading the mail or pacing back and forth about her car."

"Oh the Mustang?" Sylvia noted. "I know. She's really excited about driving it. John bought it for her although I guess I really did. Anyway, it doesn't matter. Brenda loves the car. If she seen yours though, Robert, she'd probably lose her mind."

Sylvia took a long swallow of her wine.

"Brenda's in college is she?" Robert asked.

"Yes." Sylvia said.

Her aged and withered blonde hair fell to the side in a drape of gesture that meant I'm hiding my face.

"She's studying ancient history. Currently her subjects are preparing her to become a professor in Social Studies."

"Perhaps our world will need her by the time she has a class of her own." Robert added.

"What do you mean honey?" Holly asked.

"At what point does history change? I ask that because books are constantly outdated. History was one subject I never had much faith in. Of course, I don't generally use the word faith very often. Growing up and doing much traveling, I learned that most of our children's teachings are misguided. Learning from books is like being hog-tied. Seeing the world with your own eyes, now that's history Sylvia. Nobody can disprove experience."

Sylvia looked on in awe. Robert smiled at her, and then drank some wine.

"Hopefully your daughter will make things current in our world. I found through my childhood that what they teach today is not a hundred percent accurate."

"That's interesting." Sylvia said.

"Is it?" Robert smiled. "I didn't think it would be."

Sylvia drank the end of her wine. Robert refilled her glass. She could smell him across the room. It was the smell of cedar and oranges splitting open to the sweet tangy scent inside. Enough to make you want to …

"What else has she studied involving her entry into becoming a student's guide?"

Makes you want to…

Sylvia hesitated. She watched her glass full of blood being pushed towards her.

Taste…

"She's been studying vampires."

Robert's eyes widened with interest. As if a light bulb had gone off in his mind.

"Vampires?"

Why did I think the wine was blood? Sylvia thought.

"What an interesting subject Sylvia. Was that part of her curriculum, or was it…how can I say…choice?"

"I believe it is required." Sylvia said. "My daughter is at the age where she doesn't do things without a purpose behind them."

Robert laughed. He even threw his head back, and enjoyed his guest's comments. The steaks were frying delightfully on the oven. Holly Raven joined in with the laughter.

"I'd like to meet Brenda some time."

"I'm sure you will." Sylvia said.

Robert turned towards his wife, and observed her placing the steaks on the ceramic plate.

Sylvia, who didn't like uncomfortable silences, spoke out.

"Well I must say I'm glad to have finally met you guys. It feels good to know someone in this town, especially with what's been going on."

"I know." Robert said. "It's strange really."

" How do you mean?" his wife asked.

"Well doll," Robert began, laying his long fingered hand on his short dark hair, as if heavy in thought then placed it on the armrest of his chair. He leaned back in the chair. "I don't believe this man will be caught anytime soon. I also don't believe, it's a man doing it."

Sylvia's eyes widened. Winter stopped reading her book, and looked in on her father. Her young eyes blinked with a yearning knowledge and respect for him.

"You think it's a woman?" asked Sylvia.

"No." Robert smiled. "But I do believe he's relatively young, careless in his matters concerning his endeavors just like most young people. Weather they're preparatory or not, they forget much and do very little. The same goes with murder. I think perhaps the person responsible has only started doing it this year, and perhaps likes it more and more as time goes on. I also believe he is not an amateur at all. The media and the police have said that too much on the radio and TV. This killer may be new at what he does, but being new at something doesn't make you an amateur. People have that all wrong you know. Amateurs never get it right. People believe because society tells them to believe they perhaps are good at something because of practice. I don't believe that at all."

"You don't?" Sylvia asked.

"No." Robert continued. "Practice usually in most circumstances does nothing more than provide a false sense of hope. Think of it Sylvia from a salesman's perspective. I've been around guys that have been trained to be salesman by others doing it for years. Real experts if you will. I've seen them go to seminars and classes to hone their abilities, and only to watch these same poor fools fail miserably."

Sylvia looked on in awe.

"Then," Robert continued. " I've seen guys come and go, who have never had one lick of salesman experience. Who never went to class or seminars. I've seen these people sell more than the guys doing it for years. I've seen the same thing happen in Law, when I used to be a lawyer. Some juries just became attached to the lawyer more than the other no matter what facts are presented. It's as if Sylvia, if I may reiterate an earlier discussion, people that are born into doing what they should are the most successful. They are the ones that hypnotize no matter what. They are…in a subliminal sense the vampires of society, sucking off the popularity of their own culture. It boils down to their very birth. My point is Sylvia, I believe in most cases, you are born into positions, and those positions you're the best at."

"Interesting theory." Sylvia said.

"It is." Robert added. "Some people are born into positions and are lost from them, because if you think of it as chess, certain pieces go in certain places. It's the same all over the world. If you're born with a gift or talent, it will never be seen or succeeded unless the chess piece is moved in its proper place. The source of success lies within the womb. The mothers of us all are the reasons we live, that is the truth Sylvia."

Sylvia felt a flutter in her eyes. It was the way Robert looked at her when he said *Mother*.

"I knew a boy once when I was young. A villager in this poor little town wanted nothing more than to be a best selling novelist. And to be truthful, his stories were so alluring. He was one of the best writers I have ever read, and trust me; I am very well read Sylvia. This boy just couldn't break out like the others you know? No matter what he did, no matter what help he got, his manuscripts were turned down despite the fact that he had dozens upon dozens of people that loved his work. He supported his family by making wine at a local vineyard in Italy. His boss placed him as the head winery connoisseur. He was the best wine maker in the valley, but he never saw that Sylvia."

Robert closed his fist.

"He never grasped *that* concept. That instead of wasting his time chasing a dream of becoming the next Edgar Allen Poe or H.P. Lovecraft, he was in fact, the best Wine maker in the country. That was his blessing. That's what he was made for. He couldn't accept it. His chess piece never found its space Sylvia."

Sylvia sipped her wine.

"So what do you think this young man killing teenagers was made for?" Sylvia asked.

Robert looked up from the table, as his wife placed a wooden salad bowl before them.

"To kill."

Sylvia sat quiet.

"I believe wine makers are born, rich men are born, gardeners are born, construction workers are born, bosses are born, and writers are born to be what they are. Think about it for a moment; let's take authors for an example. How many books have you read in your lifetime Sylvia?"

"I don't know." she said. "Probably fifty or so."

"Okay." Robert continued. "Let's say fifty books, and most of them you've probably liked. Yet probably a small percentage of them were memorable and even a smaller percentage have been so successful that not a year goes by without relating yourself to a character or a favorite saying contained in the novel. I think, my dear, there is only one God. There is only one Devil; there is only one Elvis Presley, and only one Stephen King. There was only one Mozart, but yet, many others follow trying to become complacent in the fact *if they can do it why can't I?* It's that human genome. That false sense of hopes that should be left behind in the wombs of our mothers Sylvia. I'm not saying a person born cannot learn many talents, but being profound in a specific talent is a whole other chessboard, a whole other diversion in fact. There is many vast athletes and writers like the wine maker I knew, but it's the ones that are *born* to be what they are that are above others."

Robert moved his face towards his guest.

"The ones that are born into things can never be trodden, no matter how much a person tries. The Violator has recently been born, right here in Carper Falls. He knows it, and so does many others. He was born to kill...for whatever reason. Look through history, I bet your daughter would understand me if not appreciate it. A great many people over our times are legendary because of their impact. Take Dracula for example. History has Dracula as the first vampire ever to bare teeth and taste blood as fine as this wine you and I are drinking. But many do not know that there is a theory he was not the first. Either way, he is the *only* because we, as a society believe it. It's not a depressing thing though, because Sylvia, if we all could throw the ball, there would be no need for a quarterback.

"I see what you mean." Sylvia said.

"It kind of makes you wonder why you're here right?"

"Sort of, now that you put it that way."

Robert smiled.

"You're here because of the womb because nobody can overcome a mother. Behind every talented individual, behind every serial killer, madman, and rapist. Behind every terrorist and mentally ill victim, there is a mother. Mothers are the righteousness behind madmen and angels, and they all go to Heaven."

Tears suddenly rimmed Sylvia's eyes.

"Now Sylvia, you tell me, what greater gift is there to a son or daughter, then the womb of its mother?"

Sylvia looked away, and Robert could suddenly see her pain like a current looming from a wave.

"Would you like a cigarette dear?" Holly asked.

"Yes." Sylvia said. "Please, I'm dying for one."

All three of them laughed, for whatever reason, as the night became a memorable time for them all. From his dress pants, Robert pulled loose a lighter, bending over the table he lit Sylvia's cigarette.

"Still." Holly said sitting down. "It makes you wonder what the son of a bitch thinks about in between his murders. I mean Dear Jesus."

"He's a vicious man." Robert said. "I don't go on within one minute without worrying about Winter because of this sick bastard."

"Dad." Winter said from behind pouring soda into her glass. "You don't have to worry about me. I'll be okay."

Robert faced her.

"In this world Winter, you can never be okay."

They feasted on steak and fresh salad as the skies opened to snowfall. Only a mild dusting was expected before Monday would bring on a full-fledged storm. After the meal, Robert spoke his good byes to Sylvia and planted a cool kiss on her cheek. She worried all at once if he could taste the caked foundation covering the bruises.

Can you hear me coming bitch?

Sylvia watched him walk into the dark of the living room, and then followed Holly to the den.

Can you hear my boots stomping? I got something for you. Something nice and tight.

76

You were over there with those fucks!

Sylvia sat down across from Holly as the fireplace warmed the room.

"I should be going soon."

"You're welcome to spend the night if you wish." Holly said.

Sylvia smiled.

"No, I think it would be best to sleep in my house."

Holly quickly changed the subject.

"I hope we stay here for awhile, with Robert's business it's hard to stay in one location at a time."

"I'm sure." Sylvia said.

"And to add to the damn stress, our daughter keeps making friends, but she never gets to really keep any because of moving all the time you know?"

"I've thought of moving myself," Sylvia said, looking down at her hands. "But...I don't think John would agree."

Holly watched her neighbor rub the back of her hands.

"This weekend is the hot rod festival you know."

"I know." Holly said. "I want my hubby to enter his Mustang, but he's still thinking about it."

"Yeah, Brenda will be home this weekend I'm sure she'd love to go."

"So bring her."

Sylvia sat dumfounded.

"No I couldn't possibly. Her fath-"

"Robert would be happy to take her down to North Shores. She would make great company. They both have something in common with the Mustangs."

"That's true, but Brenda's Father will be home then, and he promised her he'd take her out driving, so she can practice for her license."

Holly leaned forward, her mouth opened to speak, she paused, and then decided it was warranted.

"I don't mean to pry Sylvia."

"Oh?"

"This is none of my business, but why do you seem so...lost? So worn out? It can't be just from working with the horses. Is...is everything okay with you and John? If it is, forgive me, if it's not, then I believe we should talk."

"No everything's fine." Sylvia said.

Everything's fine. My asshole sometimes bleeds so bad I got to wear a maxi pad back there, but everything else is fine. I sometimes have to drive to work with ice on my face hoping my boss won't notice but hey, everything's fine. You wouldn't believe me if I told you that one time after John finished sodomizing me I went to the bathroom and was so constipated I had to hold onto the toilet paper holder like a crutch while I cried. While I thought of my daughter. My only daughter. After I was done, guess what I seen in the toilet? A piece of the wooden chair leg he broke off from downstairs coffee table. I used to think of different excuses to tell him I don't want to have sex, now I think of different ways to kill him. He sometimes for fun flips a Zippo lighter open in the dark and lights the flame letting the ring around the top get really hot, and then he holds it too my tits while I scream, but hey, everything's fine.

Sometimes I hear him moving around in the dark, or he sneaks off, but I don't ever know where he goes. *I used to think it was to Brenda's bedroom, but what would he want there? Sometimes I wake up and he's sitting in the dark naked on the rocking chair, holding the teddy bear I bought for our unborn daughter. The one he caused the miscarriage for. Sometimes he hits me over and over and over again while I pray to whatever god exists if any, to take me away, take me anywhere. Sometimes I wish the Devil would take me to hell where nothing can be worse than John Dejour. But hey, everything's fine.*

"Are you sure?" Holly asked, while Sylvia sat in a trance.

"Trust me Holly, I'm a-okay."

And that's when Holly observed red and blue lights dancing off her guest's face. Holly stood quickly and walked to the side door of the den along with Sylvia. When she opened the door to the cold winter night, a flurry of snow struck her in the face like icy feathers.

Her dark hair blew back from her head and Sylvia looked in awe behind her. Two police cruisers were parked across the street in front of the Dejour residence. One of the cruisers's had its headlights aimed towards the house. Two officers stood on the front porch. One was knocking.

"What the hell?" Holly said.

"What the hell is right? Why are cops at my house?"

Because he's coming. Can't you hear his boots? Johns coming and he's bringing a teddy bear.

Sylvia hurried, grabbing her coat and purse and walked across the street as the stroke of mid-night approached. Her friend followed her.

"Is there a problem officers?" Sylvia said. Both Policemen turned towards her.

"Are you Sylvia Dejour?" one of them asked.

"I am. What's this about?"

"Can we go inside ma'am? Talk about it in there?" the other deputy asked.

"Sure." Sylvia said, reaching in her purse for her house keys.

A blast of fear kicked from inside her stomach.

"Did I do something wrong?"

"Not at all ma'am."

She entered her house and flipped on the lights. There, instinctively and almost like a bad habit Sylvia went to the answering machine but stopped. The number 5 blinked every second back at her. It reminded her of an eye perhaps one that the devil would look upon her with.

Five messages. Sylvia thought. And I bet I can guess who they're all from.

"So what's this about?" Sylvia asked, as Holly stood in the shadows of the doorway.

"Ma'am," the older cop of the two stepped forward taking off his patrol hat, "my name is Deputy Davis, this is Deputy Washburn. We are Sheriff Turner's men and-"

"Yes." Sylvia said. "I know who Turner is, we used to go to school together. Do you want to tell me why two policemen are standing in my home?"

Davis turned towards his partner, then back at Sylvia.

"I'm sorry to be the one to tell you this Mrs. Dejour, but your husband…"

He's dead…Sylvia thought. Oh dear God he's dead, what am I gonna tell Brenda? Oh dear God no he's dead. I can't take it if he's dead. I hate him, but…but I think if he's dead. I'll miss him. What. What's wrong with me?

"Your husband was in a car accident." Davis finished.

Sylvia let out a little sigh, as if Davis noticed it, he looked at his partner. The sigh was one of relief and one of disappointment. Sylvia blinked twice, and rapidly before she felt the back of her knees give a little. They almost gave away all together. In her mind, the cop's words were slurred, but that was perhaps an afterthought.

If John Dejour was dead, she didn't know what she'd do. After all, Sylvia lived on the side of the fence many women like her live on but never climb over. The girls on the other side would cheer for the death of the cocksuckers of the world. The wife beaters like John Dejour to rot in hell. But women on Sylvia's side of the fence stay around hoping for change. Men like John Dejour don't ever change, but that hope keeps women like Sylvia alive. It's what they hold onto during those long stormy nights in bed when the sex is painful and the love hurts. Those nights when lovemaking is nothing but a distant dream, a hoax.

Women on Sylvia's side of the fence gather to pleasant discussions explaining that their husbands are good to them. They sit smiling, laughing, and lying to one another. In truth the only good man in an abused woman's life is either their father, or their grandfather, or any man on the other side of the fence. And yet some others would say, that the only good man in this world, is a dead man.

Sylvia would feel regretful of her husband's death because John Dejour was more than a wife-beating drunk. He was also the man who defended her no matter what in public. He was once the man who opened the car door for her no matter where they went. He was once the man who made love with her, the kind that maybe hurt, but hurt so good under the Christmas tree. He was the man who once brought her breakfast in bed morning after morning. The man who once followed her down the hospital hallway after her surgery and staying up night after night after night with Brenda when she was an infant.

He was the man who cleaned up her blood when the nurses wouldn't come in the hospital during a snowstorm. He was the man who stood by her side when her father died. John held her all night in his strong arms with his pleasant smell of Old Spice cologne. His dark hairs slicked back almost like Holly's husbands. John once was a man like Robert Raven. That glimmer in Robert's eyes of pure honesty and respect and brilliance mixed with a sexy confidence contained in a deep voice is what Sylvia remembered. That was perhaps the argument to Robert's theory. John Dejour wasn't born, as Robert would say to be a wife beater. No, John just became one.

There is nothing more brutally honest then that. The way a family dog sometimes grows old with a poisonous mind. The way the happy pooch grows tired of all the hands that pet, or just tired of being a dog at all.

"Is he alive?" Sylvia asked.

"Oh yes." Davis smiled.

"What happened?" Holly asked from the corner of the room.

"His truck hit another car in Pocomoke. Luckily, the car was parked. Your husband was drunken ma'am. He hit the car doing at least sixty. His head hit the windshield and he fractured a vertebra in his neck, other than that, he's got a few bumps and bruises. He's also got one heck of a laceration across his forehead. But I'm told he'll be okay."

"How long's he have to be in the hospital?"

"Don't really know ma'm," Davis said. "I believe that's a question for good ole Doctor Hobbs. He's the visiting practitioner. The State Police were the ones who found him and radioed it into Sheriff Turner. He called us while out on patrol so; we thought it best to stop by. I'd call the hospital in the morning. Don't go out tonight, the roads are slick. They're expecting it to sleet later on."

"No" Sylvia said. "I won't I'll call the hospital. Thank you both." Sylvia said.

They turned to leave and walked past Holly as she stood in the doorway.

"I'm sorry." Holly said.

"For what?"

"Your husband."

Sylvia couldn't respond, at least not at first. Instead, she looked around the room and suddenly it hit her. All the emotions swelling up like a great water balloon inside her finally burst to the absolution of sadness therein. Sylvia fell to the floor crying, and Holly ran to her side.

When she looked up again, Sylvia observed Holly holding her tight, and a second pair of arms holding her as well.

They were Robert's …

VIII.

The snow didn't reach WestPoint College, although the people living inside the brick walls wouldn't care either way. None of them were relevant people to Carper Falls save one. She was the daughter to a troubled mother who at the very moment was in devastation. At the top floor of the college along the east wing, a seeded, violent young woman studied through the night as the echoes of laughter and music could be heard outside. College parties were not interesting to Brenda Dejour.

Her professors admired her determination. Brenda Dejour was a top student. Her I.Q. was well over 180. She was not a jock although she shared a room with one. While the young adults who were to be the future of this world were all over campus finding places to fuck and get wasted, Brenda occupied her time in other ways. Brenda stayed in her room with her nose in the books. A man wrote the current book she was reading in the early 1900's describing vampirism and addressed numerous Hollywood stereotypes and other frictional theories unsupported by fact or historical documentation.

FROM THE CHRONICLE BIBLIOGRAPHY (UNDEAD TALES) VIOLATOR:

The word vampire derives from the Slavic word Vampir or Vampyre which first appeared in the 1600's in the Eastern European region of the Balkans. Vampyre is derived from UPIR, which first appeared in print from an Old Russian Manuscript, perhaps co-written by Barnabus Nodsley. In Novgordian prints, the legend more or less manifests itself. UPIR meaning (Wicked vampire) and thus, the legend commenced from there at least as bibliography.

The origin of the vampire is even more controversial; many ancients believe the word is derived from (witch) meaning one that casts from the dark. Barnabus Nodsley or Nola suggests just the opposite, which the term is pre-Croatian and means "to blow"

Although this has been modified from the Greek legends, if they were real at all in it's own paradox. The Greeks believed "To blow" is actually "To drink" and thus has become the culture in terms. In the dark ages drinking blood was often thought to be a remedy for diseases in which case the vampire was more or less a clinical absolution to illness. The vampire is also believed to be the link in a chain of a long line of inbreeding. It is the mixture of man, saint and sinner which devours darkness on a satanic scale.

The first vampire in recorded history was Lillith who was also the first wife of Adam in biblical times. She left Adam for Lucifer. In short, the bone of the quarrel was that Lillith would prefer to stand over Adam but God wanted man to rule. She in fact, wanted to take over the whole city of Jerusalem, and devour anything in her way, including children. Lillith is known as the queen of death and of demons. She is adorned in modern times by magicians and sorcerers and has been known to marry a man many moons ago and father a child. But this is perhaps myth.

All vampires are related through their blood to those that must be kept. It is unknown how Lillith spread her disease, but in fact used aggressive violation of children in the forgotten days by letting demons enter homes and take over the bodies of those weakened and deaf to God. In turn, mortals were turned into creatures that could no longer procreate.

But they could adopt...

And thus gave their souls to the damned. They must take mortal blood to survive and never tolerate daylight. In the course of the vampire, it becomes known to Barnabus Nodsley's writings that the undead become lesser related as time moves on and lesser inbred. Sunlight is part of the evolving threat, because in some beliefs a vampire caught in the sun not only is killed but their children are killed as well even while they sleep. This could be the reason for some odd occurrences of spontaneous combustion

A European vampire, one thought to have multiple wives and at times, could control the animals of this world. He was thought to be the devil and the reason for death period. A whole village suffered from disease and the disease itself very mysterious in being that none of the villagers who died from the disease really died at all. But their children disappeared.   Often times these disappearances were attributed to the undead that came to victims houses at night knocking on their doors asking to be let in.   If entry was refused, they would murder the livestock.   There is even documentation where the vampire climbed into marked graves of the dead and brought the godly back to life in an unholy embrace.   The consumption of blood was a sign and an obvious one, but also a man or woman with overly red lips and long white teeth were thought to be a vampire. A vampire corpse was disposed of in the, most awful but necessary ways. And these ways were certain.

Impaling the heart is not accurate. This is the death of a witch, but not one of the vampires. With the vampires association with appeal and death it is surprising even to a critic that the vampire is a friend of people as well as the dark. We must remember as humans still hearing the footsteps of God, the devil is a replication of all good will. A reflection in the mirror still smiling when we look away will often lead to bad things left over in the mind.   Many scholars that Barnabus Nodsley has interviewed had acquired the knowledge that more than 75% of vampires are in fact not undead, not from Satan's womb, but undeniably human with a touch of insanity.

More and more psychotics are born, and more and more unknowingly adopt the characteristics of monsters. The vampire is perhaps guarded and accepted because of its paradox with love and youth. The bonds of the vampire fascinate children that deal with virginity and first time dealings of sex, and the sexual imagery of hostility is witnessed through blood sucking and praying on the living's innocence. Barnabus Nodsley maintains that the vampire is appealing to the villagers as much as ones who are feared because they simply are "Horrifying". True horror is the next step towards the feeling of survival and subconsciously being glad to be alive at all.

Vampires are infinite, and they are, at least to Barnabus Nodsley, no more monsters than the monstrosities that make them this way. Everyone since the dawn of time has had at one time or another secret desires they push to the sides in their mind. More often then not they wish for those desires to surface. The contrast of the vampire and an angel of God are in fact, polar opposites.

The vampire is immortal, which has been the goal of man for ages and perhaps is the downfall of light in the flash. Men built pyramids in order to gain immortality. The supernatural have power over others, that is mystic blackened and magical which is very alluring to someone who has no power of their own. An abused wife, a lonely child, a town full of people wishing to be more than they are usually become a dark one's diet. The power and dominance contained in a vampire's dance with a human soul is won over in one vicious bite. The main belief by scientists and witch doctors is the context of vampire vastly differs within one psyche, which accounts from its diversity through interpretation. It could be truly said that the vampire does not exist at all, and is nothing more than a shared insanity suffered by the same type of people who believe they will eventually become immortal. More than not, the humans before being changed are sadomhastic and evil within anyway. Perhaps telling themselves they are truly incorporeal makes a man more of serial killers than a legend.

Another origin of the vampire is the paradox image of the Christ. A series of oppositions can be easily described. Blood represents life in Christian religion and the Eucharist. It's the transformation of wine into blood and bread into flesh. The vampire's total reversal of the Eucharist is that the vampire sucks the blood as Jesus gives it away. More interesting is the process of contamination by which the vampire is dividing it into new vampires, and then there is eternity. As the Christ lives through eternity, the vampire deals time against blood. The vampire is moving in an endless time, as the Christ will come at the end of all times. Christ is the energy that radiates in the universe a supernova if you will. The vampire is the end. He is a dark place where nothing comes out. Not love, not light, a constant and forever black hole where voices can still be heard.

Christ gives his life to save humanity as vampires take humanity's lives to save it. Both lay on wood before death. Christ against the cross, the haunted against a coffin. The nails of the cross correspond to the fangs of the vampire. Christ dies loosing blood from the wounds of the nails as vampires cause wounds for his or her survival. The kiss of death is but a parallel to the gift of life.

The Roman soldier who stabbed his spear into Jesus' chest is coincidental to the similarity of the perforation of the vampire's heart with a steak. On one hand, Christ lives through the divine escaping through his own wounds. On the other hand the vampire is destroyed but the god who created him, often times betrayed by love. The SUN/DOVE correspond and resolute through the MOON/BAT.

Barnabus Nodsley writes that the unholy vampire doesn't necessarily kill their victims, not the ones he has seen. It seems that they need a relatively small amount of blood from their victims. But most time, the victim dies from the constant return of dark kisses, being drained of their life. Vampires take perverse pleasure in killing their victims as they do in remaining secret, blending in with us all. Vampires can live without feeding for long periods of time, where they enter a state hibernation. They sleep in the dark, away from the sun, and in often myth, the vampire bitten is not a vampire until he or she drinks from its maker, and thus dies as if from being poisoned only to wake crawling from a grave with unhallowed eyes.

The victim is usually under domination from the master vampire, unless of course, the vampire chosen becomes the master. Only the death of a master vampire may release all victims of their curse. Barnabus Nodsley finds in some instances, this doesn't always happen, and not all vampires die in the sun. It's not widely accepted in the villages that vampires can live on animal blood. In European folklore it is widely popular that vampires have been known to assault cattle and other animals, even sheep and rats.

In society one would believe it would be easy to follow the vampire and spot them out from a crowd. By simply following a murder has proved false. The vampire is a clever creature that can easily dispose of its calamity. There is documented cases in 1812, that the vampire thought to be an ax murderer, chopped his victims into bloody chunks and ate them, what was left was fed to the dogs on a winter night. Although this would account for missing persons, it is not fact. Be that as it may, remember blood is blood alone is the vital element. A vampire cannot survive without feeding on fresh blood. As in every myth, the vampire is related to the internal struggle between life and death, good and evil, and it's the blood that bonds this together.

You may subscribe to these theories if you will, they have been stated because they exist, but there is no overly blaring fact they exist at all. There is a theory that states the hormone discovered by scientists in the body called EXP is the next stage in human evolution. A surgeon who performed an autopsy in 1894 discovered this hormone. This hormone is dormant and lives within the body, but becomes active after a vampire bite, this changes a human's physical form and in turn this new human can inject the hormone into another, a race of super human, which unfortunately aren't living anymore but still walking.

In another adjunct, vampires are thought to be the daughters of Lillith and in some belief of Eve. Sent by God on Earth to change men into the secret destroyers of cities in corruption. A walking disease that stops at nothing to destroy the evil already contained. The theory is to thwart the demonic offspring of angels, which according to Nodsley, has been known to happen and live among us. The legend of vampirism is almost undetermined in it's myths as well as doctored through legend. There were studies of ancient vampires called the Brahma Persia that were thought to be cannibals rather than vampires. They didn't don the stereotypical teeth Hollywood has recently bloated like a tick in a dog, but they did drink blood. They slashed the throats of many and carved bodies into rugs. The Brahma Persia for fun wore intestines on their heads like crowns. In 1820 settlers had killed them, when a few of their children were attacked.

Another fact is that vampires love to count. In ancient myth it is said that you can stop a vampire from leaving its coffin if you spread cloves or poppy seeds around its burial ground. It will spend the night counting rather than killing. This is thought to be a trait of psychological compulsive disorder, and may be manifested since the beginning of time. There are different names for vampires, has discovered. And different types as well.

"Strigoi" Is a common Romanian slang term for the vampire. The ancient myth of a wooden stake piercing a heart has also been blown up and out of the water. Some instances in the bibliography of ancient myth, a vampire can only be killed if you place blocks of wood

under their chin and nail their jaws shut. Then decapitate their heads from their bodies. The stake through the heart has been a glorified anvil for Hollywood to pound on. St. George's day is supposedly the holiday of the vampire, when a blood covenant is rekindled like a demon's wintry flame. In medical terms, it is thought that a vampire relies on the sustenance of blood perhaps because of the scientific need underneath.

Monocyte, for example is a chemical in the body that helps circulate. Some believe that the undead rely on the Monocyte to stay animate. Eosin Phil is another substance in the human body that creates antibodies in which cells use to attack parasites. This is believed to be a missing trait among the vampire. Legends report that the seventh child of the same sex will become a vampire. A child that is born out of wedlock, or a man or woman that has been excommunicated has more than a chance on becoming a slave of the night.

It was not only the blonde woman's acquisition into knowledge, but also what she had been doing in her extracurricular endeavors as well as that fed her. The knowledge of vampirism was a feeding in between. It kept the student free from becoming a slave to the voices for a time.

The voice in her head had grown to control her. Brenda Dejour's pretentious ways of wanting to be a legend herself had more than consumed her. It had driven Brenda mad.

The door opened to his dorm room, just as she began to think about Winter Raven.

There behind her stood the tall Asian girl named Atheos. Atheos held a young man's hand in hers. The young man held Atheos close and nudged her in the provocative yet horny way college boys and girls are accustomed too.

"What are you doing Brenda?" Atheos giggled.

"Studying."

"Studying? On a weekend?" Atheos laughed. Then her new lover laughed as well. He would grow up to marry a Doctor a few years from now. Atheos however wouldn't live past 23.

"You're always studying girl."

"Leave me alone please." Brenda said lowly. Her eyes shifted as she paused from reading.

"Here." Atheos said. "Have a beer."

"I don't drink."

Atheos rested a Budweiser on Brenda's desk. Brenda rolled her eyes then took the beer throwing it in the trash.

"What is your problem Brenda?" Atheos said.

"I said I don't drink, you know that,"

"I know." Atheos said. "I just thought maybe you'd want to have some fun for a fucking change."

Atheos boyfriend fell back on the bed drunk. It made Brenda uneasy. Her eyes swerved to the left seeing her man lying there with his denim-covered legs slightly spread. His arms splayed. His magnificent tight and bulging crotch called out to her.

"What do you want Atheos?" Brenda asked.

"Nothing. I just don't understand why you stay cooped up in here all the goddamned time."

"Because it's my time." Brenda said. "Let me have what's mine."

" Okay, okay. Damn you're such a fucking louse."

Brenda closed the book she was reading and turned towards her roommate.

"I got a joke for you Brenda."

"I don't like jokes. I don't care."

"Yeah but this one's funny."

"No jokes are funny." Brenda said.

"How can you tell when a man's satisfied?"

"I said I don't care." Brenda proclaimed.

"C'mon man, work with me here. How can you tell when a man's satisfied?"

Brenda looked on with contempt.

"Do you know?"

" No"

"Who gives a fuck?" Atheos laughed. Her physically commandeering arms pulled up on her boyfriend. Both party animals that they were ventured out into the hall and joined the congregation of laughter and partying.

Brenda slid her chair back and walked towards the door slamming it shut.

How dare they?

She thought. *How dare they venture into my domain and laugh at me? I should cut he boyfriend's throat. Maybe decapitate his head from his shoulders, and I'll make Atheos watch. And when it's all over I'll tell her, "You're right, who gives a fuck?"*

Instead, Brenda Dejour dove back into her words depicting long gloomy tales of the undead. When midnight had finally struck, she closed the book thinking about the upcoming weekend. Her father promised he would take her down to Ocean Pines and drive in the slow trailer parks or perhaps Ocean City. Once summer came she would have her license. She'd be like all the other young people driving to pick up hot members of the opposite sex. Brenda, however, would be driving behind all of them with a young toddler in the back seat. She'd laugh as the child struggled with his or her mouth duct taped. She'd listen to the radio about the police searching for the Violator. Brenda would be smiling knowing she has done it again, only now it was in her new mustang, her Nola. With fresh blood on her palms soaking into the leather steering wheel perhaps making the vehicle well on it's way into the world of being haunted.

These were utter fantasies however. She thought briefly about her younger years as she tied her blonde hair back into a ponytail. When she was five years of age, when times with her mother were good, before the shadows of her father's footsteps, and before the beast, and the rape. She couldn't remember a single memory of him that didn't contain something dark and twisted into a root of her inner self where the soil of a soul sours way down deep into dreams like a stake piercing an undead heart.

Her favorite times were with her mother. When she was five years old and had been outside playing along the hot summer, when the sun was still something of an admiring youth's dreams. Full of youth and admiration. Mom took time out of her busy job tending to the horses on Assaetegue Island. She could remember one particular moment when mom placed a kettle on her head and pretended to play army with her. During lunch, Brenda asked her about the birds and the bees and what that meant. Mom told her a long story about what a man and a woman's purpose was on this planet and Brenda told her it was hard to take her seriously with a kettle on her head. They both laughed.

But now those days are over. Brenda stared into the mirror of her lonely dorm room. A tear edged in her right eye like a lost drop of rain emerging on an insane asylum's window. They were distant memories that didn't seem real at all. What magic that was once contained in them had long since dissipated.

Brenda stood in front of the mirror and suddenly didn't see herself any longer. In the peeked reflection of a room swallowed by midnight darkness, she saw a black robed figure with violent violet eyes. Perhaps it was Barnabus Nodsley. Perhaps…it was Nola.

While out in the hallway, the laughter continued.

Suddenly, her cell phone rang.

Brenda turned away from the mirror. The robed figure did the same. She grabbed the phone and gulped.

"Hello?"

"It's me." her mother said.

"Mom?"

"Your father's in the hospital." Sylvia Dejour explained. "He had a car accident."

"Is he okay?"

"Yes." Sylvia said in desperation, "He's okay, few broken bones, so I'm told. I called up to the hospital and they said he was sleeping, so I haven't gotten a chance to really do much. I'll wait for you to come home and we can go together."

"Okay." Brenda said. "I'll leave right now."

The phone found it's home in Brenda's faded jeans. She pulled her jacket on and grabbed her wallet. Looking at her watch made her realize she needed to hurry if she was going to catch the last bus out of Lancaster to the train station in Wilmington. There she would take the Amtrak to Pocomoke. Her mother would pick her up in the morning and drive on to Salisbury Hospital. Brenda closed the dorm room behind her knowing her roommate had been lucky. She was planning to kill her and taste all she had to offer in the way of crimson.

Sheriff Turner drove to work at the small precinct off of route 50 in Carper Falls feeling sick to the stomach. At first, he believed it was hunger pains. He pushed his spectacles further up the bridge of his nose. He took a bite out his morning sandwich listening to the radio for the local news. The sheriff was still in shock from the recent murders befalling the town. This remote area of Maryland had become a great stomping ground for one evil son of a bitch. The FBI did all they could to keep the Sheriff and his men out of the loop. Of course, he would be there if they needed him, but in truth Harrison Turner knew very little of serial murderers.

The small town law enforcement official had never been exposed to anything so vile in all his years as a cop. He was what Robert Raven would call an amateur. However, he knew what the text book said about these types of madmen. At some point all of them would let their guard down. All of them at some point wanted to be caught in order to gain recognition of their work. The Violator was here to stay. Sheriff Turner would see to it, come hell or high or water, that they would catch this freak.

The chime of the door entering to the police station made the three deputies on duty jump for a moment. Bonnie Raiff, head of the call center, looked up in bewilderment. They anxiously hoped that maybe Davis or one of the other deputies would be escorting the madman into county lock up. Carper Falls police barracks was only big enough to hold three prisoners. The State Police usually sent a van over from Cumberland to transport additional prisoners to larger facilities. In the past, the police barrack never needed more than the occasional van. Carper Falls was a spoiled community, where crimes were few and far in between.

"Good evening Bonnie." Sheriff Turner said. "Quiet I take it?"

"Yep." Bonnie said. "Three people called in about where they can get chains for their tires. I told them Maryland's law about chains."

"It's not even snowing yet." Turner said, taking of his police coat and hat.

His stomach remained trim under the vanity of his bulletproof vest. A vest he has never worn in his life. Now days it was like MasterCard, whereas he didn't want to leave home without it.

"They say storms are gonna be pretty bad." Bonnie declared.

Turner poured himself a cup of coffee, as Deupty Davis walked down the lobby past him.

"Davis." Turner said. "You did talk to the Dejour woman up on Main Street last night, am I right?"

"Yes sir."

"Everything's okay then?'

"Everything's fine"

"You're a good man Davis. I want you and Harvey Dickman to be careful out there, especially if you pull double shifts. This maniac has been known to use a gun, so watch your back."

"Yes sir." Davis said, opening the door to the frosty morning air.

Turner walked onward towards his office. He wondered about madmen like the Violator. His mind went to how Devena Mirrow was found with her pants down and her guts spread out like a grotesque map to the world of cannibals. Is a serial murderer ultimately on a quest for sex or power?

Turner knew some killers would indulge in illusions of religious grandeur. He has heard once of a maniac from a small town in Garrison City Pennsylvania called Shallow Front who desecrated a whole town. He claimed to be the Anti-Christ. A lust murderer intertwines their domination and lust so tightly they bleed into one another thus making it difficult to determine where sexual depravity leaves off, and where the need for blood takes over.

Was the Violator of Carper Falls sadistic? It sure seemed possible. One thing was for certain to Turner and his men. He was the subject of all their nightmares.

IX.

Stationed like a majestic temple to some forgotten god, poised against the oncoming winter, stood the historical Salisbury Hospital. Its five floors (six if you count the parking garage) towered towards the sky in inexplicable detail. Like any hospital, only the most professional and dedicated of souls could work within its walls.

Betty Keen, the attending nurse, left Jonathan Dejour's room holding a vague thunder within her soul. After all, the patient in Room 76 was one cruel son of a bitch. He had awoken early on Friday morning before the Hotrod festival in Ocean City demanding to use the phone to call his useless wife. Betty, another attending nurse, as well as the practicing physician told him not to move. The doctor explained that he could use some rest. He needed it that was for sure. Instead John filled his urinal under the sheets and when the nurses asked if he was done he threw it across the room. John was afraid of no man, and certainly not a woman. His abuse ran high and intolerable.

The slow morphine drip brought him exciting and fantastic visions, and placed him into dream world. Some of the dreams he wouldn't remember, but all of them he didn't much care for. He dreamt of Carper Falls mainly. He dreamt of a yellow diseased sky. The yellow shimmered down like a dense fog opaque with mist. The local venues he often frequented in the real life were gone in his sleep. Everything was gone. The people that ran Carper Falls and made it what it what it was. The newsstand downtown. The post office. They were all replaced by a deep, moronic, disturbed quiet that no postcard would fit for a tourist.

John awoke in slurred speech. His right eye was closed from slamming his face against the window of his old truck and exploding the glass across the highway. Stitches ran their course along his temple. He saw himself in the large hospital room mirror near the right side of the wall. The last thing he remembered when he awoken, was the yellow skies in his dreams. They scared him although he would never admit it to anyone.

The clouds in the dark place of his mind the clouds were bleeding like over soaked cotton balls, and the blood rained down on Carper Falls like explosions in meat factories. There were people running everywhere with their mouths open trying to catch the bloodlike children try to catch snowflakes. The more the crazed people tasted the blood, the more of it they wanted. In his dream he was not one of them. Somewhere in his confusion lost by the morphine drip, he saw his daughter in the Mustang. Written across the top of the windshield were words dripping in blood. This one said ENOLA, and the girl behind the wheel who used to be John's daughter was smiling at him. He smile contained teeth like that of a cobra. They were glistening like her eyes. Her beautiful blue eyes were gone like the skies above. They were black now, reflecting the yellow of a dead sky. The Caper falls in his dreams was a place where where nothing but doom and magic blacker than a sea of sorrow dwelled, flooding the soul with blood, and leaving behind a taste for new things.

Out with the old, in with the new.

She wanted to kill John.

She wanted to kill John for hurting mommy.

In his dreams he walked closer to the mustang. The muscle car sat idling with a twisted growl from the 8-cylinder engine underneath. Before his daughter opened the car door to grab him by his drunken state and drain him dry. Before she tore his neck open and swallowed his jugular vein, like a straw to a fountain drink. John saw something in the passenger seat of his daughter's Mustang. Something lying under a towel soaked with blood.

" Wha-"

Before John could finish his words, his daughter in pigtails smiled wider at her father. She ripped the towel from the passenger seat revealing Brenda's unborn sister.

"You killed her."

John's terror gripped him.

"Daddy." Brenda said. "I've gotten what I've always wanted. I've gotten what I've needed. I'm a vampire now...*daddy*, and I came to show you the things I brought back from the dead. What you took from Mom."

Brenda lifted the mangled corpse of her sister who never had a chance at life. The sister she would have name named Enola, if mom had asked her.

John awoke on a subtle Friday morning in a daze. His heart was beating fast. His pulse pounded through his jugular vein.

You kicked her.. Daddy.

You kicked mom, with those same boots you kicked me with.

My face hurts like a motherfucker, was the first conscious thought that passed through John's mind. His eye that had been closed with contusions felt heavy and horrible. When he reached over to the right for a glass of water, he discovered he wanted to call the nurse.

There was a man in the corner.

John's good eye squinted, then widened as he tried to see what was before him. He knew it was a man because of the long thin legs covered in black dress pants. The shoes the shadowy figure wore were dressy as John saw through his peripheral vision.

"Hello John" said a voice from the shadows.

John's heart had slowed down with the revelation that his previous visions were only dreams. The new terror however was real and his heart began racing again. The voice was that of his own father, Clint. His father used to come home and beat him for no reason. He would always say hello before he did. John couldn't see the man's face, but imagined it. He could see his father's commandeering scolding look bearing down on him.

"Who are you?" John asked.

"A friend."

John tried to turn his face towards the upper body of the man, but the man's torso and face were in the shadows of early sunrise.

"What are you doing here?" John asked.

"Same thing as you." the voice said. "Trying to ascertain why I'm here at all. Do you know why you're here John?"

"I had an accident." John said. "A car accident. Are you a Doctor or something?"

"Something." the voice said. "And if you keep treating your wife the way you are, I will be something *more*."

John's eyes widened with a tinge of fright. His impulse flared. He couldn't see a face and didn't want too either.

"I'm here today to give you a warning my friend. I would advise you to listen when I say no man should beat on a woman. A man that beats on a woman is no man at *all*."

"Is that a fact?" John said.

"That *is* a fact." the shadowy figure said. "And here's another one if you choose not too take me seriously. I know where you live. I've seen the things you've done. I've heard the screams of your wife and daughter from miles away. I know the clothing you wear. I know everything about you Mr. Dejour, except the day you'll die. But if you don't take this meeting seriously, I'll know that too, and so will you."

"FUCK YOU!" John snapped.

Suddenly, the man from the corner of the room was gone.

It's just these drugs. These goddamn drugs are making me crazy!

Leaning his head back against the pillow, John looked up at the ceiling seeing the tiles and beams between. Suddenly, he wondered if it was real at all. First, the dreams, and now out of sleep he was seeing things. He closed his eyes and breathed deeply. When he opened them again the man in the corner was now in front of his bed standing under the television his face still in the dark. However, there was something new to the characteristics of John's mysterious visitor.

The man was smiling. All John could see of him was his mouth and chin. Inside the smile were pearly white teeth. The upper ones on each end were longer than the rest elongated to thin cannibalistic points, thin as bony needles. They seemed to spring from the stranger's maw at his very own dark chilling words.

"Your such a ladies man Mr. Dejour. Let's see you get up out of that bed and beat me motherfucker. You like using your fists right? Come on John come use them on me. I promise I'll let you live long enough to watch me peel your face off in the mirror. I should come over there and draw some blood for the lab myself. See how much chicken shit you have really running in your veins."

John closed his eyes. *Not there! Not there goddamnit*!

John opened his eyes and screamed. Before him, inches from lips, a kiss away, was the face of a creature talked about in movies and books. It was a man, one with a long pallid chin and stretched out ruby red lips like a leech in love. Inside its mouth were those perfect teeth, including the unusually long ones. John saw its gray eyes. The eyes of the evil in John's room were the color of all the tombstones on Cobble Avenue; including the one his name would be on if he didn't take Robert Raven seriously.

"SSSSSSUUUUCK!" The thing screamed. John screamed in terror as the vampire closed its mouth. Blood ruptured from each side of its lips, as if tit's mouth was too small to hold such brilliant teeth.

The vampire yelled into John's face.

"HOW DO YOU LIKE ME NOW MOTHERFUCKER? HOW DO YOU LIKE ME WIFE BEATER! DO YOU WANT ME INSIDE YOUR VEINS DRIVING YOU CRAZY?"

"NO!" John cried out in tremendous terror, turning away from the thing in his room.

"I'll make you sorry John." Robert said, walking slowly backwards out of the light into the dark towards the front door.

"This is your last chance. Leave her alone, or you'll die in a way you can't possibly imagine."

He saw those eyes in the dark. They backed away from him towards the door to the room.

The eyes became beady and sunken like caves filled with oil. Just before the door opened to Betty the nurse John saw those eyes tinge with reflection. It was like into a cat's when you catch them in headlights. Like looking into two dime sized mirrors. The door opened on those eyes. Impossibly there was no collision between the doorway's occupants. Betty the nurse entered with a pissed off look on her face. She wondered why the patient in front of her was riddled with sweat.

"Mr. Dejour, seriously."

"DID YOU SEE HIM!" John panicked.

The nurse stepped forward.

"See who?"

"HE WAS THERE!"

99

Betty tried to calm John down. Before he entered into John Dejour's room the attending physician heard the sounds of a muscle car booming outside the window.

That evening the Dejour women met at the bus stop in Pocomoke. The pile of cigarette butts told Brenda that her mother was smoking way too much lately. There was something in her mother's eyes that worried her. A look of thickening madness from brutality. Sylvia didn't want to admit it to anyone, especially not Brenda, but she in fact was loosing her mind.

"Hello mom."

Sylvia reached out to hug her daughter. She could feel the tears wetting her shirt underneath her jacket. The human mind can only take so much before its damns give way to the flood of misery overwhelms the mind.

"It's okay mom." Brenda said. "He'll be okay."

"I don't care." Sylvia said with sorrow, wiping her nose with an already half-used clean-ex.

She lit another cigarette.

"What do you mean?" Brenda asked concern.

"Your father treats me like shit!"

Sylvia leaned forward and placed her head against the steering wheel. Brenda didn't know about the five messages that awaited Sylvia when the police left her home.

"WHERE ARE YOU FUCKIN BITCH!" Message number 1 said.

Then a dead click.

"YOU BETTER NOT BE OVER THERE WITH THOSE FAGGOTS!"

Message number 2.

"WHEN I GET HOME SILLY SYLVIA, YOU AND I ARE GONNA TALK!"

Message number 3.

"YOU DON"T LOVE ME YOU CUNT FACE!"

Message number 4.

"I'm GOING TO-"

Message number 5 followed by the sounds of a grunt and a heavy crash.

Then Sylvia began to cry. She fell into the arms of her friends, Holly and Robert Raven. The snow danced in the doorway because as her friends called her and she called her daughter.

Fatigue began to catch Sylvia as she drove along the night passages of route 13 with her daughter. Her mind drifted from the snow filled highway.

She remembered at one point seeing someone standing in her doorway as tears escaped her eyes as she felt the warm love of new friends. Someone was standing in the doorway of her home. Snow fell behind his dark silhouette. The lurid glow of the blue streetlight cast a horrifying presence upon him. It was the Violator. Sylvia knew it. While her friend's were holding her, listening to the messages on the answering machine, the Violator had come to her home. He had come with a pair of scissors. He had come to ravish her.

But it wasn't the Violator. It was nothing more than shifting shadows of stripped naked trees. Robert held her the tightest, and looked at her with a serious gainful face. A long face, foxy and full of tight wound brilliance. Sylvia couldn't stop the tears when he reached out to hold her close again. Holly held her close from behind. Finally, Robert took her gently by the face and lifted it up to meet his. She forgot why she was upset until Robert mentioned the messages.

Robert's eyes were gentile gray. As she looked into them something happened. Something inside her snapped just like a rusty faucet bearing the weight of a reservoir. Something let loose and Sylvia spilled the beans. She told Holly and Robert what John did to her. They kept holding her close, and then closer, and then closer.

They told her it would be okay. It would be okay because they already knew.

Robert whispered into Sylvia's left ear.

"Every prayer you whisper, every wish you desire, can all be yours if you choose it."

She became lost in their loving embrace. She felt as though she could stay there forever. For once in her awful life, Sylvia felt safe in someone else's arms. When she opened her eyes again she was lying on her sofa feeling woozy. There was a glass full of ice and whiskey by her side. Under the glass, a coaster remained. Under the coaster, was a note.

. Holly sat up from the sofa. She was wondering what she would tell her daughter that day. She put off that responsibility until later that evening. She looked down at the note, which was written in that alluring poetic scripture writing like that of the candle her wonderful husband had smashed in a rage.

She looked closer at the note. As she did her long wavy blonde hair fell away from her shoulders revealing her neck, and the two puncture wounds half way up the side of the milky white flesh.

The note said:

Do you want me to talk to him for you?

Truly,
Robert.

When she went to the bathroom and fell ill. She thought about her new friends the Ravens. As she thought of the new neighbors from Vegas the side of her neck began tingling. In the mirror however the reflection shown nothing more than a woman growing used to abuse. They say the mirror does not lie. Perhaps that is a saying that remains relevant only to those of us that are still alive…

"I hate him," Sylvia said, placing the car in a lower gear.

"Mom, don't say that."

"Are you serious Brenda? Come on." Sylvia yelled, puffing away at her cigarette.

"You've seen what he's done. You've seen the things he's done to me, to both of us. How can you say don't say that?"

"I don't want to talk about it mom. It makes me crazy." Brenda exclaimed, reaching in her pants pocket suddenly feeling frantic.

All she could think about was blood and…and…fire.

Brenda groped the rabbit's foot.

"We're not a normal family Brenda. You know that. Ever since I was pregnant, John has changed. He slipped into booze and drugs while I had to take care of you. Can't you see that?"

I see it the entire time mom. Brenda thought. *Through the eyes of those whom beg me to stop.*

"Yes I know." Brenda said. "But don't force me to take sides. I can't do that."

"Sometimes we have to pick a side Brenda. Sometimes there isn't a choice." Sylvia threw her spent cigarette away

"And besides, I'm not asking you to do that. I'm asking you to see the truth, and know what's going on."

"I know." Brenda said calmly, rubbing the rabbit's foot in her pocket. "I know what you're trying to say, and I agree mother. But what do you wan me to do?"

Sylvia remained quiet. Her eyes fixated on the dark road. Her Pontiac drove along Route 13 towards Salisbury, Maryland.

"So how is school?" She changed the subject.

"School's fine." Brenda looked out the window as the cold rain pelt heavy. "I passed my Bibliography exam. I'm having a hard time with Professor White's class."

"You'll get it." Sylvia smiled. "You were always smart. Always different."

Brenda suddenly felt afraid for her mother. Looking at her was like looking at a deer, as it stood dumbfounded caught in the headlights of a car. Her mother was lost at the bottom of abuse where the long light of morning can never be found to show her bad things can change. She felt sorry for her and angry all at the same time. Why didn't she leave if it was so bad?

Because sometimes, there is no place to run to, and no place to hide. Brenda thought.

Brenda Dejour's eyes drifted down to her mother's seat seeing a block of foam padding. She inadvertently never realized it until now, that there may be something wrong with her mother. When they used to all go to the car shows together she started putting that padding on the seat. That extra padding Brenda thought was so she could look up over the dashboard. Sylvia Dejour was a relatively petite woman after all. Now Brenda felt troubled knowing the foam pad might possibly be for another reason.

They pulled into the hospital parking lot, twelve minutes after Robert Raven had left. The rain had calmed to fine ice-cold drizzle, compliments of the weatherman's lies of sunshine. The morning had burst into the winter friendly sky by the time Sylvia and Brenda had arrived.

In John Dejour's room, the television was loud. He was watching the morning show. Anchors from WBOC 13 were describing the bizarre killings taking place in Carper Falls. The news people placed all the photos of the smiling victims on the screen and in related news, posted another crime that transpired last year in Pennsylvania. The Violator had killed Dawn Ambrose in a similar fashion.

His room door opened and the tall lengthy college girl John had raped once came into the room. John loved his daughter but sometimes the lines between love and rage get blurred in life. John just never loved his daughter, until recently. He admired her. He admired her for keeping her mouth shut for all these years. He didn't love her on the day she was born, and loved hr less then his wife. But recently there was a feeling inside him that made him feel it. He guessed that perhaps it was part of the old saying you don't know what you have until it's gone. Now his only daughter was running off to college with the dirty little secret of what he once did to her on that stormy night. He admired her for that at least. Her perseverance was astonishing. John wondered where she got her motivation and drive

And behind Brenda came the bitch. The thorn in his side. The reason everything bad that transpired for the past four years. LOUSY COOK, LOUSY LAY, LOUSY HOUSE WIFE. John believed that sometimes you can beat a person bloody all you want, but stupid is very deep and will not come out with the blood.

"Dad." Brenda said.

Seeing her father lying shirtless on the bed with sheets up to his navel made her cringe. So did his massive beer belly. On his chest were cables and diodes regulating his heartbeat. In his right hand were IV needles.

"Hello Brenda." John said. "I guess it's safe to say we won't be going driving this weekend."

" That's okay." Brenda said.

She looked at the floor. Her hands were thrust into the pockets of her coat. She didn't like looking at her father this way, no matter what he has done to her or mom. His hair was all over the place. His right eye looked like a swollen plum. The doctors had to pierce the skin right under the epidermis to let the fluid drain. A bandage crossed his forehead. On his neck was a plastic brace keeping his head immobile. The top of the brace was pushed on the under side of his cheeks making him look morbidly goofy.

"And how are you Silly?" John asked his wife.

His good eye widened. Sylvia could see all the beatings to come in it. It was as reflective as the bathroom mirror.

"You miserable bitch, my wife, how's it been without me...hmmm? I bet you can't wait till I get out of here can you?"

"John. Please." Sylvia said. "We came to see you, not to fight."

"Oh." John said with belligerence. "I'm not going to fight Sylvia. I'm not going to cause any more problems for you or Brenda. I'm moving out when I get home, or I may end up doing something I may regret."

Sylvia looked over at her daughter, then back at her husband.

Do you want me to talk to him for you? Instantly sprang into Sylvia's head.

"Well, we just stopped by is all." Sylvia said calmly, her eyes rimmed with red. She looked down at the floor then back up at the man sitting in the bed like a hurt puppy.

"You both should try this shit they got leaking into my spine keeping me calm. It makes you see things be damn, things you wouldn't believe."

"Like what" Sylvia said.

"I really can't remember to tell you the truth." John said. "But I know now it was all a dream. Had to do with a bunch of people in Carper Falls and...wait, let me think. That's right, there was a man in this room when I woke up."

"A man?"

105

"Yep. He was a vampire."

Brenda's eyes widened.

"Are you serious pop?"

"Would I lie to you?" John asked.

It's a sign. Brenda thought. *It's a sign like the Mustang was a sign. Like all the children are signs. Dad's having dreams just like I used to have them. When I went back to college last week the first night I dreamt of all these balloons and they were talking to me like the voices in my head. The voices that tell me it's okay to be a vampire. I want to be a vampire more than God wants the world. There were decapitated children lying everywhere in the town square, and there heads were inside the floating balloons. They were dark blue balloons and inside were the heads of all the young teenagers I've set free. They were talking to me, asking me if everything's okay. They want me to become what I've failed to become. But I will, oh make no mistake; I will become the queen of the nighttime world.*

"Well it's almost time for Nurse Betty to come check my blood pressure. Although it's been fun, you both wasted my time for nothing." John said.

"It's okay tough." John added, looking at the two women in his life who were staring back in disbelief.

"I'll be coming home soon sweeties." He smiled as both women turned to leave.

Outside in the hall, Sylvia walked facing the floor. She cried all the way to the elevator. She would never see her husband again. Brenda stayed behind only for a few minutes and was promised by her father that they would take that Mustang out for one spin as soon as he got out of the hospital.

X.

Sylvia slept soundly that night. Her daughter did not.

Instead, she climbed out of the window as she often done. Slowly, carefully descending down the backside of the house till she could jump free to the ground. She was in old jeans, and a jean jacket. On her hands were tight leather gloves. Normally she would have slept, but this was one of those nights like all those nights years ago that started the fires. The voices of Enola wouldn't let her sleep. They were the cries for the Violator.

It was two in the morning as January neared its end. The Violator walked on towards Main Street as an ice-cold wind kept her awake. Her feet were thundering with every step. Her mouth was dry with the anticipation of something ...

Out with the old, in with the new...

Something that would take all the headaches away and leave behind sweet validity. She didn't know where to start and worried as if her mother would awake and check in on her. Mothers had a habit of always worrying about their babies. The Violator felt a cool calm newfound brilliance. She wondered if Billy Owens's mother felt the same motherly impulses. She smiled thinking that his mother slept peacefully knowing her son was safe in the next room. Something about that made Brenda Dejour feel gratified. It made her feel that this was well worth coming out in the cold for. It was all worth the stained jeans and the latex monster mask she was wearing.

This isn't Halloween. Brenda argued in her mind.

Everyday is Halloween Brenda. And there is never a holiday without a funeral.

She wore the tight mask all the way to Maple Street. Somehow she remembered where Billy Owens lived. When she used to deliver newspapers Billy had been an infant. Now he was a charming five years old boy. Brenda was thrilled by the fact she was able to wear the mask right up to the front without being caught. That was part of the game. The initiation into becoming a vampire was seeing how much guts you had when it came to taking chances of being caught.

The devil mask peeked into the window and there was little Billy Owens, lost somewhere in his dreams of crayons and chocolate fun. Not understanding, evil, or knowing what murder really was. His little form called out to her. His small body rose peacefully from the breathing. Brenda stood in the dark wearing the mask and felt powerful, new, and strong with the desire to kill.

She stared at the sheets covering Billy Owens while his parents slept in the room across the hall.

Maple Street, which ironically has no trees on it, went on for five miles and was around a bend lost in the dark. Along the bend, a lane cut sharply through the woods leading to the train tracks several hundred yards behind it. Eventually a stream appears out of nowhere and near the streams origin, is a half-kilter shack.

This is where Brenda Dejour dragged the young toddler still in his pajamas, kicking and trying to scream. Brenda already had sliced his right ear clean off, but the little fucker had so much fear. Billy Owens tried to scream for his mother, but those screams were at most muffled in comparison to what her other victims had been. Billy Owens little tightly wound terrified face was filled with a horror no person or words could describe. The man carrying him was not a man, but a woman. Billy believed it was the boogieman for sure. The thing carrying him with its arms around his neck was the monster of all monsters. Billy saw the face of what held him. It was the face of a demon long and stretched with jagged teeth and flaring nostrils. It was the cross between the Chinese parade dragons seen on television and a deadly diseased witch who perhaps took the time out of life to vomit razorblades.

Into the dark both of them had gone. Into the void of fantastic terror, where the Violator spent the next two hours talking with the young boy and playing all kinds of games.

Sheriff Turner received a call from Rachel Owens, Billy's mother, that her son was missing. It was the first call of the morning and one that would be the most remembered. It took the sheriff several attempts to calm the woman down for him to understand what she was saying. Turner sent two patrolmen out to her house. They were given a letter Rachel found in her mail slot. Apparently her son's abductor had come back and delivered the note. Officer Davis placed the letter in a plastic baggy, and commenced with a statewide search for the missing Owens boy. The rest as they say, is history.

Sheriff Turner delivered the letter to Brad Corbin, head of the crime division investigating the killings in Carper Falls. Grim faces looked at the folded piece of paper realizing that the letter would contain nothing hopeful. It was carefully examined for fingerprints. The only prints found were Rachel's. There were bloodstains on the letter, which were compared to Rachel's and tested positive on her DNA. The letter was something new to the investigators of Carper Falls. This killer was jumping around in his relative characteristics. He had never written a letter before and the FBI had wondered why he felt compelled to do it now.

Billy says hi and goodbye. I brought him to the train tracks just north of the Valley Woods Preserve. You'll find him there. I'm sure you know the place. I've been here before and I guess so have you, am I right? There is a shed that stands alone not far from the train tracks. I stripped him naked you see. I tied his hands and feet and gagged him with a rag I picked up off the ground. Then we talked while I burned his clothes. Once the clothing is gone from a person, only then do you get down to <u>wear</u> it really makes sense. My father taught me that. I took an old leather strap I found in the shed and whipped his behind. I believe little Billy was a bad boy. I was once a bad person too, but I'm different now. I found a way to live forever. To become immortal. It's through blood of the young. I've been baptized in the magic of other women's offerings from their wombs. Children are such easy pray, and taste soooo good. To live forever is the oldest human desire. It's an ancient secret that one has to become vampires to live forever.

I cut off his nose and ears. Then I slit his mouth from ear to ear while he begged for me to stop. While he begged for his mother. I gouged out his eyes with my thumbs and left him there in the dark for a while. I left him blind and guessing what I'd do to him next. I stuck a knife in his little belly and held my lips to the hole and drank his blood. Then, I cut him too pieces. I put his nose, ears and a few slices of his stomach in the fire. I cut off his head, his feet, and his arms and ate them. You hear me motherfuckers? I ate them.

    Truly,
Enola...
Or, The Violator as you badges call it.

The law enforcement officials read in silence. All were mystified at the sheer insanity and brutality of what they had just read. The maniac they sought was methodical and all feared that it might be impossible to catch him with little information as they had available.

That Saturday morning, a knock fell on the door of Sylvia Dejour's home. Low and behold, Robert Raven was there to greet her in broad daylight. He stood tall and ravishing in the morning sun. He six foot two at least stance. He was wearing those black Ray Bans in which Sylvia could see her frail reflection.

    "Hello"
    " Good morning." Robert said. "Mind if I come in?"
    "Not at all."
    "Coffee?"
    "No thanks." He smiled.
    "You don't mind if I have some then?"
    "Not at all Sylvia." Robert smiled. "It's your morning."
    Sylvia walked away suddenly wondering how little she knew about the stranger in her house. It occurred to her while she poured the coffee that Robert Raven could very well be The Violator. Briefly she thought about her husband. She already had gotten used to the idea of him coming home next week and leaving forever. Hopefully, John wouldn't lie about what he said.
    When she returned to the living room Robert was eyeing the television. Local news crews were down in Ocean City. Jennifer

Pastenelli was standing amongst concession stands talking about the hotrod festival that would begin at noon. It was still two hours before the hotrod festival would quickly become a thing of the past the worldwide media would be consumed with disappearance of yet another youth in Carper Falls.

"I hope the snow holds off for the festival." Sylvia said. "Later I may take Brenda down there, get our minds off the bad stuff."

"That's actually why I'm here." Robert said.

His face tightened into a bright-eyed seriousness.

"It is?"

"I was wondering if your daughter would like to drive there with me this morning. I know you mentioned it before that her father was to take her test-driving this weekend. Since he was in an accident, maybe I can help."

"What are you asking me Robert?" Sylvia said.

She took a sip of coffee.

"I'm saying that bad stuff can be thought about later. I wanted to help you and your daughter get your minds off of things happening in this town."

"My wife is taking Winter in about an hour. I thought that maybe Brenda would like to drive with me. We can get to know each other. I like being the neighbor, especially in trying times."

"I'm sure she'd love that." Sylvia said. "I hear her upstairs now."

While they talked, Brenda stood in the shower. A hot spray of water ran down her budding breasts rinsing the blood from her lower face and chest down to the drain in the floor. She was smiling in the steam, thinking about Enola. Thinking about the vampire books she's been reading. The blood mixed with soap ran from her curvy body, down into her pubic hair, and rinsed clean. She closed her eyes and thought of Billy Owens. How his little fingers tasted between her teeth when she bit down to hear the bones crack almost made her burst out laughing. Through her midnight escapade she had bitten into her tongue. It stung and blew pain throughout her mouth. She lifted her face towards the ceiling where the voices were loud in the shower.

111

"I can't." Brenda said. As what was left of Billy Owens ran down the drain in one gurgling liquid scream.

"I can't kill her." she whispered.

In a few minutes, the door opened downstairs. Brenda Dejour walked down them. Her hair was still damp, but she was in a fresh t-shirt with the words CURVE written on it in purple lettering. She was wearing tight jeans that were no longer stained with baby brains. She stopped at the base of the stairs. There in front of her sat a man in her father's favorite chair wearing a dark leather jacket, and a black turtleneck sweater underneath. His face was pale and his eyes were a deep gray. His black hair was cut short and pushed forward into a widow's peak. Perhaps this man was a cop. His eyes squinted when he observed Sylvia's daughter stop. His eyes became exploratory.

"You must be Brenda." Robert stood holding out his long fingered right hand.

"I am." Brenda said shaking it.

"It's a pleasure. I've been talking with your mother contemplating the idea of going to the Hotrod festival. I was curious if you would like to come along with me. Your mother was going to drive with my wife and daughter."

"You own that old Mustang don't you?" Brenda said, as it suddenly came to her.

This was the guy I saw downtown at the newsstands.

"Yes." Robert said. "The one everyone seems to bring up in conversation now and then. 1970 Shelby Cobra raked in the rear and mean as all hell. I was thinking you could go with me to Ocean City. You can drive if you want."

What Robert said shocked both the women.

"What?" Brenda asked. Her eyes were blinking fast.

Robert smiled, which was something he didn't seem accustomed to doing.

"You can drive us down there. Tell ya what I'll do. I'll drive down to the old Antique Store out in the outlets. It's deserted. Then you can practice there. Then when you have it down, including the shifting, you can drive us to Ocean city."

"Oh boy." Sylvia said. "I don't know about this."

"Mommmm." Brenda said.

Sylvia looked into her daughter's eyes and realized this was something her daughter needed.

" Okay, just be careful, both of you."

Along the way, Brenda Dejour sat in the black Mustang. The car was equally as dark inside. Inside the car the two sat on the black vinyl seats when suddenly a slight vibration occurred as the car sprung to life. The Mustang roared along the cold grounds of Carper Falls, while people looked on in envy. The muscle car was all Brenda ever wanted. Robert reached behind her, flipped open a plastic case and withdrew a CD. He inserted the CD in the dashboard player which was something not invented in the 70's. They only had 8 tracks back then. Those people that had any experience with them knew in fact that 8 track players were not worth a fuck in the snow.

KISS came on the speakers. That's when Robert looked over at his neighbor that. The girl was only a few years older than his daughter was. He gave her a smile of adoration, pleasurable, and bewilderment.

"So…Brenda, I hear you're studying vampires?"

Brenda's eyes widened in surprise. She turned to look as the man with the dark sunglasses. Suddenly Robert smiled.

"Can't keep anything from mother you know."

"Yeah." Brenda smiled. "I'm fascinated by them. I actually did a report, well, more of bibliography reports on demonology. Part of it was research on the history of vampires."

"Yeah." Robert said. " But correct me if I'm wrong Brenda, you're a bit passionate on this subject, are you not?"

Brenda didn't respond.

"Vlad?"

"Excuse me?" Brenda said.

"Vlad the Impaler?"

"What about him?" Brenda asked with a smile, rolling down her window to catch a breath of fresh air.

" I've done a lot of research myself. Vampires were fascinating to me when I was young. I suppose they still are."

"It's a bit funny. You have a Mustang. I have a Mustang. We both have studied vampirism. Although I've studied vampirism, for a much longer time."

"For college?" Brenda asked.

But Robert responded with a blank look to the road ahead.

"It's as if we are one in the same. Except for the fact you are a woman, and I am a man. Perhaps we are from alternate universes."

"Now that's something I don't believe in." Brenda Said.

"Why not?" Robert asked as the car thundered along.

He downshifted, as he approached the vacant lot. Brenda not only admired the fierceness of the Mustang but the components therein. The shifter knob was a chrome skull with light-up red eyes. Robert's leather driving gloved hands wrapped around it and smoothly transferred the gears. Finally they came to a halt in the empty parking lot.

"I don't randomly believe in something I don't have proof exist."

Robert laughed at the young woman.

"You mean something you don't care if it exists."

He lit a cigarette.

"Brenda, I believe you know very much, and are in fact a bright young woman. You're gonna have to forgive me when I say this, but why haven't you called the police?"

Brenda sat back against the leather seat. A sudden fear burst inside like a head in a balloon.

"About...what?"

"About your father." Robert said. "Come on. You didn't think we were coming all the way out here just to practice driving did you? A woman as smart as you can pick up driving within five minutes and retain it forever. Shifting won't take you but a few blinks of an eye. I came here to talk to you about your father Brenda. I have no business in asking, I barely know you. I barely know your mother. What I do know Brenda is abuse. It can affect the whole goddamn family. It's worse than any disease my friend. Someone like your father can haunt you forever. I can help you Brenda, but you have to help me. I can help your mom too but she's a hard person to talk too about things like that. I can see it in her eyes and they are calling out for help. I can almost read her mind."

How did he know my name?

I'm not wearing my nametag.

"All I know is what she has told my wife. And to tell you the truth my dear, it scares me a lot more than that psycho that's been going around killing children. At least he's doing it out in the open. Abuse is a monster that hides within us all."

"I don't want to talk about this." Brenda said. She wanted her rabbit's foot, and suddenly remembered she left it on the dresser from last night's excursion.

"Why?" Robert shut down the Mustang. "Because you really can't or never had too before?"

"Both." Brenda said with attuned firmness.

A solid wind suddenly slammed the car.

"That's a bit, I don't know...nondescript wouldn't you say?"

"I wouldn't." Brenda said.

She reached for one of Robert Raven's cigarettes which Robert didn't mind letting her have.

"I know it's not the reason you're looking for Mr. Raven, but it's my reason. Let me have what's mine."

Let me have what's mine...

Enola.

Robert leaned towards Brenda just as the clouds passed over the morning sun. As he spoke, remains of smoke bellowed from his bright red lips.

"Do you know what your father does to her?"

Suddenly, for the first time since she had murdered someone, Brenda Dejour was afraid.

"I've seen things...yes." Brenda said.

"Things hmmm?" Robert said.

He drug on his smoke. The cherry was glowing brightly. Brenda felt uncomfortable and wanted to get out of her car. Instead, she reached everywhere in her jacket for a light as the cigarette dangled between her lips. Robert revealed a silver lighter. It was bright with a pewter dragon wrapped around it. When he held his thumb on the dragon's head the mouth of the beast opened and let loose a lucid green flame.

"All you need to do is ask." Robert said calmly lighting Brenda's cigarette and smiling warmly. "And I don't mean about the cigarette. Do you love your father Brenda?"

"Yes."

"Your eyes tell me different."

"My eyes never lie."

"Maybe not." Robert said. "But they veer from the truth. How many times has he hit your mother?"

"Robert." Brenda said. "I told you before, I don-"

"How many times has he hit…you?"

They both sat in silence and then gave one final look to one another. Robert exited the Mustang. A cold winter wind blew ruffling his hair. He and Brenda switched sides and spent the next two hours driving.

As Brenda drove, she saw Robert had a picture of his daughter tucked in the metal of the speedometer.

"That must be her."

"Who?" Robert asked.

"Your daughter." Brenda said. "Winter. That's her right?"

She looked at the picture seeing a buxom young girl. A girl with bigger assets than her and already prettier than Brenda could ever be.

"That's her." Robert said. "She's the reason I live."

"I bet it's hard to sleep at night when you have kids, especially with what's been going on."

"It's not easy." Robert said. "Whoever's killing young children and their parents will never forget my name if they come to my house."

Brenda looked over at the man in the passenger seat, then slowly back to the road.

"Everything in this town seems short lived."

"How do you mean?" Brenda asked.

"You know…boring, under the curtain if you will. I hear the summers are most enjoyable."

"They are if you like the clubs, the night scene and such."

"I like the night scene. " Robert smiled.

Brenda Dejour finished her cigarette as he made another pass in the parking lot. The shifting was as good as she would get in the parking lot.

"I believe you madam are ready for the road." Robert said, placing his cold hand on the young woman's' right knee in a congratulating gesture.

"I love this car." Brenda said. "It's so powerful, so-"

"Enchanting?" Robert finished. "Yes, I must admit it keeps me smiling in the morning when I have nothing to feel good about."

"You're a very different man Mr. Raven, where are you from?"

"Originally" Robert began, " I don't really know. I know that sounds funny, especially to a college student, but I don't remember anything until I was five years old. Like my daughter I was adopted. And like you it was by parents that were disposed of normal upbringings."

"You were adopted?"

"Yes." Robert said as he lit another cigarette.

"All I can remember was moving from family to family. I was out on my own when I turned seventeen. My adoptive parents were heavy into drugs and the bottle Brenda. They were just like your father, except it was both of my parents. I don't know why my real ones didn't want me. Quite often growing up I understood why, especially when I would fail in life. But my adoptive parent's were quite abusive, and only recently have I started to understand that.

In a family Brenda, especially a bad one, you grow very use to things. Your heart beats within your mothers but it beats in your father's as well. You grow use to things and start to believe that this is the way it is, the way it's done in everyone's family. My Mother used to throw me down the stairs. She used to do so many drugs that for many days I was malnourished. She fed me black licorice till I shit green for a month. She often would do LSD and then afterwards have visions I was so dirty she would draw hot baths for me that were scalding. My skin would blister and peel. She once tore every one of my finger nails off thinking they were too dirty for me to attend school."

117

Brenda was stared at Robert.

"And she used to rape me."

"My God." Brenda said.

"No." Robert noted. "I'm afraid he wasn't there then."

"Shortly after, my adoptive parent's gave me up to a good family, a hearty family. My thoughts became more focused, more tightly wound. As a family we ate together, played games together. We did all the things that families should do, or at least what you think they should do." Robert tossed his cigarette.

"My Mother and Father were killed by some lunatic. Someone, who I don't think about much, but believe in him none the less. I remember his face, and I remember my parents. I remember the man responsible standing in the living room smiling with big beautiful teeth. Some of them were as long as a cobra's. Yes Brenda, I too know vampires."

"But they're not real." Brenda said frantically.

Robert smiled, and there was something dark within that smile.

"I learned many great things growing up on my own. Many arts, many ways of life and death, some without a sense of light showing from the other side."

Brenda looked on, nonplussed.

"Look" Robert concluded. "All I'm saying girl, is no matter how resilient you are to abuse, it never goes away. Sooner or later the screaming and the hitting fills the cup with tears and it keeps filling in your mind if it hasn't already. Then one day, perhaps sooner than later, the cup will runeth over my friend, and then all will bless the ringing bells of the angels when you find yourself in my shoes."

"I didn't know." Brenda said.

"Of course not." Robert replied. "Nor should you. I don't just tell anyone my business. I found the man responsible for killing my parent's and I made him pay Brenda. I made him scream, and then I made him pay."

"Was he scared?" Brenda asked.

Robert turned towards his new friend.

"Shitless." Robert said with a small but noticeable smile.

"I met Holly much later, my wife and brought her tragedy to my own. I brought Winter into the circle of things, her father was also like yours and mine, along the list of many others. Even if you know he was wrong about the things he did, you do better to stay silent. It was like being a chess piece rather than a person."

He actually understands. Brenda thought. Then suddenly she observed Robert smiling as if he suddenly could read her thoughts.

"All the talk shows and the discussion groups on television can say whatever the hell they want. But when it boils down to it, where the water is hot and the blisters burst, no one can understand pain until they've felt it themselves. I know what you're going through, and I want you to know, I'm here if you need me."

Brenda exited the parking lot, as a tear edged the cusp of her right eye.

"Thank you." she said.

"You've always been welcome." Robert replied.

With that the wind followed, and the roads ahead and the ones left behind were theirs to cherish.

XI

The Hotrod festival had begun getting crowded by noon on Saturday. There were custom hotrods with flaming paintjobs, any imaginable color fit for a street king. There was a rainbow of muscle cars at the event. Camaros, Corvettes, Chevelles, Mustangs, you name it and it was there. Holly called her husband so they could find each other in the crowed scene. Holly, Winter and Brenda's mom met under a convention stand where they were selling magazines and giving balloons away to the kids (the kind without heads inside them). Brenda stood beside Robert and they all agreed to get something to eat before exploring the festivities.

"I'm thinking a cheeeeseburger." Robert said as his wife gripped his arm. "Burgers are always better for some reason at places like this. The meat is different."

" I know what you mean." Brenda said.

Winter was smiling at her, and appeared like a flirtatious girl that would grow up to fuck all the boys Brenda wished she could have. Brenda thought Winter was much older than her age. Brenda didn't know if t was typical or not, but she was slightly taken by her attractiveness.

"You want to come with me and waste some money on some games?" Winter asked.

Brenda thought about saying no, although the voices in her mind, the voices of Enola were telling her to go ahead. She didn't understand that feeling at all. It was like being invited to your own birthday party and saying you have better things to do. What could be better than a conversation, especially one in the dark?

"I guess so." Brenda smiled showing dimples.

"Aren't you girls hungry?" Robert asked.

"No not really dad." Winter smiled.

"Well, all right, but I want you both to meet us back here in an hour." Robert handed his daughter a twenty-dollar bill and one to his newfound friend.

"Oh no Mr. Raven, I couldn't."

"Take it." Robert said. "I owe it to your mother. She'd want you to have it."

Brenda took the bill and stuffed it in her tight jean pocket. Although embarrassed by the man 's generosity, she felt oddly comfortable around the dusky haired man who brought his family to Maryland from Las Vegas.

"We'll be back by then." Winter said as she turned to leave.

That entire day Brenda Dejour could not take her eyes from Winter Raven. When they went to the cotton candy stand and shared a bag, Brenda could smell the delectable aroma of her perfume. It was a high sweet consummate mix of shampoo and new cotton, far from the smell of blood soaked clothing. She liked winter. Although she was afraid to admit it to herself, perhaps a bit more than a friend. Brenda didn't like those thoughts. She felt Enola was reading them and laughing. Vampire wannabee is gay? May not. She liked to fuck men but liked to be with girls in different ways. Closer ways. She liked to see the way different girls moved. Perhaps, she was Bi sexual. Maybe that was why she killed her first fuck in Pennsylvania. The lover who choked on rat poison while Brenda watched in excitement holding a pair of scissors in the ill light.

However, Brenda was much too old to convince a girl like Winter into a sexual experiment. Besides, she had much better things to do with her time then think about puppy love. The voices were growing louder, day by day. The voice of the Violator screamed as Carper Falls called her. The voice of Enola. Some mystical entity that was once a vampire slayer, who wrote a series of novels she's been reading in the public library called to her. The latest of which, called I Want to be a Vampire, was overdue. Brenda was being successful at pushing Enola to the side. Enola, the voice who sometimes came as Barnabus Nodsley, sometimes as The Violator of Vampires. This new novel was how Barnabus made a mistake and became one.

Winter occupied the human side of Brenda's mind, and the monster within her grew from the soul. She enjoyed the company. They walked together, often times quietly, until something caught Winter's dark seductive eyes. They were passing out hot cider by the

121

Agricultural stand at the festival. Beside it was a game stand, where many giant stuffed pink elephants hung. The game was ring toss.

"I want that damn thing." Winter said.

"What?" Brenda asked.

"STEP RIGHT UP!" The game attendant announced to the passing crowd.

"Step right up and be a winner! Only takes one ring! Only takes ONE! Throw one and pick your prize! There's a lucky someone out there tonight! Look at this young lady!"

"How much." Winter asked.

"4 rings for a buck."

"Okay." Winter said.

She reached in her small handbag. It was pink like the elephant she yearned for. A hand came down with a five-dollar bill in it.

"Wait." Brenda said, tossing back her blonde hair. "I'm good at this."

Winter hesitated, and then looked at her with those freckled face and dark eyes. Brenda wanted to blush. The rusting sun fell apart behind her deep in the sky like a bullet exploding a fiery skull. Brenda suddenly felt something crack inside her. The block of ice around her heart broke. She looked at Raven and blinked quickly. A lock of crow colored hair hung across her face, long and silky.

"You'd do that for me college girl?" Winter asked.

"Well." Brenda blushed. "I just…just want you to save your money is all."

Winter smiled. Dimples formed on her cheeks, and suddenly Brenda could see her future in them. She could see driving her Mustang out to California with an older Winter. She'd still wear that dark lipstick. She'd still wear that makeup Brenda favored, and still wear her dark hair the way she wore it now. Brenda would be smiling with her, and they'd both be vampires. They would drive to Los Angeles where all lost angels are found.

The sun would go down behind the Mustang and it would sink into the night and glow in both their dreams like new ideas for murder. Brenda would smell her just the same as she smelled her now. The smell, which is sweeter than candy, adrift with fantastic, and adoring cotton. The smell of roses cut deep and shredded among lily. She would lean her head against hers as they drove along a lost highway. She would think about the future. Think about everything brilliant and nothing dark. There would be no town to go back to. No murders under her belt. Girls like Winter made everything bad that happens turn into nothing more than distant dreams. Girls like Winter Brenda could perhaps be lovers. These thoughts were just fantasy. An attempt by Brenda to find fascination with something other than the undead. For Brenda Dejour favored men mostly and even if could leave home with Winter, the knife would almost certainly follow.

One ring was thrown, missed, second, missed.

"Don't you lose."

Third ring, we have a *winner*.

Winter jumped up and down like a much younger girl. Brenda stood surprised. She didn't expect to win. As a matter of fact, she never played this game before. Her father didn't believe in games. Games were a waste of time and money in his opinion. Brenda was too busy liking her new friend to even wonder how her blood would taste from a kitchen kettle.

"THANK YOU!" Winter screamed joyously grabbing the taller college student. She gave Brenda a tight wound lovely hug.

"No problem." Brenda smiled.

"Which one will it be?" The attendant asked.

"The elephant." Brenda said.

"Elephant for the lady."

The attendant leaned down, smiling with smoke stained teeth. His breath smelled like everything else at the festival. It was a mixture of peanuts, hotdogs, the occasional foray of beer and fried doughboys, all wadded up into a tinge of some young things spill of puke. His breath smelled like vomit spewed from some ride that didn't look nearly as menacing or fast as it was once you got in. Which was very much like the plain Jane girl before Winter.

"I can't believe you won."

"Trust me." Brenda said. "I can't either."

"What now?" Winter said, hugging the stuffed animal as they walked together among nightfall.

The lights from the rides made Winter think of Christmas and Brenda think of monster eyes. They were both on a crash course to nowhere.

"I'm getting sort of hungry."

"Me too." Winter said. "We have to check in with my Father though."

"Yes I know." Wonder what they're doing?" Brenda said.

"My dad's probably is driving someone nuts talking about his car."

Brenda smiled. "It's a nice car Winter."

"I know." Winter said. "But to me, cars are cars."

They walked along the screams of the children at night. They passed by a large scale but instead of numbers this scale had bright red letters depicting all the months.   Another dial underneath depicted the day you were born and yet, another depicted the year.

"Step right up! Give you twenty dollars if I can guess! I've never been beat! NEVER! Can guess WHEN you were born! Step on up and win a prize!"

Brenda suddenly thought about performing that man's job as they walked by.

Brenda would say:

Step right up! Step right up! Hey there Mister! Step right up! I don't know when you were born but I know when you're gonna die! Wanna take a guess? I'll tell you! Right FUCKING NOW!

"You okay?" Winter asked.

"Yeah I'm okay why?" Brenda replied

"I don't know you look a little pale."

"Naa" Brenda said.

She rubbed the back of her neck.

"I just got a lot on my mind."

Winter smiled then placed her hand on her new friends denim covered arm.

"I'm so glad I've met you."

Brenda's eyes widened another crack broke in the ice.

"You are?"

"Yes." Winter added. "I think you're very nice. Dad always says nice people are not to be trusted Brenda, but I trust you."

"I see." Brenda said. "You're dad's a smart man. I admire him."

"He's very respectable." Winter added. "And he's a good judge of character. He can see the evil in us all. I think most people can see evil, especially in men. What do you think?"

Brenda kicked a stone with her high heel boot. It flew off towards a tent exhibiting old cars.

"I think you're right, at least to some degree. But people that are evil themselves can be blinded by it can't they? What you're talking about is what I call absolution."

"The Violator?" Winter suddenly said stopping Brenda in her tracks.

Kill her now. Do it here. She just said our name. She knows Brenda. She knows who we really are. She knows about Enola and the others. The voices of the vampire to be. Take her behind the tent Brenda. Take her there and devour her innocence with a hunger that would make the world sick

"What about him?" Brenda said.

"How does absolution fit in there?"

Brenda turned towards the young girl as people passed by about their business.

"I suppose it doesn't."

Winter came closer.

"He scares me, mom too. Dad say's the police are looking in the wrong places that the violator sits right under our noses. My dad says revenge is the only thing sweeter than blood."

"Your dad must be a poet." Brenda smiled. "What if the guys the cops are looking for isn't a guy?"

"What do you mean?" Winter asked.

"What if, just what if, the person doing all these killings...is a woman?"

A chill flew upon Winter's spine.

"What do you think your father would say to that?"

125

Winter didn't respond. Instead she took the lead as both women walked towards the park entrance.

"We better head back." Brenda said.

Before Enola awakes. Enola will awake and it won't care how sweet revenge is. Enola doesn't care about revenge. Enola only cares about violation. Enola cares about the red.

Something bothered Robert about Brenda. Something he couldn't at first put a finger on. Robert was good at reading peoples' auras especially bad people or folks that were hiding something. Quite often people say they can see through others when they are lying and such. Robert's keen senses went far beyond theirs. But Robert couldn't see through Brenda. He had tried to read her mind when a group of people stood idolizing his Mustang, and he had told the people what the license plate letters stood for. CDLMKR stood for CanDLe MaKeR. He had tried all evening, even on the way home. But never once could he see Brenda's colors under her soul. He even tried to use his car.

The Mustang had it's own abilities it seemed. It was something other than a car. Brenda knew this. The CD player was installed after production but the unnerving powerful music coming from it wasn't. KISS was heard bright and loud. The eminent sounds of the rock band with painted faces were never too far away. Robert wondered if Brenda knew that. When they had all gone to leave the festival, the car had started on it's own. Robert didn't have one of those electronic key fobs, or a kit to hook the old car up to. Brenda knew the car somehow, someway started on it's own.

Monday morning, the snow began. It came down in droves drifting down among the pines and sands of Carper Falls. To Winter Raven the snow reminded her of ashes. Winter stood in the living room looking out through the curtains. In the background, she could hear the television blaring out the events of what was gripping the town with horror. Although WBOC 16 news mentioned little of the letter, they did mention the Violator's recent victim. Little Billy Owens was not yet buried and not yet at peace. The mentioning of it amongst the silence of her surroundings scared the young teenager.

She turned from the window and stared at the enormous pink stuffed elephant in the corner of the living room floor. At least she felt some peace knowing she had a friend like Brenda in her life.

There are vast places in Carper Falls with miles of wooded lands far from the reaches of any beach. Winter was thinking about the woods near her home. She was thinking of a young boy being held captive by some terrifying monster. She was sipping warm hot chocolate from her favorite mug. Her dark hair astray and her freckled face in a tangent of wonder thinking of these places. How did men like the Violator exist?

Winter tried to push the thoughts somewhere that she would never see them again. She would be soon sixteen years old. She would soon understand the nature of boys and realize something she always suspected. But boys were not what she wanted recently. Girls seemed to touch her, although she never openly thought so until now. Winter found the secret place to keep thoughts like the Violator's purpose and startling facts about her own sexual personification. Her eyes were set on Brenda Dejour. Up until the past weekend she had a crush on Carter Felix. Some things aren't meant to be while others fit right in their places like chess pieces. Even still Winter understood the desires within her soul. Suddenly to her unknown surprise, the girl next door replaced Carter the violin player. Winter was attracted to Brenda.

Her father has been there for her while she. Robert Raven had taught her much of the world that teachers and books could never touch on. She felt blessed to know that she had parents who could guide her throughout all the obstacles life would bring to her and a father strong enough to protect her from any of the world's boogiemen.

Rachel Owens had checked herself into the mental ward that Monday evening just when the snow begun to fall. She told the emergency room doctors that she no longer could live without her son. When the nurses seen she had failed at drinking bleach to commit suicide they took her in. Sheriff Turner wondered what she would do if the media released what the Violator actually did to her son. How much does it take to drive a person over the edge?

Revenge is sweeter than blood.

That evening, she wasn't the only one who entered the emergency room. A man, with the firm intent on making sure things would change had silently retreated somewhere in the hospital and waited for the midnight hours. He thought about things in his hidden domain. He thought about the woman across the street and how last evening at the festival Sylvia Dejour broke down once more. She received a phone call from John when Robert and Brenda had been practicing driving. The call home had been vicious in its certainty. John had threatened to kill her once he got out of the hospital. He was coming home for good. He told Sylvia if anyone was packing his or her bags it was going to be her because Silly Sylvia would be the only one who is sorry. Only this time, the bags would be packed for the funeral home.

Robert and Holly watched Sylvia cry. Her eyes begged to be let free like dark birds from rusty cages. Brenda and Winter had gone on the Ferris wheel and were becoming fast friends. The girls talked about the killer in their town. They looked into each other's eyes as the freezing winter wind brought tears to their eyes. And they brought their words closer, long enough to feel each other's lips without ever revealing a kiss. They wanted too however. They wanted to kiss each other while Brenda's mother cried far below knowing what was coming home to show her who was once again boss.

In the room of John Dejour, darkness had cultivated the vastness of space. Finally he had gone off to sleep with the firm notion of having no more dreams. The nightmares had left a caustic taste in his throat like cheap whiskey. John was only disturbed once when the nurse came into the room at midnight to check his pulse and blood pressure. Then John drifted into the deep dark cavernous realms of sleep. This dream had offered nothing to John but black. He would need plenty of rest because soon, he would be getting out of here. Soon, he would be going home with his right eye still black and blue, but open enough to see what must need done.

Outside in the quiet hallway the nursing station remained calm in the silent tranquility. Albert Joper, the old night watchmen and security guard, walked along with a song inside his head. One he didn't know the title too. He smiled when he passed the three nurses. The dark haired raven-eyed beauty in between the older nurses really caught his fancy. He didn't know her name, but in his fantasies he knew much more than that. Albert made it to the hallway elevator before something came out of the bedroom behind him, looming above it seemed. Albert's eyes slowly looked at the linoleum floor and saw the shadow stretch like a black triangle along the baseboard. The shadow was of something flickering like black fire moving among stone. The flickering turned into the shadows of dragon wings.

Albert's eyes widened, as he turned slowly behind him.

Nothing...

However, the broom closet door, which normally was closed, stood on a crack. He pressed the down arrow on the elevator, and waited it to open. Above him, Robert Raven crawled across the ceiling in his own shadows of apocalyptic evil. Like some purported spider from another time. The nurses never noticed, even when he entered John Dejour's room without a scent, or a whisper.

John Dejour's breathing was calm. A silent rhythmic method of peace came out of him. In his subconscious, John Dejour had felt something. A wet fluttering of a bizarre passage that began to bring him back into the norm far away from the safety of the land of dreams. As if a mist from a crashing waterfall brought him slowly out of the darkness. When his eyes fluttered open, including the badly bruised one that under Doctor Gooding's assessment would take quite awhile to heal, his vision open captured the darkness before him. Jonathan Dejour winced, and moved the whites of his eyes towards the flickering of light casting dancing shadows around him. Like partying ghosts of some seniors dying ballroom suicide delirium. At first, John forgot he was even in the hospital. When he saw his the tall raven haired beauty standing still near the far side of the wall he was brought back to reality. It was his attending nurse. The one he had told since his admittance that he would love to fuck. As he soon as he left his useless wife, he would. Even more so, he didn't have to leave her at all. John could have the best of both wo-

Her eyes were wide with terror. It didn't frighten John the way she looked as much as it made him curious. She was standing like she was in shock or perhaps dead but still on her feet. On the small table next to her a candle burned bright. It was one of those like the ones his neighbor made. Like the one he had thrown across the living room into the kitchen wall making his good for nothing wife scream. He tried to move, and couldn't. His head was turned to the left and he noticed his arm had been stretched out against the bedpost. His wrist was tied firm with strands of speaker wire. He turned his head to the right and observed his other arm in the same state as his left. He tried to move his legs and felt both of them tied as well.

"What the fuck?" He whispered.

John turned towards the nurse named Lana.

"What are you doing just standing there bitch?" he asked. "Help me!"

But Lana needed help herself. Something had her throat clutched in its powerful right hand. The hand had long fingers and long yellow nails. The man from John's dreams was holding her by the throat. His face was down hidden from John sucking on the nurse's jugular. Blood ran like lightning down the front of her white uniform from her shoulder. John could hear the sucking sounds in the dark sounding like a low-pitched evil giggle.

" What the fuc-"

Before John could finish the dead nurse dropped to the floor and the man from John's dreams slowly moved back into the dark shadows. Before he disappeared the monster grinned showing the blood stained lips smeared across it's face like a clown's greasepaint. The flicker of dancing flame from the candle illuminated terrifying shapes in the room. John closed his eyes asking himself to wake up.

But John was awake.

Very awake.

"Hello wife beater." the darkness said.

It drifted to his ears like a haunted chant from an old cave containing undead choirboys. John forced his eyes to look down at the floor. He saw Lana slumped into the corner like dirty clothing. Her eyes were open and glossy, staring into his, reflecting the candlelight. There were two holes punctured in the side of her neck that went along in a long large rip down to the purple vein still throbbing and bursting with blood beneath.

John could see what stood in the darkness in her dead eyes. It was like a shadow slowly becoming a man. Its face was white and cold. Its eyes were silver like the handles found on morgue drawers. The thing turned towards the dead woman's eyes and smiled knowing John was looking at them. The smile was long and stretched for a thousand years. It was the smile only the devil could trust. It had an unholy clarity brilliant and white. The thing opened it's mouth wide and closed with one vicious snap on it's own tongue. Blood sprayed across the short room peppering the dead nurse's face. A piece of the man's tongue fell to the floor.

"Now that I have your attention wife beater, I'm sure you know I am serious."

"Yes." John begged like a child. "Oh dear Christ*!* *Yes!*"

John closed his eyes, wondering what kind of monster was hiding in the dark. Suddenly, the thing moved closer. Its face was hidden all but its pale bluish forehead and black widow's peak of hair.

"A man has got to know when he is defeated Jonathan Dejour. He can wake up every morning believing he has won but only the mirror will show him his defeat. The reflection never lies John. Now if you look above you, you will see what I mean."

John's eyes crept above him slowly as he lay on the bed like Jesus nailed upon the cross.

"I cannot see my reflection wife beater." The vampire said. "What can you see in yours?"

John's face trembled. His lips became cold with horror. There above him somehow glued to the ceiling was the giant mirror. In the mirror he saw darkness at first. Then the dancing candle flame let him see everything. In his reflection all the answers to why he had awoken came true. He was lying on the bed, dissected. Carefully with a surgeon's skill John saw himself sliced open from his Adam's apple to just above his balls. The skin was folded over on each side pinned with ten-penny nails as if John had become a display model for a science class. In his reflection John could see his internal organs bloody and grimed with bodily fluids. His intestines lay nicely fitted in the way they were supposed too. Everything was wet, bloody, and gray.

"No!" John yelled.

His eyes filled with terror.

"I see you find me serious now because you and I are talking without blinking. This is good John.   The eyes of the dead don't blink."

"No." John whispered in hoarse terror.

"I wouldn't advise trying to sit up John. Things could fall out of place." The vampire noted stepping forward out of the shadows of the candle.

Suddenly the lights to the room came on and John could see his own evisceration more clearly. In his reflection he had become a living nightmare like a frog on a student's dissecting table.

Once he seen the man move fast towards him, he no longer cared for his reflection. The vampire stripped the air like a ghost without remorse for the flesh it once or that of others. Robert Raven stopped inches from John's face.

"OH GOD!" John screamed.

"God is in the forgiving business Mr. Dejour." The vampire said. "I however, am not."

"Please…" John begged.

His twisted hair was riddled with sweat.

"Please put…put me back together!"

"I can see your heart Mr. Dejour." Robert Raven said.

Blood leaked down the front of his chin in a thick perfect crimson line. The vampire was grinning and his blood stained teeth appeared menacing and inhuman. The fangs were elongated and came to points like hospital syringes. Roberts's eyes were black; the pupils were silver like mercury in a thermometer.

"I'm going to crack your chest open and *squeeze* your heart John." Robert said.

"No dear God…"

"I'm going to strangle your heart like you've been strangling your wife's for all these years."

"NO!" John screamed.

"What do you see in your reflection John?" The vampire asked.

Veins began to spider across his forehead.

"Do you see death yet?"

"PLEASE!" John screamed. "I DON'T WANT TO DIE!"

"But you must."

"NO! PLEASE! I'LL NEVER HURT HER AGAIN!"

"No." Robert said. "I guess you won't."

"I'M SORRY!" John screamed. Tears leaking from his eyes. The vampire leaned forward towards his throat.

"You're always sorry."

The vampire bit down into John's throat and tore out his Adam's apple. Blood spurted out of the hole and across the man's open chest. Before John slipped into darkness forever, Robert released him from the bounds. The speaker wire came free. He grabbed John with both hands and made him sit up like a baby with his internal organs falling out all around him. Those perfect intestines unraveled and fell to the floor like wet towels. Blood splashed from them and more from the hole in John's throat. When Robert finally let the dead man fall back against the bed his arms draped to the sides his chest and his stomach was nothing more than a hollow cavity of gore. There would be no more abuse. In a few days Sylvia would become one of the family. A family that as growing stronger, darker, and larger.

A family of vampires.

Out with the old and in with the new...

We never blink.

XII.

The snow fell in long drifting gusts on Carper Falls without mercy. The community had gone to the local hardware stores and Food Lions emptying the shelves of all their can goods. The local residents like Southern Gale and Freddie Hurst bought cell phones the day before at the only cell phone store in town, Fairs Cingular Wireless. Everyone had prepared for the snowstorm and prayed their preparations would be in vain. They weren't prepared for the Violator or the other man who had come to town. Not since 1976 has Maryland braced themselves for such a storm.

The local news that new morning depicted a brutal murder had taken place inside the Salisbury Hospital. Mark Paparelli, the local news anchor declared the killer brutally attacked a patient and killed one of the nurses. The reporter was unaware whether or not the killings were the same patterns of the Violator. Investigators had been at the hospital all morning when the blizzard began to slam the eastern shore. Brenda had gone back to college, or so her mother thought. Sylvia had gone across the street to relax with her newfound friends. Robert Raven and his wife Holly sat along the red velvet living room couch listening as the storm outside screamed like demons in a church choir. The fireplace cracked and sizzled eating the bark of the woodpile. Winter lay upon the easy chair, her hair tied in a bun, with a video game controller in her hand and a steaming mug of hot chocolate at her side. Beside her was Sylvia Dejour who, despite her ignorance to the fact the man sitting across from her had murdered her husband looked relieved, less stressed, and years younger.

"This is crazy." Winter said. "I won't be going back to school in like, forever."

"Snow melts." Her father noted.

Holly smiled.

"Can you believe what happened at the hospital?" Sylvia stated. "I should call John and ask him if he knows anything about it."

"I wouldn't bother." Robert said. "Just in case he does."

134

"Dad." Winter started. "What do you mean?"

You know damn well what he means. Winter thought. *Just like when you were twelve and those older boys bullied you because you were overweight right? Remember? You went almost six months keeping it all in, but your new Father knew. Your new father named Robert, because your old father disappeared long before your mother Mary died. She was found dead on the floor with a meat clever buried in her back all the way up to the handle where that little ring dangles where it used to hang it on the wall.*

Your new father seems to always know. When he stands next to you *there's a feeling in your mind like something is not ordinary. Something pinching your thoughts although it doesn't seem real, it feels very real. But that's what it is and it's very real. Your dad can read mind but he can't read everyone's. He knew about how your parent's were abusing you and what your brother used to do things to you when he and his wife Holly came to the rescue all those years ago didn't he? He knew about the boys and how one of them felt you up while you screamed in the alley and the other two laughed while the one went groping for your barely budding breasts. He had wandering hands and shifting eyes. Didn't you ever wonder why the boy that bullied you and pinched your iddy biddy titties was found in the dump? The seagulls eating at his eyes? The coroner revealed his neck was broken and his throat torn out. But what made you wonder even more, Winter, was that the boy was found with his hands cut off.*

And the more you sat there all those years ago trying to wonder if it was normal to feel good about it, you knew all along didn't you? Just like you know it now. Your Dad's gone and done another one of his famous favors. What he feels is right to do. And he's sitting on that sofa the same way he sat all those years ago watching evidence of his own handiwork on the television.

"I'm just saying maybe it's better sometimes not to know everything." Robert finished.

Of course Sylvia Dejour knew he was right. Just like she knew something had been happening to her since she had broken down in her darkened living room a few days ago. It was the side of her neck where she had been injured. Since it has faded she somehow felt different. Sylvia felt woozy and found herself succumbing to dark dreams. Dreams of a high sweet evil only a mad man could listen too.

She had slept last evening and awoken with a fever She was up the rest of the night until the early hours of the morning. Recently up her gums bothered her. Robert and Holly had bitten her while feeling sorry for her. She had been having visions since the biting. She was sharing memories of Robert Raven. Visions of darkened skies and fields of hollow wheat that buckle and slope spanning out for.

These fields lead to distant eclipse of a land forgotten by time and remembered by madmen of our history. A great and giant castle lay in the north of the slope of weeds. There the land dips and rises like the sexy curves of a mistress lying on her side nude in the dusk. The castle seen in Sylvia's mind brightened from striking lightning in the night sky. At the entrance was a moat filled with crocodiles yearning for flesh to devour. Before this was a great pasture filled with black roses growing in a blood soaked ground. The roses bloomed through the eye sockets of skulls and in an instant were plucked by the new and disastrous teeth of black demonic horses that stood. The horses had darkened eyes and red pupils and blew hot steam from evil nostrils. They stood on two legs to gallop showing long, grisly, twisted, and wretched teeth. Mend and women wearing black robes rode them showing only the color of their eyes, which were dangerous liquid silver. Pupils like shiny bee bees. Eyes of the damned.

She awoke with an empty feeling in her stomach and mind. Those empty feelings people sometimes get in-between prayer.

"You killed him." Sylvia said, as she closed her eyes to sleep.

She had fainted among friends. Robert watched closely. He rose and gently touched the sides of her face with the back of his hand.

"Soon." Robert said. "Soon, you won't care about any of that."

"Dad!" Winter yelled, standing to her feet. "What did you do?!"

"It's what she wanted!" Holly intervened. "Can't you feel that?"

"Honey." Robert said. "Your mother's right. It's what she wants. I could feel it inside of her. She wants to be free. Needs to be free."

"Than why am I not one of you?" Winter asked.

"Because it's not your time." Robert said. "It's a gift many people want but end up regretting once they have it. Winter, you can live free from all of this with your mom and I."

"But I want to live forever too Dad."

"No." Robert said. "You don't."

"I want to be a vampire."

Robert sighed. He looked at his wife and back at his daughter.

"Forever is too long. Trust me on that. Time becomes your enemy. Forever is much too long."

"Then WHY HER!" Winter screamed.

"Because she has nothing else." Holly said. "Now stop getting upset."

Winter stormed away from them, slamming the door to her room. Tears feel from her eyes as the slow blanketed the town.

Along the snow caked roads a young woman walked wearing jeans and a hooded sweatshirt. The hood was pulled up over the back of her head hiding most of her features. In her ears were headphones. They hung not connected to anything. It was how she believed she could hear the voice. The voice that took over what was once a rational thought. She believed she could hear the voice better using the headphones. She believed she knew who it was. It was the voice of Dracula. You must end this with another the voice said. Brenda trudged along Baker Street. The sidewalks were heavy with snow. It came from the sky swirling and blowing with drifts. No one in his or her right mind would be out in this shit, yet, here she was.

The place will be ready. The terrible voices yearned.

She could not lie to that. Brenda waited until her mother left and walked from the bus stop while the snow continued to spread across the East Coast that morning. She took the long hike eastward across the Valley Woods Preserve near the route 50 bridge. Someone the night before murdered her father in the hospital. She did not know of this. All she knew was that her feet moved as if possessed.

The walk had been cumbersome, but filled her with new and fantastic ideas. The night prior, she slept dreaming of her mother. They had found a house in the middle of the woods somewhere where dreams perhaps cannot reach. The house was brilliant, beautiful and while she stood with her mother, she observed the house in her darkest moment was not a house at all, but a great castle. The walls made of staggered brick the color of Robert Raven's eyes. Inside someone was standing near the top wearing a black robe with silver eyes. Brenda knew who it was and was glad to have finally met him. Even in her dreams. It was the legend. The one she was reading about. She observed the hooded figure holding a long pole with his right hand while the other end rested upon the ground. At the top of the pole a grisly human head remained impaled. Flies swarmed around the head's sleepy and shrunken eyes. The thing in the hooded robe raised its hand and pointed towards Brenda's mother.

She's one of them Brenda. Not true blood...but...turned.

Brenda awoke in a sweat. Her breasts perked and nipples hard and erect excited by the notion that her mother was a vampire in her dreams. To think that her mother was lost to a dark sided embrace of something inhuman and unholy where not even God could not save her. A hint of jealously, loneliness, and terror came across Brenda.

That was hours ago. Presently Brenda trotted through the snow life fluid moving through the veins searching to recapture hear innocence through brutal interactions with those innocent at heart. However in Carper Falls no one is innocent and none were safe.

She passed where many old cabins and closed down military bunkers were. She trekked past an old rusty water tower standing tall among the forestry. The snow made a terrific and bright backdrop. As she walked onward Brenda found answers to why she did things. Why did she eat Billy Owens? So Billy could become alive inside her. Doing so would maybe stop the voices or, if nothing else humble them in the dark.

She tried to block out the things in her mind and focus on normality. She thought about the first time that she had found love and how she killed him with rat poison. The first time that she ever reached orgasm was not with him but while she was pulling open Devena Mirrow's insides. The first time Brenda achieved ecstasy was like a wet, thick, veined, dull fleshy arrow piercing the pagoda of her most intimate and lustful dreams.

Brenda moved onward passed the rusty old tower and into the area of dense pine trees that remained deciduous all year. The pine trees made a tarpaulin against the following snow as she walked under the married branches twisting among one another to an opening in the clearance ahead. She reached a boarded up old shed much like the one she had killed Billy Owens inside of. This shed however was bigger, painted a dull yellow, and shingled with a carpenter's precise hands as if it was meant to be something grand. And to the Violator perhaps it was.

"Is this good?" Brenda asked. The crop of blonde hair moved around along her forehead. Her bangs blew back from the wind as if it contained an answer.

"Thank you." She said trudging forward further towards the shed.

A stack of wood already was cut outside. It sat piled neatly and in concurrence to the front door that remained half-rotted from the weather's unforgiving promise. She could smell the sweet arid burning of sap and wood drifting from the makeshift chimney above.

"I know there's someone inside." she told the voice.

It was Enola. The voice of Enola crept inside her thoughts and strangled what was left of her sanity.

Brenda peeked in around the front window. Her path became hidden, blanketed by the winter storm. In her view was an older man resting in a rocking chair. He was amid a half drunken state it seemed. He wore greasy long johns and wader boots amongst a camouflage vest. An orange hunting cap loaded with dirt rested upon his slurred thoughts. His haggard face jostled every so often as sleep took hold of him. Age perhaps was narrowing the old man down to a forever sleep six feet under. The can of Budweiser in his left hand was slowly slipping out.

Before he had decided to drink the rest of the first six-pack he had bought last evening he had been chopping wood outside his cabin. This is where many men like him came to hunt deer or ducks, or just to get away from the "Sand People" as he sometimes called them. "Sand People" was the term for the tourists who came to dip their toes in the polluted ocean water. The drunken man had forgotten to bring in his groceries from outside where his jeep was parked. He also forgot to lock up the shed adjacent to the cabin that was growing hot from the makeshift fireplace.

There were tools in the shed reflecting a time when a productive man occupied the premises. There was an axe, hedge clippers, and a chainsaw, which had been resting by the woodpile. It was one of those bright orange-handled ones that said STHIL in all the fluorescent glory. The axe was brand new too and so was the machete lying near the woodpile amongst a splitting mall and a dropped pack of matches. The old man had grown busy before deciding to call it quits. Brenda the Vampire looked at the plethora of tools which would be useful in her trade. Brenda considered herself an artist who had been chosen to turn the tales from books into reality.

The door to the shed opened and a winter breeze invaded the overly warm shed. Brenda smiled seeing that the shed was big enough for the night's plans. The cold breeze woke the man. His mind slurred. A headache suddenly overcame him. He realized he forgot some things outside. Frustration overtook him as the old man realized he must have forgotten to lock the front door. The old man noticed the can of Budweiser had fallen from his hand. When he reached down to pick it up off the floor he observed the woodpile outside where he had last been. He saw he had left his old flannel shirt lying across the sappy pieces. He remembered at one point becoming sweaty from swinging that goddamn axe and went over to drop the shirt down to his vest. That's when he put the axe down and decided to use-h

The chainsaw was gone.

The old man who was born as Dorman Chester, one of the last workers of the old shoe mill in Baltimore that many folk believe is haunted. Dorman squinted his eyes and retrieved his reading glasses with an old leather hand from his vest pocket. He observed the woodpile. That's where he last left the orange handled chainsaw.

It was in fact a very bad thing that he misplaced it, because someone else found it for him. Someone coming up fast behind him who pulled the rip chord before Dorman Chester registered the sound in his old ears. The growling chainsaw, which became overbearing in the small shed of a cabin, screamed as the woman holding it raised it into the air. Exhaust smoke from burning oil made ghosts of odorous vapor. Brenda Dejour's eyes were maddened and raw, red rimmed and berserk. Her teeth were snapped closed like a devil doll. Her tongue was hot for the taste of blood it was a dry sponge in her mouth.

Dorman didn't get a chance to scream. As the sky outside emptied its frosty guts all over Maryland Brenda Dejour emptied Dorman Chester's guts all over the floor. The chainsaw came down in one vicious ark. The old man instinctively reached out to defend himself with his hands. The new saw cut through them like grass. The fingers blew off in shreds of flesh as Dorman let out a life ending hurtful gasp. The pain shot up through the top of each shoulder. Brenda rammed the saw into his guts and the blade reciprocated as the blood poured onto the floor. As it sprayed across the room, Brenda was smiling as Dorman's blood dotted her face. She pushed the saw in and out slowly like a lover new at sex. The chain eventually stopped when it got caught up in too much gore. Dorman's face was a sunken in a terror mask. The woman holding the saw was shaking with hate and rage. She was drooling from her lower lip. Brenda backed away as the oil smoke bluish and white began to dissipate.

She dropped the saw and ran her hands through the blood smearing her face and into her blonde hair, slicking it back and making it tinge with pink. She turned around observing her surroundings and saw a tiny bathroom ten feet away. She walked slowly into the bathroom and saw the mirror. She didn't like mirrors because she could still see her reflection in them. Her father couldn't see his anymore but Sylvia still could. She observed the tub to the right. The bathroom oddly didn't support a toilet. Her mind suddenly ran wild with the thought of her neighbor Winter Raven. She was only 4 years younger than her.

Why would anyone live in such a shit ? Brenda thought.

Brenda's mind went to Raven and the time they had shared. She looked at her surroundings again.

You had him here for a reason. Was this was the place I was supposed to find wasn't it? Brenda asked the man in her mind.

He stood there at the top of the black castle in his robe. His mouth dropped open like a drawbridge showing teeth pearly white and jagged. His eyes were glowing like purple fire. Brenda stood possessed by evil staring at the ceiling. Her thoughts went to a chapter out of the book written by Barnabus Nodsley, the vampire hunter who eventually became one. She thought of the book, *I Want to Be a Vampire* and a sickening, poisoned, flu-like feeling came over her.

Read another chapter oh sweet young college girl. You have an exam to pass after all. There is no other grade than, A. You must take the test to become one of us.

Read another Chapter. There is no ending. Because in reality Brenda, a book is never finished is it? Only our parts in a book have endings. Now it's time for you to embrace this evil and write your part. You can feeeeel us in your dreams can't you Brenda? You can feel us in all your desires. We are the devil's horns lifting up your nightgown. We are the teeth that allow you to enter the veins of all that deny us. We are Enola.

"Enola." Brenda said in a trance.

Brenda suddenly realized it wasn't the name of her snow covered Mustang after all or her unborn baby sister. It was the name for Barnabus and for the Violator.

Enola...

Brenda turned in her stance. Her hiking boots swung up on the heels. She held out her arms as if she were a puppet on a marionette. Some invisible source of evil was pulling her strings. She walked towards the body of the old man who was still pooling blood all over the floor. Her hands hooked into claws and her blue eyes widened. The rabbit's foot in her pocket was in her thoughts. The foot was a bookmark holding the place for Brenda to come back too.

You will soon be one of us Brenda. Brenda could hear someone else talking amongst the robbed figures in her mind. The robed figures were the Violators of ancient times. They were ENOLA. The robed figures were the servants of something greater.

It's you isn't it? Brenda asked her mind. *Oh please tell me it's you! I serve you! I love you! Once a month Dear Dracula, I bleed you!*

Brenda didn't get a response. She suddenly had the feeling that the Enola were somehow the women of Dracula. Or perhaps they were like dark monks from a time long since passed. They existed in her mind for now but they wanted to be set free. Brenda pulled with all her skinny might. Using all the strength her 20-year-old body could muster she drug the dead man towards the bathroom.

You must bathe in his blood, just like Elizabeth Bathory. Bathe in blood to be young again.

Brenda propped the old man up as blood poured from his ripped open abdomen. She kicked the bathroom door shut. Ten minutes later she opened the bathroom door and stepped out wearing nothing except panties and her jean jacket. She stood breathing heavily. Exasperated dots of blood freckled her face. Her arms dripped with warm crimson from the elbows down. Her lips were smeared with it and she drunk some of the old man's throat wine from out of the bathtub. She propped the old man up on his knees and slashed his throat with the machete from outside. What blood he had left spilled into the tub. The voice told Brenda to bathe. Bathe to feel young again. Bathe so that the vampire inside of you will finally open her eyes.

Brenda had just learned to bathe in blood of the old to stay young. Out of her jean jacket Brenda pulled a Polaroid camera to add to her scrapbook. The camera was a gift from her mother last Christmas. She took several pictures of her handy work to place in her scrapbook filled with newspaper articles and other trophies.

Brenda sat in the old man's chair. She saw the cooler in the corner. Brenda went to it and found a warm six-pack of beer. She pulled one loose from a plastic tab ring and sat with her milky white breasts barely peeking through the opening of the jean jacket. She was speckled with blood. Her mouth and chin looked like the result of a bad lipstick fight. Blood dribbled from her chin. She was thinking of

Mustangs and the snow. The winter itself had brought much more snow than usual this year. The winter had brought something much colder than evil.

Out with the old, in with the new.

Before she finally fell asleep Brenda walked over to the bundle of clothing she left in the bathroom. There the small novel she brought with her peeked up at her.

The rabbit's foot was about halfway in the center serving as the bookmark. *Violator* was the name of the book. On the page that was opened with the bookmark there was only one word very large. Underneath it was the following message:

To see what the word below really means, hold it in front of a mirror.

ENOLA

XIII.

Liam Griffin, otherwise known as Duke, stood in the sheriff's department with binoculars that same morning the Violator struck again. This time she killed out of necessary. Law enforcement officials realized the Violator needed a new place. The police had already began investigating the train yards and all the old sheds to the west. Duke watched the deer cross Juniper road and run into the bushes behind Cobble Street just east of the graveyard where Brenda Dejours's Father would be buried.

Sheriff Turner called off sick the night before as well Deputy Davis, as well as Betty. It seemed all three of them had been running fevers and probably the flu. Betty was the last caress of old technology and did things the way it used to be done handling 911 calls. Today a much younger girl ran the switchboard. It was obvious she was new at it. Vicki paused each time she was asked a question. When dealing with emergency dispatch every second was precious. Seconds add up to minutes, which can seem long when on the other end of the phone being held at gun point. But today, it was all Duke had. Turner's other deputy, Becker Washburn, was out in the 4 wheel drive. The chains were on the tires due to the heavy snow. Both deputies had few worries on anything happening in the town of Carper Falls today. The snow would cancel everyone's plans including a serial killer's, Duke imagined. He was wrong.

Duke stood about 5 foot 8 at the most and was very thin with even thinner black hair. He didn't expect any calls that morning. For several hours all that came in were calls as to where to buy rock salt. He told Fernanda Wise, the Mayor's wife, not to worry till the storm was over. Camen Mogan's wife, who turned the balls at the fire hall for bingo, was worried her roof would cave in on her little home on Race Track Road. He told her not to worry about that either. It had to snow a real wallop before there would be a danger of that occurring. Duke remained fixated on the front of his boss's office.

Sheriff Turner had tacked many newspaper clippings to the wall about the attacks on Carper Falls. He even had a zoning map laid out. Despite the FBI taking over the case of what they called the "Vampire Murders" (although they dared never call it that publicly), Turner still kept up with the case. Turner and his men wanted to be more involved. This was his town and how dare the FBI get in the way. But he knew his duty and that the best thing for the people of his town was for him to stand aside and let the real professionals had the case. Let them catch the motherfucker and let him die slowly the way he had made others.

Duke lowered the binoculars again. The deer was now out of sight. He placed them down on the table and reached for a cigarette on his boss's desk. He struck a match lighting a Marlboro and stepped outside. The wind had died down but the snow still fell in heavy downward spirals. The streets remained so quiet you could almost hear the snow falling. The streetlights stood on blinking yellow. Not a single car had passed for the past two hours. Duke could see Bright's pharmacy near the end of the street and Fairs Cingular where the roof has been covered with over 8 inches. The quiet surroundings made Duke feel a bit awkward and unnerved. Usually the street adjacent to the Police Station was jammed with traffic

Just as Duke came to the end of his smoke he saw something coming around the corner of the Avenue. A car with overly bright headlights was brightening the street. Duke lowered his cigarette and squinted. A loud rumbling of something wicked and strong drove like demons howling from hell came down the street. Duke watched in amazement as the 1970 Shelby Cobra drive along the snow and ice. The car did not slide one bit. The four-wheel drive on the police vehicle was barely able to go out in this shit. How was that a rear wheel drive hotrod doing it?

Must have something under the hood, Duke thought. He watched as the taillights disappeared into the ending snow.

Moving away from the precinct we find that the streets have been covered by snow and stops signs have been bent from a winter's choke. The train tracks that cut through the town are glazed with ice. The roofs of the houses all along main streets are like the scenic beauty found in a wonderland. Sylvia Dejour awoke with a thirst that hurt.

146

She gulped madly. Her throat was on fire. In her peripheral vision she observed the dark haired fifteen-year-old-girl smiling at her. Sylvia's eyes came into focus.

"How long have I been out?"

"All day."

"Where are your parents?"

"Mom's upstairs taking a bath. Pop's out driving too the candle shop."

Sylvia turned to look out the window to see the icefall.

"He went out in this?"

"My dad's got a strange work ethic, what can I say?" Winter smiled returning to her cocoa.

Sylvia sat up. Her mind felt fuzzy. Her head was spinning. When she moved her eyes in their sockets it hurt. The dreams she was having were beyond phenomenal. It's as if her brain became haunted by someone else's imagination. Sylvia stood up and immediately fell back on the couch.

"You shouldn't do that." Winter said. "It needs to take effect."

"What does?"

"You're one of us now." Winter said smiling. "My parent's gave you the gift, something I can't have."

"What gift?"

"I can't tell you." Winter said. "It's better for dad to say."

The wind howled in gusts as if God had caught asthma. Sylvia took a step towards the bathroom and fell back on the couch.

"You need to rest. I've seen others go through this before."

"Others?" Sylvia asked.

Winter smiled. She then opened a magazine. There was a celebrity on the cover.

"I'm so sleepy." Sylvia said.

"You'll be okay. Shut your eyes and dream awhile. When you wake up my Dad should be home. If not I'll make you a hot cup of tea."

"Winter." Sylvia sighed with her eyes closed. "You're an angel."

"Not really." Winter smiled back and watched the woman slowly become lost in her dreams.

Winter's mother fell asleep as well. Her Father drove in the safety of his Mustang through the piles of snow. Her Dad's Mustang was more than a car to him. It was like he was driving in the company of an old fried. Winter drew herself a hot bath. Before she knew what was happening the girl hiding upstairs in the corner of the shower stall grabbed her and cut her hands with a machete.

When Sylvia awoke she felt much better. A cold wind blew in hard from somewhere. Her eyes flicked open. She lay on the couch staring at the living room ceiling tiles above. Hours passed. The fire crackled and the fireplace worked hard at keeping the home warm. Outside the wind died. Snow fell heavily outside. Sylvia sat up this time feeling great, wonderful, and

Reborn…

Of night and time…

Out with the old, in with the new.

She turned her head to the right. She saw the vanity mirror in the living room and wondered where her reflection had gone. There was nothing but the couch, a cup of cold tea, and her clothing in her reflection. Suddenly she grabbed at her hands and her face unsure as to whether she still existed.

"What's going on?" She yelled rising to her feet in horror.

It was as if she was looking at an invisible woman wearing clothing or perhaps a ghost in the mirror.

"The mirror does not lie." A dark voice said.

Sylvia turned towards it and saw nothing.

"Who's there?" She asked in a voice she barely recognized.

The teeth in her mouth had grown lounger, stronger. Her eyes now found new sight under the color of madness. She sensed a vibe, a presence that was wonderful and at the same time frighteningly strong.

Something made her look over to her left and observed Robert Raven standing tall in the living room wearing a black leather jacket and blue jeans. His fists were clenched. Sylvia saw the look on Robert's face. She could only associate the look with an unknown and magnificent terror.

"Robert?"

"Where is she?"

Sylvia leaned back against the couch. If she were still alive perhaps her heart would beat out of her chest. Instead she looked at the man who before her was not the same man she seen with human eyes. Now she was-

One of them.

Enola

Robert's face was sunken in. The ridges of his cheekbones were purple, livery, and deeply chiseled. His eyes were gone. Complete black invaded their space, and the black was alive, like smoke. It looked like Robert's insides were filled with it. His forehead depicted purple veins. They were slivering progressively from his temples to his cheeks in an undead manner. Robert's nostrils flared with his words. When he opened his mouth to talk Sylvia wanted to die. His teeth were so long that she couldn't understand how they could possibly fit in his mouth.

"Where's my daughter?"

"Is this a dream?" Sylvia responded

"Does it feel like a dream?"

"No."

"Does your reflection tell you it's a dream?"

"No." Sylvia gulped, seeing only her clothing in the reflection.

"Now Sylvia." Robert said, stepping forward, "I've answered your questions, now answer mine

"What are you tal-"

Robert didn't let her finish. He stepped forward with inhuman speed and with one hand grabbed Sylvia by her throat lifting her to the ceiling. Her mouth snapped open into a gagging scream. Her new vampire teeth stretched out like a cobra's.

"WHERE"S MY DAUGHTER!"

Robert shook her. His eyes filled with more darkness. Sylvia finally screamed as Robert opened his mouth longer, wider and Sylvia understood all too well what she had become. Robert's eyes weren't gone anymore, now they were there for the viewing. She couldn't see her image in the mirror but she could see it in the vampire's eyes. His

149

long fingered yellow nailed hand wrapped so tightly around her neck the force brought her back to life, if only for a moment

Robert dropped her to the sofa.

"What do YOU want!" Sylvia screamed in a panic. If she could have she would have cried tears. Instead only the notion came.

"I gave you the gift you bitch. You whore. I gave you the release, from your husband. You mortals are such fools."

"What are you talking about Robert?" Sylvia slumped to the floor terrified.

"Blood." Robert said.

His new teeth getting in the way of his articulate speech.

"I could've had anyone, but I chose you Sylvia." Robert screamed in a rage. "I chose you over HER!"

Sylvia turned just as the hand propping her up became soaked with wetness. She turned her hand over and saw blood, deep and rich with iron. In the kitchen Sylvia saw the chair she once sat in when she met the Raven's and the dining room table, the oven, the dishwasher, the sink, the little figures on the wallpaper. She remembered schoolchildren riding bicycles and walking. She saw Holly Raven lying in a pool of blood on the floor. Her arms were stretched out towards the ceiling as if she was grabbing for God with both hands. Her fingers were crooked, broken, and bent. Sylvia's ghostlike eyes focused on the only friend she had anymore. Holly's exquisite face had been ravaged. Someone singed an X in her forehead before cutting her face in two with a meat clever. Robert had taken her teeth. Her vampire teeth.

"The ultimate disrespect. Is to take the teeth of a vampire after they die." Robert said.

He lowered his face. His eyes were blacker than midnight's forgotten. He tossed Sylvia his dead wife's teeth.

"Oh my God."

Robert came forth grabbing Sylvia Dejour again. His dead, cold hands were strong and firm.

"My wife is of no use to me without my daughter Mrs. Dejour. She was the only thing human I had left in this world. She was my heart. I find it humorous that I kill your husband and now come home to where the heart no longer is. And I killed my wife in a rage my daughter's missing. Don't you understand what's going on here? I cared for you when you were nothing more then a pet. Food for the Gods. That's why I made you what you are. Your life was going nowhere. I saw you in my life. You were to be my wife's replacement. You were strong, had to be living with John for all those years waiting without hope. You wanted the grave and I saved you from that."

"WHO ARE YOU?" Sylvia cried.

Robert stood back, the fireplace crackled behind him. He brought his hands up together hooked into claws. The back of his leather jacket blew out like an exploding curtain. Sylvia watched in astonishment and horror as the vampire sprouted long, colossal and monstrous wings like that of a bat. His face elongated and melted into a twisted manifestation. His eyes became orbs of purple swirling lights. His teeth lolled out and became forked. Sylvia saw the end of his tongue and it had a tooth. As for the rest of Robert's teeth, they grew perfectly straight, and the fangs grew longer than the rest. Sylvia heard Robert's jaw crack and unhinge like a cobra's. Robert smiled as the teeth in his mouth went on forever. The thing flapped its wings and laughed in an angered scream before the wings exploded into burning black feathers that died like embers before drifting towards the floor. They disappeared into ashes of another wrecked dream.

In a microsecond the vampire was behind the couch standing between the sofa and the wall impossibly. The couch was tight against the wall but Robert Raven stood behind it all the same. His arms were wide, long fingered, clawed. Sylvia turned around to scream. As she did, Robert spoke.

"Your daughter has my daughter." He said. "It seems Brenda is the answer to all the murders. And it seems Mrs. Dejour, that I am that answer to all the innocent's prayers. I'm going to visit everyone in this town until I find her. I'm going to find your little girl, Sylvia, and I'm going to wear her face to your funeral."

"NO!" Sylvia screamed as the vampire grabbed Sylvia's head and jerked it back exposing her long thin neck.

In a speed like a starved animal Robert responded by biting into the side of Sylvia's throat with a force that blew out all the windows in

151

the room.   The glass showered the furniture. The fireplace extinguished. What blood was left in Sylvia showered the wall behind her and the couch. Robert's black Mustang came to life on it's own, as if haunted, as if it responded to its master's anger.

Robert devoured Sylvia's throat ripping out the one side in an empty half meaty moon. His pale white face became a goatee of gore. He slid out from behind the couch as Sylvia fell over on her side. Blood spurting from her neck like a park water fountain. The shadows of evil made idiot and hapless shapes on the wall.

Robert gently closed Sylvia's eyes with two long undead fingers. Her blood popped with his words and ran down his lips.

"Such a tragedy."

Outside the snow fell silently. The door to the house of doom opened to a tall man with blood on his face. He walked briskly to his muscle car. The vampire backed his car out into the winter night trying to outrun death..

Sylvia Dejour laid on the couch she opened her eyes once more as they began to fade to darkness. She had one final thought as her eyes drifted to the wall and she drowned in death. On the far side living room wall Winter's coat still hung. It was that fake fur coat she adored. Her dress boots lay underneath. Above the coat as if painted by a professional were words dripping in blood.

I'VE GOT HER MOM

"Brenda?" Sylvia trembled in disbelief.

"Brenda?"

She could only think the words because her vocal chords were now gone. They fell out of the hole her killer has made.

BRENDA!   She screamed in her mind. Thereafter Sylvia Dejour slept forever.

There was no coming back a third time.

XIV.

The smell of something deep, horrid, as if gone but not forgotten lingered like death in the air. Her eyes were open but yet she could not see, not until she felt fingers sliding under the blindfold she was forced to wear. Winter's eyes came true and she found herself wishing for her father because he was the only one who could save her now.

The Mustang rumbled along snowy roads almost getting stuck twice. The driver wearing the latex mask designed by some fantastic artist cared very little about life. She cared little about getting caught without a license. There weren't many people out in the blizzard that night. Her dark 1999 Mustang drove discreetly with Winter in the passenger seat beside her. She knew who it was she was riding with and felt apprehensive knowing that the driver was once someone she thought she knew.

Brenda Dejour drove her Mustang into the Forest Woods Preserve where she had murdered so many others. This was where the voice in her head told her to go. This is where she wouldn't be bothered. This is where her macabre dealings with the evil in her mind set her free. Winter remained in her seat crying and whimpering. She had better shut up or the young woman sitting beside her in the frightful Halloween mask would slap her again. She looked down by her side. She saw the deep cuts on her hands and saw something else in between the seat cushion. There was a copy of a novel. The cover was dark with purple lettering.

VIOLATOR.

There were bloodstains on it. Brenda Dejour gripped the steering wheel tightly driving like a madman.

Her eyes drifted in the murkiness of it.

"Where are you taking me?"

Brenda switched the radio to KISS. The face painted band blew out a song. She turned up the volume listening to King of the Nighttime World. The voices of vampires in black robes riding haunted horses filled the void in her mind.

I'm the king of the nighttime world, or should I say...queen?
The Mustang rounded the ravine of a region in Carper Falls dotted with
new construction. She drove up the snow-covered lane into the woods
as the stroke of midnight blossomed like a dark rose. Brenda gunned
the engine, shutting off the music as she drove as far into the preserve
as the Mustang would allow.

"I know it's you Brenda."

"I said be quiet."

"Please, don't talk to me that way. I can help you. "

She slammed on the breaks. The car slid three feet forward and
almost made both of them fall from their seats.

Slowly she turned her head to the right. Winter observed the
horrid mask. It's gray wrinkled latex nose. The twisted paths of fake
cuts in the face. The cuts made from a repulsive fake grin. It was a
witch's reflecting the end of all things sacred.

"Don't talk to him." Brenda said.

"What?"

"I said don't talk to him. Do it again and I'll cut your throat."

Winter turned away from the woman she thought of as her
friend. She began to sob, terrified knowing that the girl she trusted,
hell the girl she was even attracted to, was the Violator. Everyone
thought it was a man doing these killings but they wrong. Winter
began to cry heavy. Tears fled from her eyes in torrents. The woman
driving the car was crazy, this much she knew. Her intentions with
Winter were a complete mystery to the captive.

They soon wouldn't be.

"Why are you doing this?"

"Are you deaf?" Brenda said hoarsely. "SHUT UP!"

A hand came out grabbing the young girl by her hair. She
pulled her down slamming her face into the dashboard. Winter
screamed.

"ARE YOU GONNA SHUT UP?"

"YES!"

After a moment Brenda let up.

"Please don't kill me?"

"Oh you're going to die bitch. You're going to scream."

The door opened to the cold winter air as the madwoman stepped out into the snow. Quickly Brenda rounded the other side of the car. The fake hair on the latex monster mask she had worn to kill Billy Owens fluttered in the wind. A wave of damp winter air shook the car as the snow ended. The Violator opened the door.

"Get out."

"Please Brenda, you can't do this!"

"I said get out Motherfucker!"

She grabbed the girl by her pajamas and threw her into the bite of the snow.

"I don't have shoes!" Winter sobbed.

"We don't care."

Winter stood in the cold snow barefooted. T he wet raw spell of winter bit into her tender young feet. Brenda placed a pistol into the center of the girl's back.

"Try anything funny bitch and I'll color the snow."

"Please dear God." Winter begged.

Brenda Dejour nudged her with the gun. They walked calmly towards the shed where she murdered the old man hours earlier. Darkness fell over Carper Falls like a dirty curtain as she trudged along closer to the shed. Someone painted it an ugly mustard yellow. She cut that someone with the bad taste into firewood. Brenda moved quickly forcing the young girl in front of her towards the shed.

"You'll never hurt mom again." The woman under the mask grunted.

It wasn't what she said that terrified the young girl, as much as how she said it. Brenda was seeing her father in her mind. She saw all the hurt he had caused her mother. Then she saw him dying in the hospital at the hand of the thief that deprived her of her retribution.

Duke saw the both Mustangs while sitting in his office. Something wasn't sitting well with him. Maybe it was his cop's instinct. Sometimes we just get bad feelings no matter how much we try to ignore about them. They are there like voracious animals biting at our sides. Duke holstered his gun that evening before the snow ended. He

155

pulled on his winter coat before Sheriff Turner called him and asked if he'd pull a double. Duke agreed. He didn't have a wife or anyone to go home to like Turner did. What he did have was his police mind, carefully turned over years of being a cop. It was no surprise that evening when he seen the 1999 Mustang sliding and swerving through the snow near Sundown Boulevard that he felt suspicious. There was something else that caught his eye. The driver was wearing something over his or her head.

Could be a hood.

Duke was sure it wasn't. Ten minutes after the Mustang passed the Police Station turning down Sundown, Duke decided he had sat long enough. He called Deputy Coulter Jones on the radio and told him to head back to the station. Together they were going to comb the streets. There was more than 8 inches of snow out there. What would be so important that someone was driving in this weather?

Coulter Jones pulled the 4-wheel drive Isuzu Trooper up to the Police Station. The wipers were swinging heavily. The snow had stopped falling but now the wind picked up with a hellish Antarctic fury. Coulter stepped out of the Trooper just as Duke met him at the door.

"What's so important sir?"

"Come on. We're going to find out."

Jones got back inside the warmth of the Trooper as his superior officer got in beside him.

"It's a goddamn blizzard out there."

"Yes I know." Duke said. "Teddy Lawrence and a few others will be in at 2 am. There'll be no one minding the telephone lines until then, but I don't expect many phone calls.

"Sir." Coulter said. "We're not supposed to leave the station unattended. Someone has to stay behind to-

"Just Drive Coulter. Never mind the bullshit."

"Where am I going?" Coulter asked.

He was a young deputy, only two weeks on the Sheriff's team. He couldn't make the State Police but has no trouble getting on with the Carper Valley Township Authority. The town was much too small to have an entourage of more than 8 cops or so. Coulter was the newest addition.

"Head down the boulevard, I want to see something."

Coulter did as he was told. The Trooper drove on with disco lights turning as the worst winter in Maryland came to a head.

People slept peacefully despite all they had heard. Some of them resound in the thoughts that the FBI was there searching for the psychotic killer. Freddie Hurst had been watching baseball reruns on television and fallen asleep an hour prior. The last thought in Freddie Hurst's mind was how he had taught his son how to throw a curveball, before his son went off joining the softball league. Freddie's specialty was throwing curveballs. It was one of the few things he was still good at.

Across the street from his house he saw the muscle car that often refueled at the station where he worked. The car was a Mustang.

All he puts in that baby is hi-test.

Freddie sat up in his bed looking out the second story window to his home. Down on the snow-covered streets nothing was alive. People were either inside their homes trying to sleep like him, or maybe they were up playing cards as the hours wound down into dreams. Whatever the case, Freddie seemed to feel a sense of oddity when he observed the hard green luminescence of the light pole transfix it's ghostly aura down on the muscle car. The 1970 Mustang COBRA sat with snow blowing around it. The glowing green of the pole light made the car look evil, deranged. A black eye to some old an ancient curse. The windows were tinted. The exhaust billowed from the powerful engine. Short bursts of fuming power came from it like growling dogs or rabid beasts.

"What the fuck is he doing?" Freddie whispered in the dark.

The car was idling. The windows were all blacked out like the eyes of who drove it.

"How can a rear wheel drive car drive in this shit anyway?" Freddie asked.

He reached over to the night table. He grabbed his spectacles and placed them on the bridge of his nose so he could see further into the night. The Mustang's headlights cut through the darkness into the snow-covered road before it. Suddenly the door opened, and out came the stranger he had come to know little or nothing about other than he had a few bucks. Must have. How else could he afford living uptown and restoring such a muscle car?

The stranger stood still for a second. He then turned his head slowly to the left. He took two steps forward and stopped sensing something new and profound.

Darkness. Cold, horrid, darkness.

Freddie clutched the bedroom curtain and lifted it back just enough so he could see. What he saw was a middle-aged man who looked very good and youthful. Freddie thought anyone with hair that dark without any gray in it must have no problems in this world. He in fact thought the man's hair looked like the hair on a doll. He was looking up at him. The man was staring right up into Freddie's eyes perhaps trying to find the thoughts behind the windows to his mind.

The man wasn't blinking.

Freddie looked on as fear clutched his heart like a sponge and began to squeeze. Under this would rather go drown in the bathroom tub rather than look into those eyes ever again.

The man was still staring.

The dark man's eyes were absent of shine. As if they were filled with smoke. Hollow eye sockets devout of humanity. Freddie could see a sparkle become eminent in both. A glistening. A sliver of sun hitting a mirror like liquid silver. The man's eyes were filled with a wonderful conception of evil and doom, as if he had come back from the dead, from the grave and has brought with him the gifts of whatever lived there.

The dead don't blink.

Freddie would rather swallow a bullet then see those eyes again. He looked away. Then he looked back.

The man with hollow eyes was smiling. A mouth full of teeth shined under the streetlight as if the man below Freddie's window was reading his mind and liking what he found. The fear, the horror, it fed this vampire's soul with a kind of dark and brilliant magic.

He signed his name...with only one letter. A single letter that was not found in the name Robert or Raven. That letter is...

D

Freddie watched the dark man smile wider as he walked closer to the house not looking away from the man sweating upstairs. Somehow the vampire's teeth had grown with the smile. Somehow, someway Freddie broke away from the evil walking towards him and closed the curtain. He fell back on the bed frantic and fearful.

Then he heard knocking. A slight soft but urgent rapping. A full five seconds passed between each knock it seemed.

RAP...RAP...RAP...

Freddie went to the closet sliding open the door and he pulled a tin box from out of the darkness. Quickly with damp palms he opened the latch and flipped the top. The gun inside was oiled clean and ready. Freddie dropped the cylinder out of the revolver to make sure it was loaded. It was.

You're going to need all six shots Freddie. You're going to need all six because the dead don't blink. They come for you Freddie. they eradicate, they eat, and they violate. He's coming Freddie, knocking, probably licking his own lips curious about what your veins are going to taste like. He's going to drink you dry Freddie, because this guy only uses hi test.

The knocks came again, this time faster.

"GET AWAY!" Freddie yelled from the top of the staircase down into the dark.

The front door was hidden by shadows and remained still. Freddie could see snow flurries from the top of the door where a moon shaped window remained. The knocks came louder, harder, and more forceful. It made the chain on the hasp lock bounce and jingle.

"I'M WARNING YOU MISTER! I'LL PUT A BULLET THROUGH THAT DOOR! LEAVE NOW! GOD DOESN'T WANT YOU!"

Silence. Freddie didn't understand why he said that last part. But he didn't feel bad for saying it. He flipped on the light switches from upstairs. The staircase light illuminated a cut of the living room then the front door. Freddie saw the bottom of the door. The threshold was drifting with what looked like cigarette smoke. Fog or mist came from under it like a great and fantastic fire was alive on the other side.

"What in God's name?" Freddie said with terror aiming the pistol at the door.

He descended down the stairs slowly. He could smell the smoke coming under the door, and it reminded him of moldy basements and damp leaves rotting under houses. It was the stench of decay, gone over with bad blood and of rot only orgies of rats would enjoy.

"LEAVE ME ALONE!" Freddie screamed firing two shots into the dark.

The lights in the house went off everywhere just then. He stood alone, barefoot, shirtless and in the shadows. The gun was becoming wet in his right hand and his black skin pimpled with fear.

Then, all at once, he heard a muffled moan from a man hiding in the dark. How did the man get in here without opening the front door? The answer to that question would be found in insane asylums. It was a moan of a bum that hasn't eaten in days. Before Freddie turned to run upstairs he saw the eyes of what drove the Mustang come alive in the dark. They were festering with brilliant light. A liquid silver with purple shadows coming to life inside them. The silver turned darker and began to glow like neon, the color now a full lurid purple and the color of bad roses and poisonous blood.

"Freddie." The darkness said.

The unblinking glowing eyes moved in a trance like embers to a brilliant fire.

"Freddieeeeeeeeeeee."

"Get out of my house, you're not welcome here." Freddie said.

"But I am welcome Freddie." The voice said.

It laughed. Whatever it was it laughed. Then it and cursed and laughed some more as if something inside the human portion crossed the street and began to hurt.

"Where's my daughter you old fuck?" The thing hissed.

"What are you talking about?! Good God LEAVE!"

Another shot from Freddie's revolver rang out. This time Freddie shot at the eyes in the dark, but they were still there, still moving towards him.

"I'll ask once more before I pry off your head and see for myself where you're hiding her. Where is my daughter?"

"What are you talking ab-"

The vampire cut him off. It had had enough. It let out a scream of evil like Freddie had never heard in all his life. The scream faded down to a low growl. It sounded like the Mustang outside idling to a twitch of the accelerator. The lights came on, all at once, even the ones he never turned on to begin with. Upstairs, downstairs and outside. In that instant Freddie saw what owned those eyes in the dark now standing there in the light. It was a man, but not a man at all. It was taller than before, not inches, but by feet. It actually had to kneel a bit from keeping its head from going through the ceiling. Its face was sunken and its pale white cheeks were cesspools of throbbing jowls. Its lips were redder than the last whore Freddie had bedded from Pilot Town. Freddie dropped his gun and the thing moved forward. It's long arms were outstretched and hooked into claws as they came out of the sleeves of the leather jacket it was wearing. The jagged fingers twitched as they moved. Freddie screamed as it opened its mouth over extending its jaw like a snake would do. Freddie could see it's long and perfectly white teeth.

"I'm going to suck Freddie." It said. "I'm going to suck and suck and suck until you know where she is. Until you all know where she is."

Freddie managed to move his legs; at least enough to run upstairs. Behind him the thing laughed and loomed forward. It drifted across the floor as the tip of the dress shoes it wore drug across the hardwood. The vampire floated forward like a living ghost. It was laughing, and Freddie could here its fingers twitching through the laughter. Ten it screamed in hate after the gas station attendant. Freddie looked back over his shoulder as he saw Robert Raven pick up the dropped pistol. He held it in his hand. The vampire's black leather jacket was tucked up and ruffled in the back making it look like a cowl and made the vampire look even more authentic, as if he wore a cape instead. Dracula was not the first. And he was not the only.

Under the leather jacket that hung open to the bare white t-shirt underneath, Freddie could see a massive dark stain of blood in all its goriest glory. It was frozen dry.

"I'm going to drink you until you turn sour Freddie." The vampire said. "Not even God will want you then." The stairway lights shined off his face in a kind of idiot Halloween orange.

"Sour." Robert Raven whispered, revealing those teeth again through middle aged dimpled smile.

Freddie made it to the top of the stairs and turned left wanting to run. He didn't know where he'd go but at the end of the hard wood hallway was the bathroom. There was a window leading to the cold winter night outside. If he managed to escape he would surely freeze to death. But still that was better than the alternative. Freddie ran with everything that he could as the arthritis filled his bones with horrible knots that burned and unwound like barbwire on the bone. He made it all the way to the end of the hall just as the vampire stopped at the top of the staircase and turned towards him.

"I'm going to make you wish you killed yourself Freddie! I want my daughter you motherfucking piece of shit! I will FIND HER! And you will wish you shot yourself!"

The vampire raised the pistol.

"Like this." Robert said lowly.

His face lowered in the shadows. The tiny pupils trapped Freddie's eyes like headlights to the Mustang catching a deer. They were dots of mercury in a land where the temperature rose and fell like heartbeats. The vampire raised the pistol not at Freddie, but instead placed it into his own mouth and smiled.

"Oh dear Christ." Freddie whispered.

His lips quivered. An unimaginable thing happened. The vampire started running towards him, pistol still in its mouth. It came charging, drooling around the barrel of the gun, that liquid silver in its pupils had now taken up everything in its eyes. It was crying tears of silver. Just as it came inches near, Freddie slammed the door on it. From the other side of the door the gun went off in a deafening.

Freddie swore he heard droplets of something splash against his new hardwood floor.

"Jesus." Freddie gasped. "What the fuck?"

He knelt down in his own fear as he heard only the slight wind from outside reminding him he was still in a slight predicament. His chest heaved in and out, as the old man became breathless. He was going to have an anxiety attack if he didn't stop. Never in all his years had he observed a man kill himself. But Freddie knew what was outside the door lying there dead was not a man. It looked like a man, and probably even was a man long ago. Back when revenge was not as sweet as blood.

Freddie was sweating profusely in the small bathroom illuminated only by a blade of winter moon. The coldness of the tiled floor numbed his ass and he slowly stood back to his feet trying to imagine what he'd see once he opened the door. He carefully placed his ear against it, listening, trying to hear the blood still running, perhaps dripping softly from the ceiling like a slow leak in a faucet. Stepping away from the door, Freddie decided against his own wishes. More than ever he needed some kind of ladder. The drop from the bathroom window was at least forty feet. If he were to jump from that height he'd kill himself or shatter all the bones in his. And there he'd lie in the snow with his eyes open wondering what went wrong as drifting snowflakes would flutter into his open eyes. He'd wonder why life sometimes threw you a curveball.

He turned from the window paced quickly back and forth, his hands pushed the sweat from his forehead into his gray and black hair. The spectacles on the bridge of his nose slipped to the tip from the sweat. He was cold all over but not from the weather. The terror had come quick and merciless as anyone could imagine. His white undershirt had become drenched with sweat. He looked down at his watch as if concerned with the time. It wasn't the time he was checking on but it was his sanity. After all, he had just witnessed a man run down the hall after him with a gun in his mouth and pull the trigger right outside the door.

Freddie wanted to look. He needed to see and some way somehow he was getting out of this. He needed to make it out of here and to the white Buick in his garage. He'd drive through the snow to the Barracks and Harrison Turner and his men would come back with shotguns. Freddie grabbed the doorknob. His whole arm shook. He could almost hear it in his teeth. He pushed the glasses further up his nose and wiped the frustrated tears from his eyes. If he'd live to see dawn he would never be the same.

He turned the knob, closed his eyes briefly, and then gathered what was left inside him. With his eyes closed he saw the vampires silver eyes disembodied. He opened them as hallway light cut into the bathroom and that's when he observed the hand on the floor as if someone was propping up with it. Freddie opened the door further on a screaming creak and felt the horror leap from his chest. The vampire was slumped against the hallway railing inches from the bathroom door where he had fired the gun. Freddie saw everything else in a flash like something out of a madman's nightmare. The vampire lay decreased; it's mouth open, and the razor sharp teeth still there like a hung shark's mouth. The hollow sockets where its eyes should be made Freddie realize it was real after all. He saw the top of the vampire's head and the gun smoke billowing from the hole. Freddie heard drops hitting the floor as bloods dripped down hard and fast, some of it into the vampire's mouth.

Slowly, Freddie stepped out into the hallway.

No! Freddie thought. *He'll grab you! And then he'll go for your throat! He'll bleed you dry and when you awake again all you'll know is that feeling of hunger and it will run inside your body always and forever, and you'll know nothing but murder.*

The body on the floor suddenly let out a giant hush like a doctor when he tell you to breathe in deep. It was the hush that made Freddie scream like a girl before the vampire's hand grabbed him by the ankle. The hole in his head was still steaming from the exit wound.

"I just *love* dying Freddie." It said. "Every time I kill myself I come back with something new to share with everyone. I see things you wouldn't believe Freddie."

Freddie was caught in mid scream, as the vampire stood tall. Its dark hair now astray and wadded from the blast of the bullet. The vampire's eyes widened as it smiled and it threw Freddie through the half-open bathroom door with such a force the door blew apart into fragments of splintered wood.

Freddie landed on his back and smacked his head against the porcelain basin. Freddie was aware of the pain but observed the thing coming for him, it's hands twitching again. The leather jacket it wore now barely fit it. Its head was lowered stinging of blood and gun smoke. It talked, and some of the smoke spilled with its words.

"Never grow old Freddie." It came forth. "Live forever, and death becomes a game for chess players."

How is it still alive? How is it still able to think with its brains still falling off the ceiling?

Freddie thought of this and screamed louder. He wanted the gun now. He wanted to put in his mouth and pull the trigger. Only he didn't want to come back. He didn't want to go where Robert Raven went every time he died. The vampire advanced, teeth clenched like a dog's. Freddie hoisted himself up at the last second and dove into the tub. The shower curtain came down around the vampire, and it stood like some tall ravished child's dream like a ghost under a bed sheet, one that was plastic and pink. It tore the vinyl curtain free from its body and draped it over Freddie as he lay in the tub screaming. It pulled the plastic down tight around Freddie's face and it leaned down biting the nose of the owner under it. Blood jetted along the wall of the shower stall. It then pulled Freddie out of the tub while his nose hung from his face like a broken chain lock. The vampire flung him back against the doorjamb splitting it up the center and dislocating Freddie's spine. He then cracked Freddie's face, leaving it bruised and bloodied after smashing it against the porcelain sink. Over and over the vampire went on to shatter every bone in Freddie Hurst's face. He finally lay on the cold tiled floor. His eyes bruised shut. His face crushed. Spine broken. His right leg twisted. The vampire stepped over the top of him smiling.

"Now I will show you pain."

"Oh God no." Freddie said, blood ran from his lips as the vampire picked him up like a mannequin in a store display window.

It stood behind Freddie with its arms stretched like Jesus on the cross. In it's hands were Freddie's own. Freddie's were also stretched.

It was as if he was going to dance with him by turning him around to tango. Instead, Robert ripped Freddie's arms from their sockets while screaming his daughter's name. Freddie Hurst fell to the floor to his death.

XV

Someone wise once said; All's well that ends well, but in this case, most likely, that would be a lie. Southern Gale was in his apartment above the gas station when a rumble of a Mustang made him stir from his sleep. He awoke much like Freddie Hurst, except with a woman beside him. And now, that woman was awake as well.

"Gas pumps are closed asshole." The woman named Rachel heard her much older lover whisper in the dark. He was standing by the window in his robe looking out through the ending blizzard. The frosted glass held his breath that he wiped it clean. In the dark early morning hours he heard the car gun loud. A throaty power surge from the engine sliced through the night. There outside in the snow was the Mustang, and wouldn't you know it here came the man it belonged to. There he was trudging through the wet snow with his hands in his pockets. The man Freddie knew only as Robert ducked under the awning below that depicted the sign SOUTHERN LAKES.

"What's he doing?" Southern asked.

"South." Rachel cooed. "Come back to bed."

"In a minute." South said with urgency. He pulled on his bib overalls and winter coat. Next he walked past the entrance to his bedroom and down the stairs that led to the inside of his dark gas station. He didn't see the vampire already inside hiding behind the corner of the staircase making his way upstairs to Rachel.

Southern pained his own bones to walk. Each step riddled with age much like his friend Freddie Hurst, although Freddie no longer worried about pain. The store was cold and closed to the winter night. Flashlight in hand, Southern aimed it at the front glass door where he was sure Robert Raven was standing for whatever reason.

And that's when he heard his lover scream.

The shed was the bloody awful yellow color Brenda remembered. A color that looked hot as if a sickness lived there. The young girl who would turn sixteen tomorrow was pushed inside, forced by the barrel of a gun. The gunman (or gunwoman if you prefer) followed and shut the door behind her.

"Now." The violator said. "Take off your clothes."

Winter turned around, hands still in the air. She couldn't believe that the words the other woman spoke were her own. They couldn't be. This wasn't the same young woman she had shared cotton candy with and who won her the pink stuffed elephant. This wasn't the same young woman she was curious about having a lesbian fling with either.

"Take off your clothes bitch...now!"

"I can't Brenda...please."

"Sure you can." The violator said. "Don't be shy."

"Please."

The Violator stepped towards her friend she once knew.

"You see that fireplace over there?"

Winter turned towards the fireplace.

"Yes."

"I'm going to put you in it if you don't take off your clothing. My father wants to see you. The way you really are. What's underneath is what really matters."

"You're father's dead."

Brenda stepped forward and struck Winter across the face with the heel of her hand.

"Don't you lie to me! DON'T YOU LIE TO ME!"

Sobbing deeply, the teenager held the cusp of her hand to her bleeding nose.

"DO IT NOW GODDAMNIT!" The Violator screamed.

Winter hurried stripping free of her pajamas down to her panties. They were purple with yellow tulips interwoven throughout. Her arms folded across her naked chest. Her hair was in a nest, wet and mangled from snow.

"Those too." Brenda said.

"No." The vampire's daughter whispered. "I will not reveal myself to you, I can't."

"You will." The Violator hissed.

The woman in the Halloween mask suddenly came forth with the pistol aimed high and shoved it in the girl's mouth.

"You're going to take off your panties now. If you don't I'm going to make you wish you had."

Pulling back the hammer on the pistol Brenda Dejour smiled. Winter gagged on her tears.

"Will you do it?" She asked, pulling the gun from her mouth.

"YES!" Winter yelled. "Dear God yes."

"Good girl."

Brenda stepped back. The fireplace flickered as it continued to burn Dorman Chester's body parts. The fire crackled and sizzled from melting gristle and bone. The firelight cast shadows off the fake latex shine of Brenda's Halloween mask. Winter thumbed her underwear and dropped them to the floor. She now stood with one arm across her breasts and one hiding her private areas.

"The Father wants to see everything." Brenda said. "Enola says turn around."

Winter closed her eyes, turning slowly in her naked stance. She didn't know what to expect when she opened them. The heat from the fireplace was strong, and the buzz of flies in the bathroom made her crazy with the desire to scream until she died from heart failure. There was blood all over the shed and Winter knew hers would be next.

"You can have me Brenda, just don't kill me." She whined.

Tears fell.

Suddenly, the young killer behind her pulled her mask from her face dropping it onto the floor. Brenda's face was a bright pale blue-eyed horror, wearing dark smeared lipstick outlined in brown. Her blonde hair ran with strands of dried blood and pink stained crimson. Under Brenda's eyes were dark purple slashes of insanity, as if she were drained and replaced by something new and alive underneath.

Brenda spoke.

"You're a whore, like all whores. I bet you're sorry though aren't you? Sorry and silly."

She tucked the pistol in the belt line of her jeans. She was still shirtless under the jean jacket that hung open showing the cusps of well-endowed blood stained breasts. In the far corner Brenda could see

Enola as she always saw him. A black hooded figure tall and broad, never with a face, but with skeletal hands and silver diamond shaped eyes swimming somewhere underneath. They were the fortune to all that was horrible. Enola rode on haunted horses, Mustangs, into the night and the black robes would never fall away to what was underneath. Barnabus Nodsley grabbed by her hair and pulled her head back as she stood naked and sobbing. But it was really Brenda Dejour grabbing her. A young schizophrenic with multiple personalities that sometimes got in the way.

Abuse.

"Do you see him over there?" She asked. " Over in the corner? He likes you Winter. He can smell your virginity. They call him the Violator and you will kneel before him on this night while I give you to him. He will make you suffer and make me what I've always wanted. To be true and not turned. And when that baby begins to grow inside you I will kill it, like my father killed my sister."

"No." Winter sobbed. "Brenda you-"

Another vicious crack with the gun.

"I will be *forever*."

Winter saw nothing but an empty corner. In her mind she knew Brenda was sick and knew it was her that murdered all those people.

"My father's going to kill you."

Brenda turned, faced the young girl, and swatted her across the face once more with the back of her right hand. She fell down hard, as the thing in the corner laughed. It beckoned and told Brenda to violate. *Oh we must violate Brenda.* It's how Barnabus Nodsley became Enola. He would kill all the vampires before he was the only one left. Until he was the only.

The image Brenda observed in the corner was her own subconscious. For Brenda had a dark mental illness rooted and twisted right into a brain stem deep where surgery was not permitted.

Schizophrenia.

"You're Father can keep his goddamn Mustang." Brenda said. "I've got my own."

She stepped over top of her, grabbing the machete and a length of rope Dorman Chester kept in the garage. She returned out of the dark into the living room and tossed the length of rope over the exposed rafter of the shed. She grabbed Winter by her right ankle as she tried to kick and scream.

"If you don't stop I'll gut you like a fish. This is what Enola wants."

"Please Brenda, you can't do this....you can't do this!"

She smacked her again. This time blood was drawn and for a moment, the young girl looked like her own pleading mother.

"It's not your fault. Your Father did things to you."

Brenda stopped, suddenly as if Winter was an island and the eye of the storm had just passed over, giving a glimpse of hope and freedom. Somewhere in Brenda's psychotic eyes, she could see the young girl she would have shared a kiss with on the Ferris wheel. The thought only lasted a quick fraction of time and left as quickly as it had come.

"It's too late for us angel." The Violator said. "It's time to make your wings." Brenda said, pulling tight on the knot around both ankles.

The Violator grabbed the other end and pulled fiercely lifting the naked young girl from the floor into the air upside down. Brenda pulled the rope raising the daughter of who very well could be Dracula towards the ceiling. The girl swung wildly as she hung upside down staring at the bloody floor. Things became alive with eyes in Brenda's mind.

The Trooper splashed through slush making its way down the path of Forest Woods Preserve. Coulter Jones drove bright eyed and bushy tailed.

"May I ask you a question?"

"Shoot."

" Why are we in these woods in the middle of nowhere?"

"Something's eating at me."

"What do you mean?" Coulter asked.

"These tracks belong to that girl's Mustang. I think she drove down this lane for a reason, and I think the reason's in the passenger seat."

"Drugs?" Coulter asked.

"Doubtful." Duke said. "I think it's something else. What could be so important to be out in a blizzard like this?"

"True." Coulter acknowledged. "How far in should I go?"

"As far as you can Coult." Duke said. "As far as you can."

Southern Gale ran upstairs, flashlight in hand and saw his lover lying on the bed, her head hanging off the side, arms apart. Both wrists yawning with rips bled dry. Her eyes rolled to the whites in the dark, throat slashed from ear to ear in an Italian Smile. He took a gasp and a step back in shaking horror as shock seized him. As whatever killed his lover stood in the corner of the dark living room smiling.

"Dear God." South said. "Oh sweet Jesus."

Suddenly, his young lover let out a sigh, a gasp of air as if still alive. Her white eyes rolled back to new colors, gray and dark. They swerved over towards her lover who stood in the sweeping shadows.

It's just air escaping, air passing through. My Mother used to work in a nursing home and when the folks there died they sometimes-

Rachel sat up in bed, her head still half hanging off her shoulders staring at Southern from behind her. He suddenly thought of Veronica, who Robert Raven had destroyed before coming here. He had nailed her face to her husband's with the same nails he used on the car salesman that promised revenge and now lay dead in the candle factory. Veronica had said,

She was sitting up. Margaret Hither was sitting up staring into the medical examiner's eyes. He died of a heart attack when he saw that.

Its just air passing through.

"No." South screamed, as Rachel stood on her feet, her neck snapped back into place, eyes lowered, hair hung low. Before she came all the way to life as a vampire, her master grabbed her from the corner and twisted her head off like a light bulb.

"This town's running out places to hide old man." The thing said dropping the head on the floor.

South could still hear Rachel scream right up until her face met carpet.

"Wh…what do you want?" South asked.

The vampire stepped from the shadows into the hallway light cutting through the bedroom. All South could see was the lower half of Robert's face.

"I want my daughter." It beckoned. "And I will bloody every street in this town untill I have her. The blood will run bridal deep Mr. Gale.

South pressed his back against the wall, chest heaving. The thing smiled as if it could sense Southern's fear. It smiled in that crooked, bent awful way.

"I…I don't have your daughter." South said.

"That's good South." The vampire smiled. "You'll die feeling better about that at least."

And in a second, no more, Robert was behind Southern biting down on his neck. The vampire raked its nails across his face in valleys of blood before South fell to his knees. His blood sprayed his dead lover's decapitated head. Robert wiped his mouth on his jacket sleeve and was gone along with tomorrow.

The blood rushed to the hanging girl's head. That's what happens when you hang upside down for long periods of time. Winter's naked body swayed back and forth. The rope cut off the circulation of her legs. She observed Brenda Dejour come from the bathroom with one of her famous kettles for collecting blood. Hey, every house has one. She slid it directly under the girl as she screamed in terror. Tears dripped from her eyes into the tin kettle making faint pings! This drove her all the more crazy. She begged for her life as she hung like a bat suspended from a rafter. She squirmed knowing that Brenda was somewhere underneath consumed by the monster of insanity.

Brenda wasn't human anymore. She bled red. She had skin, but underneath it all was a young girl who decayed from her father's

173

touch. Everyone deals with abuse in some form at sometime in their life. It's the aftermath of that abuse that matter. The feeling after the violation.

For most it's being ENOLA.

Or as the mirror would reverse that word, it's being... ALONE.

Brenda raised the machete slowly.

"NO!" Winter screamed as the Violator grabbed the girl's hair as she hung upside down. She pulled down making her victim as still as a tree branch on a windless day.

"No PLEASE!" Winter screamed, as the Violator ran the side of the smooth blade down the center of the young girl's still growing breasts.

Brenda looked into the girl's eyes and suddenly planted a long kiss on her girlfriend's lips. A kiss left behind on the Ferris wheel was found here finally, and true.

"Alone." Brenda whispered.

She plunged the blade deep into Winter's neck. Blood gushed out splashing Brenda's arms. The blade emerged from the back of Winter's neck. Brenda turned the blade and ran it slowly across slicing through her jugular and carotid. Blood sprayed into the kettle filling it to the brim in a bright colorful instant.

Brenda stood, as the young girl hung dead in the air her throat slashed open. She raised the kettle with both hands slowly towards the ceiling and closed her eyes.

"Dracula." Brenda said. "I want to be a vampire."

She tilted Winter Raven's blood-filled kettle and dumped it on her own head and face. It brought brilliant blood soaked clarity. She kept her mouth open savoring every drop. Just as she indulged herself the shed door burst open and two sheriff's deputies entered with guns drawn. Brenda turned towards them quick, blood running down her face and soaking the blue of her jean jacket.

"Holy mother of God." Duke said. He gasped, as his partner stood with his mouth open.

"Hands Up!" Duke yelled. He stepped forward slowly with his gun aimed at Brenda. At first Duke couldn't tell if what he was looking at was a woman or a man. Snow flurries filtered into the open doorway like ashes.

"GET EM UP NOW YOU FUCKING BASTARD!" Duke screamed seeing the girl hanging from the rafters.

All he could recognize was the young teenage girl hanging there. She was pale, freckled around barely budding breasts. Her pubic hair was as dark as the dreams he would have the rest of his days alive on Earth.

"GET EM UP NOW!" He yelled once more.

Brenda dropped the tin kettle; it clattered along the ground spinning. She raised her blood soaked arms towards the ceiling and shown the cops that she was unarmed. The look on her face showed she didn't care much. She was smiling.

"DON'T YOU MOVE!" Duke growled.

He reached behind him, one hand found the handcuffs and he threw them at Violator's feet.

"That's right you sick fuck, put em on. I ain't even gonna waste my time. You better put em on quick or I'll save us all a lot of time and trouble."

Brenda didn't speak. She did as the cop asked. Her bloody hands slipped on the chrome of the cuffs behind her back, but Duke heard the m lock.

"TURN AROUND!"

Brenda turned. Duke observed the cuffs were closed. He reached out slowly shaking not wanting to touch blood, and gave a yank on both metal bracelets. He wiped his hands on his patrol pants.

"Is that girl dead?" He heard Coulter ask

Does a hog have an ass?

"Yeah." Duke said.

His face was grim seeing the gory mess on the floor. Internal organs lay strewn about. Winter's heart was laying dead center on the dirty shed floor still beating.

"You're under arrest." Duke said, placing the gun to the back of Brenda's head. Of course you guessed that already haven't you? You're under arrest for all the murders in this town, and I'm taking you back to headquarters. The state police can take you from there. I should shoot you in the back of the head you fucking psycho. I f you try to escape, I'll hunt you down and run you over with my own truck. You understand me ma'am?"

"Yes sir." Brenda said smiling.

"Something funny?"

"Not a thing."

"What's your name?" Duke asked.

"I...I..."

"I what?"

"I can't remember."

Duke put the gun away, just as Coulter coughed aloud.

"Well we're going to find out." Duke said, and pulled harsh on the cuffs the killer was wearing.

"I can't stay in here sir. I'm going to hurl." Coulter said.

"For Christ sakes Coult, go outside!"

"Yes sir!"

"Now you. You just step slow and careful to the truck. We'll talk about this down at the station."

Duke wanted to kill the person before him, but decades in law enforcement taught him to do what his duty demanded. Maryland's laws were strict on murder and this killer would probably be dead before long anyway.

Duke reached for his shoulder and pressed down.

"K to K twelve, this is Unit 4, do you read me?"

Betty the voice responded

"This is Base K to K, go ahead."

"I got him Base, or should I say, her."

"You got who?"

"Who we've all been looking for."

"Oh boy."

"Call everyone in Base, we're going to need em I think."

"Affirmative." Betty responded.

XVI.

By the following day everyone in town was dead. Becker Washburn, one of Carper Falls only black deputies, didn't know that when he entered Route 50 and drove through town. The young deputy was still suffering from the grip of flu. The other deputies who lived in Ocean City and Berlin didn't know it either. Carper Falls was completely wiped out. Obliterated, one by one by an ancient evil still suffering with an unending thirst. Freddie Hurst murdered. Southern Gale murdered along with his new lover who was found decapitated. The local Newspaper runner, Curt Hollis, was disemboweled while his family had to watch. Several others would be found and some would never be found at all. The last visit by Barnabus Nodsley was to the local Sheriff.

Turner was in the shower trying to revitalize his temperature when he heard the sound in his bathroom. At the same time his thoughts drifted to the FBI. After the snowstorm there would be a massive search for the Violator. Turner and two of the eight deputies he had, along with the State Police, and together along with the FBI would track this killer to the reaches of outer space if need be.

Harrison had been a cop a long time and his wife understood her husband's aspirations to solve this crime. Wilma Turner was edging the retirement age herself. At least that's what she believed as she slept soundly with curlers in her hair. The warmth of the heater made the windows of the bedroom wet with condensation as the outside temperatures narrowed below freezing. In the bathroom of his home, which was only a block away from the town precinct he ran, Harrison Turner let the hot water run off him in soothing placidity. His eyes were closed and nose stuffy. He thought about all the children who had died recently, and how he had gone into Devena Mirrow's home and found her dead along with her boyfriend and her baby.

That's in the past now. He thought, but knew that was a lie. The past was right out in the open killing the citizens of Caper Falls. When you're a cop the past never let's go of you and often it's often the drive needed to solve crimes. This however was the first time he found himself investing such a ferocious killer.

Turner was always a good guy cop. He was likeable and dependable. His first few years in law enforcement involved him directing traffic for the local children at the bus stop. During his first decade before becoming a Sheriff he had been on several drunk driving accidents. He was always the first to arrive at the scene and stayed long after the meat wagon left. He would stand there for hours just shaking his head.

His mother was still alive back in those days. He remembered his mom worrying that her grave would sink in like her face under the moist sandy soil of Carper Falls. It was Jimmy Myers (who once was caught by his wife giving himself a blowjob with a vacuum cleaner) that told him it was going to be okay. He had the Fairmount Cemetery ship a truckload of dirt from the Preserve where the soil had less sand. Jimmy Myers, the caretaker, was visited by what was a bout to visit Sheriff Turner in the bathroom. Jimmy, a confirmed drunk, answered the door at two in the morning and was bitten over 40 times in his face, hands, and that special place on the neck, where most women love to be kissed. Something awful and dark finished Jimmy off by driving nails through his hands and genitals.

Harrison Turner reminiscences in the hot shower. His mother, Margaret Hither died last summer in a traffic accident out in Baltimore. Harrison had his doubts on it being a traffic accident at all. Blood was found in the car as well as on Margaret's neck. There were many people that summer day blaring on their horns thinking the old woman had maybe lost her mind. One of those people sitting at the intersection was an old 1970 Mustang Cobra colored black to the gills. In it was the man responsible for the end to Carper Falls.

Sometimes Harrison would swear he saw his Mother standing there in the shadows of his bedroom. She would touch his face with her cold dead hand and whisper; *Come outside Harrison. Come outside and see where I'm buried.*

Harrison would awake screaming. He would see his Mother's hand coming up from under the bed still wearing the ring he gave her on Mother's Day the month before she died in traffic. And from the autopsy report, no one still knows how.

They say the janitor in the morgue found Brian Lanes, medical examiner, dead on the floor. The old gimp had a heart attack. Great with the hands as a pathologist but guess what? Guess why he died? You heard from loose talk that one of the cops in Baltimore told his partner about it. Old Margaret Hither was sitting up on the drain table looking right at him like a snake. Some even say she was smiling.

Harrison Turner lathered up with soap, as the toilet behind him churned and bubbled. He drew the vinyl curtain back, hearing the bubbling spray of the nozzle. His head was a calamity of stuffed rags. He's been blowing snot for hours and was barley able to walk, but the bubbles in the toilet were long and different.

Damn air lines, it's doing it again, it's air passing through the pipes.

Air passes through-

She was sitting up smiling Harrison.

He turned off the valve. The nozzle released its pressure to a slow drip he stood for a moment. Harrison realized he forgot to rinse his hair. He turned the spray nozzle back on as the clear water of the toilet filled with blood, and then into a purple substance.

Upstairs, his wife stirred in her sleep as she cozied up to her pillow.

Harrison Turner finished rinsing the shampoo out of his hair as a hand rotten and peeling came up out of the toilet dripping with water. The hand gripped the side of the lid, and then another. The skin was pale white and slimed with gore. Its forehead was white. It was stretched with varicose veins purple and horrid. The crest of its eyes came of the water, reflecting the bathroom lights in their clear hideousness. Harrison drew the vinyl curtain back finally finished with his shower. This time for good.

He was staring at his dead mother, her arms out as if she wanted a hug and her face was folded and stretched with wrinkles as if all the birds in the world had walked across it. Her eyes were as black as crows, glossy, wide and aware.

"Son." It said with a smile, its lips split in the center, embalming fluid trickled like demon tears. Her mouth wrinkled back sending her age all over her face. In between its teeth Harrison couldn't believe it but stitches ran their course along the gum line. Apparently the coroner had cut her face in half to keep the brain from swelling.

" Son." It said again.

This time Harrison died inside.

"I miss you."

The thing that looked like his mother was half in the toilet, half out. Its arms were apart awaiting its son's embrace. In a cop's mind every situation demands questions as to why a situation occurred. A normal person wouldn't have time for questions in a terrifying situation like this. A normal person would be too scared. Harrison Turner had plenty of room for them. He questioned not only why his dead mother's torso was sticking out of the toilet, but how?

"Don't you love your mother?" It said and suddenly it brought a dead hand up to its mouth and lowered its head like a mischievous child getting ready to laugh.

It did laugh, but it came out like a cough. It burped blood, which burst out around its hand in between its fingers and up its nose. When it took its hand away it was like a magician moving a wand over the top of a hat revealing a bunny rabbit. His dead mother was no longer in the toilet, nor was she ever. Something else was however, something that wanted Harrison to see her.

"She misses you boy." Robert said. "To tell you the truth, I don't know why."

The vampire stepped out of the toilet, water running from its jeans. Harrison backed up into the tiled wall of the shower as the thing advanced. And yes, the whole time it was smiling...

Just like Mom.

It stepped in the shower stall and closed the curtain behind it. There, it swallowed Turners eyes as it bit into the Sheriffs neck and bathed in his blood until the Sheriff no more.

When Wilma Turner now a widow awoke twenty minutes later, she was the last person on Main Street to die.

Only a block away, the Trooper drove against the fallen snow. It came to a stop sliding near the precinct entrance. Liam Griffin, otherwise known as Duke, opened the door to the Trooper and got out with Coulter Jones. They walked to the back of the Police vehicle and in the darkness, lit by bluish translucent streetlights, escorted the serial killer out into the snow,

"Come on you sick bitch." Coulter said. "Sheriff's gonna want to talk to you I'm sure."

"Let's get this psycho inside Coult. She needs to live long enough to stand trial."

"You're going to pay for all those people you killed." Duke said.

He grabbed Brenda Dejour and spun her around. She was smiling. Her eyes lost. The blood on her face from the vampire's daughter was frozen and coagulated. Brenda was maddened by the burdened spin of a tale that had gone too far. The cop raised the novel she had in front of him.

"This book, where did you get it?"

Brenda didn't respond.

"Who was that girl you killed? What was her name Brenda? You can go in easy or hard. I don't give a fuck."

Brenda's eyes remained filled with streetlights, blue and lost.

"All right asshole, your cho-"

"Dracula?" Brenda said.

In a vicious turn of a screw gone awry in Brenda's mind, she turned her face to the left looking out towards the barren snow covered streets. In her view she saw dozens of robed figures on haunted horses, amidst her own self, smiling with new teeth of a new length.

Out with the old, in with the new.

"DRACULA!"

"Jesus, get this freak inside." Coulter said.

"DRACULA! DRACULA! I TOOK WINTER AND MADE ME ALL OF HER! I AM NO LONGER ALONE!" Brenda laughed, and the two police grabbed the young woman fiercely escorting her to the precinct.

Robert looked up from Wilma Turner's dead body, blood dribbling from his chin. He heard the words of a woman calling a name he had forgotten about. But one name mentioned was one that he remembered. It was the name of his daughter. He gripped the curtains and peered outside seeing the two police five blocks away bringing someone in, in handcuffs. He knew it then. Whoever that was knew of his daughter, and she had taken her. He closed his eyes and focused on the telepathy brought forth by dark angels. It was she. The police had found Sylvia Dejour's daughter.

His dark eyes full of silver streaked with a lonesome gaze, hollow like a ghost's, and as dead tears ran from then. The vampire's face turned into a rampant smile. Spittle flew from his lips as his voice lowered into a demonic overtone that made God shudder and Satan laugh. He stepped away from Wilma Turner, blood still pouring from her throat. She died right there as the thousand-year-old thing stood with arms raised screaming its daughter's name into the night.

He growled with his head raised towards the ceiling. When he lowered his face purple phantom light spread out from its eyes.

"I will bleed this world dry again and I will avenge you my daughter. For revenge is the only thing sweeter, than *blood*."

The vampire turned towards the bedroom door and screamed till the windows exploded and the door blew off its hinges. From Wilma Turner's bedroom came forth hundreds of bats, all flying in unison down the staircase and out into the winter morning. As they flew, Robert Raven's Mustang came to life by itself and followed the bats across the street where they gathered, circling, forming into a cyclone of darkness, fogging into flesh and raining blood.

Robert Raven stood in the place where the bats had been right outside Precinct Thirteen in Carper Falls. His fists were clenched and his undead heart beating with ghosts.

In the Police Station the clock above the waiting room struck 4 a.m. The sun would soon break across the dawn and spread orange wings of fire light into the eyes of everyone. Or basically no one since everyone was dead (all except for a few local cops most of whom soon would be). Darkness however was the now. The bloody woman escorted through the door by the short officer and his deputy in handcuffs didn't care about time. She was the Queen of the Nighttime World.

"Hey Harvey." Duke said.

Harvey turned around from the water cooler seeing the young woman in Police custody, still smiling with a terrifying grin. Her face was plastered with blood, blond hair long and slicked back with blood for hair gel. Her jean jacket looked like a towel used to deliver a baby. Harvey Dickman was taken aback by the grotesque image.

"Put this son of a bitch in cell 4. We'll hold her for the State Police." Duke said.

He pushed the prisoner a few steps forward.

"Yes sir." Harvey said.

He grabbed Brenda by the arm. Coulter Jones carefully walked behind them, his hand on his gun holster.

"If she tries anything, shoot her in the head."

Coulter nodded at the commanding officer. Betty stared in awe at the cop before her.

"That's him?"

"Her."

"You know what I mean."

"Yep." Duke said. "Brenda Lee Dejour. Never would have guessed in a thousand years that the Violator was a woman. Caught her up in the Preserve. She killed a young girl. I need you to run a file on her for past convictions. Everything before the murders. How many deputies we got coming in?"

"They're all here sir."

"Good job Betty." Duke said.

"Except Turner."

"What?"

"The sheriff isn't answering his phone nor his wife. I've been trying for the past hour."

"Jesus. Someone needs to go back to the crime scene and secure the body for the State Police! Did you page him?"

"Yes sir." Betty said, her thick glasses made her look like someone's old aunt. "I paged him, called his cell phone, nothing. I know he's sick but that's not like Turner at all."

"No, I know." Duke agreed. "He wouldn't want to miss this."

Duke poured himself a cup of coffee.

"What are you going to do sir?"

"I don't know just yet." Duke said. "I can't really follow procedure because the roads are closed off 50. The State Police would need a Hummer to get here. For the time being the crime scene is cut off."

"You're going to leave her there?"

"Betty what choice do I have?" Duke asked. "I feel bad but there's nothing we can do now but wait the storm out. I suppose this morning it will be clear enough."

"Sorry sir, I didn't mean to-"

"I know what you meant Betty." Duke said. "It's not your fault."

Coulter Jones had his nine-millimeter semi automatic drawn and aimed at the back of Brenda Dejour's head. Harvey Dickman opened the sliding bars of Cell number 4 and nudged the young woman inside.

"Get in there woman."

"I have rights." Brenda said. Both cops looked at each other in amazement.

"Yeah, you have rights all right. Liam Griffin explained them to you in the car. You have the right to keep your fucking mouth shut you understand?"

Brenda walked into the corner of the cell. Coulter followed taking the cuffs off the serial killer. When he did, blood was smeared all over his hands.

"Jesus." Coulter said. "This is some sick shit."

"Shouldn't someone clean her up?"

Coulter looked amazed.

"You go head my man, be my guest. I ain't touching her no more than I have to. This bitch ate a little boy."

The side door to the precinct opened and down the long hallway came Deputy Davis who Duke told Betty to call back. Duke wanted everyone available to guard this murderer. When Dickman saw Davis both of them looked troubled.

"What the hell's going on?"

"Duke captured the Violator."

"What?" Davis said.

"Damn straight, there she is, sitting in there." Dickman said.

Officer Davis peered at the blonde woman covered with dried glistening blood. It glimmered in the jailhouse lights.

"She?" Davis said.

"I know. We were all a bit surprised by that ourselves."

"What the hell is that she's got all over her?" Davis asked.

"Blood." Coulter intervened. "We found her over in the old sheds out near the Forest Preserve. She killed a girl over there."

" Jesus H. Christ." Davis said.

"She was bathing in the girl's blood. Like some goddamn vampire." Coulter lit a smoke. "I never have seen anything like it."

None of us have. Coulter thought. None of us have seen it or were prepared for it either. Look at her in there just smiling staring up at the ceiling like she's having a personal conversation with God.

Just then, Becker Washburn rounded the corner seeing the three deputies staring at the killer in captivity.

"Hey troops." He said. "Duke wants to have a meeting in the lobby."

In that lobby the five Policemen huddled around each other drinking coffee.

"All right boys." Duke said. "We got this son of a bitch, pure and simple, no problems. There isn't going to be anyway of her getting out of there and no one's coming to get her either. Her name is Brenda Dejour. No criminal history. Her Father Jonathan Dejour, local foundry worker. We can't get a hold of him on the phone by the listing in his records or the perpetrator's other parent, Sylvia Dejour. It isn't too far away to assume that this is because she may have killed them or very well have killed others."

"Is it true she killed some girl?" Davis asked.

"Yeah." Duke said. "I don't want any of you to focus on that though. I also don't want you guys going down there talking to her. Be professionals. I know we're only small town cops, but we still wear badges. Do I make myself clear?"

The crew nodded their heads in unison.

"There's something else as well. I contacted the FBI. They will be here in a few hours to take this woman into custody. The sooner they get her the better."

"Why did she do it?" Coulter asked.

"Jones." Duke started. "Once again that's not for anyone else here to figure out. The facts are she's caught and the bad stuff happening in this town has ended. As soon as I get a hold of Sheriff Turner he can brief you guys further if he wants too. All I can say is she is one evil twisted son of a bitch. She cut that girl in the woods like a hanging rack of meat. Do NOT go near her under any circumstances. D I make myself clear?"

"Yes sir." Davis said.

Harvey Dickman was the first one to see the end. It was his time just as your time will come too. People believe that cigarettes are killers. It wasn't the fact Harvey Dickman decided to have a smoke as it much as it was stepping outside that killed him. He stood with the lit cigarette as the frosty night blew in all directions from a terrible wind. Snowdrifts blocked most of the cars from leaving if they had too. He observed the darkened sky from the front door as he propped a butt can against so he wouldn't lock himself out. That butt can, a useful tool to all the deputies that smoked, was the cause of his death. In many ironic ways that meant very little, smoking killed Harvey Dickman after all.

He was thinking of the Violator, of that young woman in cell #4. She seemed every bit as innocent as those she had killed under all the caked up blood. He never in all his life heard of a woman serial killer. He didn't understand the morality of human beings anymore. He turned to his right to flick his cigarette into the snow instead of the butt can. His world became slow motion. He watched the glow of the cigarette fly across the winter air like a tracer bullet. When it sparked from hitting the chest of a man standing alone in the snow watching him, he finally become clear in his notions to scream. There was a man standing only five feet away, who wasn't there before. His eyes were glowing in the shadows of blowing snowdrifts and trees.

"Who the hell are you?" Dickman asked.

The man stood still at first until Harvey had asked his question. In response, the vampire smiled, snarling like a dog. It charged Dickman in animalistic fury, hands out, fingers splayed.

"Let me show you." The thing of ancient years proclaimed.

It cursed as it grabbed Harvey Dickman and ripped his right cheek open with its teeth before Harvey could reach for his gun. When Harvey fell to the snow, his gun was drawn. He fired two shots from convulsing. The vampire bit down onto the top of his head and with his other long fingered hand ripped his lower jaw off tossing it into the snow. As it flew through the air, droplets of blood trailed along the snow. The vampire stood in front of the door as the other officers came running into the lobby after hearing the gunshots.

If Betty would have she would've told everyone what she seen couldn't have been real. But when she saw the front lobby doors swing open to a tall man with arms soaked in blood and glowing purple orbs in his eye sockets real or not she pissed her pants. The man's mouth was running with gore, and Betty saw his face. It was bony despite his size. His ears were pale like his face and pointed. Betty pushed her chair back when it grabbed Becker Washburn with one hand lifting him to the ceiling. The sheriff's hat tumbled off his head and the vampire was grinning. Purple fire burned in its eyes as it grinned.

"PUT HIM DOWN, NOW!" Duke yelled, his gun drawn, behind him Coulter Jones and Deputy Davis were aiming their pistols at the vampire.

"WHERE IS THAT LITTLE BITCH!" The thing hissed.

Suddenly it changed. Long silver hair grew from its head, as if it was older than Christ. Its forehead bent inward and grew bulbous, elongated as if it suffered from some sort of brain deficiency or injury. Its chin split and came to a hardened pit that curved, the dead bone underneath shone through like a bad paint job. It was crying silver tears from its purple eyes. It was crying mercury.

Deputy Davis wasn't aware that his bladder also had burst in his pants.

"WHERE IS THE VIOLATOR!!!" The vampire screamed.

Its mouth stretched open and Duke could hear its jaw snap. Monstrous teeth grew and not just the ones on each end, but all of them. Its hand wrapped around Becker's throat tightened into an incredible god like grip. In one swift devastating sound, Becker's eyes burst from his face like over blown balloons. Blood splashed onto the floor.   Pieces of his eyes littered his uniform. Becker was still screaming with no eyes. The vampire hurled him across the floor as the other cops opened fire. The bullets went into the vampire's body with a soft squish. Like sticks striking mud. Becker slammed into the far side of the wall and broke his neck. He fell to the floor eyeless and lifeless.

"YOU STAY RIGHT THERE!" Duke screamed. "DEAR GOD! What are you?"

The wrecked evil before them snorted talking around it's teeth and swollen mouth.

"I am Robert Raven, and I am afraid my friends that God is not listening today."

Duke stepped forward firing bullet after bullet as the thing laughed instead of dying. The vampire stepped forward and with the speed of light. The three policemen tried to follow him but the human eye was to slow for such a trick. Coulter's eyes moved to the right though just in time to witness the vampire slip behind him and jerk his head down to the right. Robert bit down into the deputy's neck as blood sprayed every wall in the waiting room. Wads of spittle and foam flew from Coulter's mouth. His eyes rolled to the whites. Inside his body, his veins emptied, his heart became a stone. In seconds the vampire dropped him to the ground. Next he looked slowly up at Duke who stood in terror. Deputy Davis had his necklace off and his gun on the floor. The cross was tiny, but Davis hoped the land of movies were real, because this guy certainly was.

"Step away from us spawn of the devil. Bow before the might of the…"

The vampire interrupted with laughter. Dark blood oozed from its mouth.

" There is no Satan and this world is mine!" The vampire gloated.

Davis screamed.

"Tell me why all you mortals seek religion as your savior, when in fact you don't believe it no more than you believe your bullets will stop me?"

"I believe in God!" Davis stepped closer, his eyes closed. "Oh dear God, take this evil away. Take this evil away "

Robert Raven began to levitate off the ground, inches from the floor. The vampire spoke and it sounded throaty like the muscle car it brought into town.

"Mr. Davis." The vampire said. "Open your eyes."

Suddenly a hand seized Davis. The crucifix fell to the floor with a soft clatter. The vampire looked into Davis's eyes then dropped him. He bent down and retrieved the crucifix. The vampire slowly opened his mouth, laid out his tongue, and placed the crucifix on it as it singed and burned. The vampire's eyes rolled into his brain and he smiled as he swallowed.

"No." Davis shrieked.

His lips quivered. The vampire's face filled with surface veins that moved under the skin as if they enjoyed the blood it drank. Robert's pout red lips looked like a harlot's on Friday night. They stretched and widened into that razor-bladed smile. It dropped it's mouth open and Duke closed his eyes. When he opened them again Davis was falling to the floor blood spraying from his severed throat like a kinked water hose finally being let loose in the summer. Duke saw it was holding the deputy's head in its hands, and then it dropped it onto the floor. The vampire pulled off his leather jacket and threw it to the floor in a rage. That's when Betty the voice screamed. It turned, went for her and Duke charged it from behind only to be grabbed with one hand and thrown through the front police doors exploding 4 sheets of three inch glass. He landed on the snowy ground in a blood soaked scream wishing he were dead. The vampire turned back towards Betty who was cowering on the floor.

"My family just wanted to be like you, to live in a home. You couldn't except that."

"Please." Betty begged. "Please, I have children."

The vampire turned towards her, his eyes widened.

"Yes Betty, I sense that you do. So when I drink the blood from your veins that has aged like fine wine you will believe me when I say that I won't hurt them won't you?"

"Please?" Was the last thing Betty said, as the vampire grabbed her right arm and bit into the purple vein in her wrist.

The vein was so close to the surface that Robert didn't have to bite so hard, but he did anyway. On this night, Robert was going to bite anything that stood in his way. There he drank from her until his rage was full for a moment. When he dropped her dead to the floor, he turned towards the long hollow hallway where he saw one light coming from one cell. He floated part of the way until he reached cell three. The long silver hair parted down the middle flowing behind him like banshees made Robert look terrifying. The vampire walked a few steps coming into view of artificial light.

Brenda Dejour was praying to ENOLA, which in the mirror spelled ALONE. The mirror doesn't lie, not for anything or anyone. She wanted to be a vampire more than anything. She was praying when something stepped slowly out of the darkness and into the cell light right outside the bars. Its face was in the dark, but its eyes were silver, hinted with violet light.

"Hello Brenda."

Brenda's eyes grew wide. Under all that blood her eyes looked like spooked orbs of infinity. She slowly stood from her sitting position. The blood had dried on her face completely now. Winter's blood. The vampire's daughter's blood.

"Oh lord of flies." Brenda said. "It's you isn't it? After all this time, you've finally come to grant me everlasting life."

The man with his face hidden in the dark came forth into the light gripping the cell bars. Its eyes were completely black with silver pupils outlined in a purple like poison.

"I've come to kill you Brenda."

Brenda's smile turned into a serious glance drifting towards fright.

"You killed my daughter." Robert said in a low voice. "You murdered the only reason I choose to live. You've taken the only thing that kept me in check, the only thing that calmed the storm."

Brenda took a step back in her cell.

"You killed...my daughter Brenda." The vampire hissed. "Powerful and brilliant Violator, wanting to be what, one of *us*? Wanting to be a vampire? How sweet it will be Brenda. I'm going to take my time with you. The closest you'll ever get to being a vampire, is my *teeth*."

"No." Brenda said.

"I killed your father Brenda. I killed your Mother too, and for the record she would have made a better vampire than you."

"NO!" Brenda screamed. "I Don't BELIEVE You!"

"You soon will Brenda." Robert Raven said. "I'm going to send you to her. She begged for her life Brenda. She begged for me not to kill her. You should have seen the look on her face. I counted your Father's heartbeats when I tore it from his chest. We vampires *love* to count."

"GET AWAY FROM ME!"

"Sylvia said she's sorry she never gave you a sister."

"NOOO!" Brenda screamed in agony, as Robert slipped through the bars.

"And when it's all said and done, the Violator is nothing more than a goddamn child killer."

Robert Raven was now inches from his daughter's killer, standing tall before her. Brenda Dejour dropped to her knees in front of the terrifying entity.

"Before you kill me, tell me my mother wasn't scared. Tell me that please. Your daughter wasn't."

Robert's eyes grew with darkness.

"Was my mother scared?" Brenda asked.
The vampire smiled, teeth long and striking grew in front of her.
" Shitless." It said.

XVII.

Winter's Father carried her body through the snow. The morning sun emptied across the sky in a broadened deep cut of horizon like a bursting bloody orange. Tears ran from Robert's eyes. Newfound tears of forgotten heartbeats. The frail body of his daughter wrapped in a blanket would never be forgotten. The never-ending thirst accompanied by pain felt by Robert Raven left its mark in Carper Falls. This place was a dead zone. Hope for the future had been cast down into the dreams of the town's last night of existence as the jagged shadows of an immortal that has passed through, for his revenge was merciless and unknown to the rest of the world. Robert Raven would be a remembered name, for he was the first vampire to walk the Earth. Son of Lillth, queen of the dead. His daughter's arms hung loosely towards the ground as gently he loaded her into the back seat of the hunted Mustang. The car drove onward that Tuesday morning with a whirl of snowdrift following it. Destination, terror, next place anywhere, perhaps even your town.

The FBI came that afternoon as a group of government workers began plowing the streets of Carper Falls from Berlin, a neighboring town going into Delaware. Seven plows, there bright orange trucks with blazing flashing lights cleared the entrance to the beginning of Route 50 which led into the dead heart of the houses that remained quiet unlivable and damned. Charles Moatan led the snowplow crew. The radio still played the mayor's report that schools would be closed and the State of Maryland under a snow emergency. It was under an emergency all right. One, Charles wasn't aware of, not until he seen the first stop sign on Broad Street and Sheriff Turner impaled on it. The signpost jutting through his chest and protruding through his mouth. Turner's eyes were lost marbles in his head. He was naked, blood had frozen to ice on the rim of his mouth and the head of his cock. When Charles and his crew saw the impaled Sheriff he stopped his vehicle, got out of the snowplow, and let out a sound that put all the blonde stars of horror movies to shame.

Three of the eleven plows that entered Carper Falls that morning went down two other streets one of which was the only gas station in town, Southern Lakes. None of the state workers would know South was killed upstairs and his much younger girlfriend was brought back to life just long enough to die again. They didn't know that a block away, Freddie Hurst lay killed in his upstairs bathroom of the home he had purchased decades ago. By the time Charles Moaton found his first body and ordered the crew to get out of Carper Falls the other crews had ran across twenty. At least twenty people were found impaled on road signs, some of them with missing heads. Others were in a much-worsened condition. One, which will haunt a state worker, named Clifford forever. He found his old first grade teacher Mrs. Gabel Dither hanging from a frozen tree by her own intestines. They were wrapped around the tree branches like vines. Clifford and his boss sent the other crews away from the area to get help while he plowed through the gas station all the while feeling the killings were the work of that mad man all the cops in the East Coast were looking for. The Violator more than gave Charles the creeps. None of the workers slept again for several days.

They found the police station and it looked very bad on the outside. There they found Liam Griffin who everyone called Duke. He was cut to ribbons but still alive. When Charles walked towards him as the morning sun bled across the sky beginning to melt the worst of a fallen blizzard his bow legged knees trembled. Not all of that was from arthritis, or the sharp bite of winter. He knew something had gone horribly wrong here in the past few days. He didn't understand what he was seeing all over the town. Most of it was shock; some of it was because he didn't want to believe it. He'd seen enough to haunt his dreams for his remaining years. Duke was talking mostly gibberish. Clifford went to his side, asked him where the other police were and what happened. Before Duke could answer he died. His face was cut all the way to the tendons and veins that pumped blood in jets and rivulets. He died with a mouth full of glass. When Clifford peered into the front triple glass doors of the precinct he didn't need a badge to realize what had happened. Someone had thrown him through every door.

Clifford and Charles walked into the Police Station. They would never forget what they saw. Clifford died a few years later but Charles still talks about it usually to his grandson or his friends at Halloween. Some stories are worth repeating. Others like most novels have no real ending. In real life a story never ends, a book is never closed, don't let the illusion of a cover and a binding fool you, even as both men walked into the precinct seeing blood, glass, and bodies thought the end of Caper Falls ended a story.

Charles kept his composure, a cigarette dangling from his lower lip. The hollow wind of a winter's fix blew down the hallway from the broken doors making sounds like demons singing through instruments made of bone. Clifford was sweating profusely in the cold. T hey both stopped outside of CELL # 4. Charles was staring at his reflection in the half frozen puddle of blood. Both of the State workers turned their heads at the same time and saw the young woman.

Brenda Dejour hung upside down arms apart, feet together, she was nailed to the wall like Jesus, but upside down. Her face was skinned clean, all the way down to the bone. It was as if someone had taken her face. Clifford's eyes went a little further up and saw that the woman's throat had been slashed open. A gaping strand of flesh hung from her throat and it was in that instant that Clifford screamed. Charles on the other hand never made a sound, not even when he seen the message written across Brenda's bare breasts and chest. A message written in blood.

REVENGE

Clifford and Charles left that morning and never returned again to Carper Falls or any town surrounding.

Several days later the FBI commissioned to have the whole town of Carper Falls closed off. The first documented case of an actual town being the crime scene was archived. Head investigator Gabriel Bixby led the public to believe the Violator was caught based on one document. The Sheriff Department's 911 secretary had documented in the police log the arrest of Brenda Dejour, believed to be the serial killer involved in the murders of more than 12 victims. Bixby was undermined in his investigations however when a team of homicide detectives tried to ascertain what exactly happened in Carper Falls. Someone else murdered the Police Bixby believed which was obvious by the murder of Brenda Dejour. Perhaps one of her parents went crazy and killed the police wanting justice for their children. It was however very strange that such a small town would have two serial killers. In any case, blood had become sweeter then revenge.

Francine Bowry became famous in an infamous way. She was the manager of a local business that sold cell phones. Fairs Cingular was up and running in a few days. She was also the local librarian who talked to Brenda Dejour on a regular basis. She went to her sister's house in Ocean City the night the storms came through never knowing that had saved her life. She went on television, WBOC 16 to be exact, two months after the incidents in Carper Falls. During the interview she was asked what it felt like to be the only known survivor of a massacre that claimed an entire town. She couldn't answer. The reporter asked her about Brenda Dejour.

"She was always a nice young girl. She never made noise or acted out in the library. She checked out vampire books and would sit for hours reading them. I never would have guessed she killed all those people."

As far as the books there was one more thing the Local Herald Newspaper found out. During a report he made on serial killers he found abuse was a common factor. He discovered that the book Brenda Dejour was reading in the library every day about Barnabus Nodlsey was one she made up. *Violator* was a diary, and one Brenda had been writing. There was no Violator tales of the undead. There was no Barnabus Nodsley although Brenda believed in him. Barnabus was thought to be Brenda's pen name just like ENOLA. A word that spelled out ALONE in a mirror. Adam believed that perhaps ENOLA and Barnabus were one in the same. In fact, Adam knew Brenda believed Enola was real and described him in a manuscript she kept in the library secretly from others.

Each chapter depicted brutal killings and how she had eaten Billy Owens. The last Chapter was left blank only minor poems and writings about her infatuation with Winter Raven remained, and a metaphoric rationale of wanting to be human again. The book was titled *Violator*. Some of the pages were written in blood. Whose it was remains a mystery. The book itself is being held at the FBI building in Capitol Hill and is still under investigation. The last footnotes in the novel depict that whoever reads the novel will be visited by the undead and murdered.

The cover of the book was black and purple, dribbled with real bloodstains. The book's author drew a very faint image on the cover one that looked like a stretched out Halloween mask. The mouth and eyes were hollow, maniac looking hair took up the entire books border. In the darkness of the mask's eyes children were screaming.

The Violator.

Bixby didn't understand why this woman left the last chapter blank perhaps because she was caught before she could finish.

EPILOGUE

Two days after the massacre of Carper Falls, and long before the discovery of Francine Bowry the Librarian, Dexter Lovery a pathologist was brought into the mix. This case would forever change him. He was an expert in criminal pathology and had helped the Feds solve more than one case in the past. Before anyone would be buried Doctor Lovery examined the bodies most of which were drained of blood. He didn't know if there would ever be another holiday celebrated in this town ever again. The holidays however were far off, and there were no holidays without a funeral.

He examined over forty people found murdered. The local Sheriff's wife, Wilma Turner was taken into a separate division of the morgue because she was one of the few bodies not hacked to pieces. It appeared she had died of a heart attack brought on by an intense fear. Whatever the case, State Police found her dead and with a crucifix clutched in her hands. Dexter Lovery had to pry the religious icon out of her death grip.

On the second day of autopsies Dexter came to work on that chilly morning still in a perplexed shock of brutal murders. Along the way into the Medical Science building, Lovery carried a cup of coffee in his hands. A clipboard and laptop were at his side. He was hoping that once he opened up Wilma Turner he would find traces of something maybe a clue. In most killings, serial killers are caught because of the things they leave behind. Traces of things that allow the dead to speak in unforgiving ways. Dexter saw enough in his 26 years of playing in brains and guts to know this fact. The double doors opened to the morgue. Dexter was in a lab coat with a respirator over his face. He stood by his office desk and wrote down notes concerning Wilma Turner's apparent death and the beginning of his investigation therein.

The silence of the room shrouded his soul as he walked towards the morgue drawers containing the bodies. Their shiny chrome reflected the overhead lights and he slid the tray out all the way till it clicked onto a drain table. On the silver slab a body lay covered in a white sheet. It jiggled slightly from the disruption of movement. Dexter hesitated. He pulled the top of the sheet down to Wilma's wrinkled breast. They were as corrugated as she was like drooping saddlebags hung over a camel. Dexter pulled the sheet down further rolling it as he went stopping just above the body's navel. He turned away from the body, grabbing his examination tray filled with wicked instruments, shiny scalpels and things that would make the untrained eye squint in bewilderment. Doctor Lovery grabbed the scalpel and turned around to make his initial incision under the left breast in an angular lateral cut.

Wilma was sitting up staring at him.

Lovery let out a scream as if he was a schoolgirl finding a spider in her hair. The dead woman was sitting up smiling and her eyes had gone over into darkness. The pupils were gray like that of an overcast sky ready to snow. Dexter's heart pounded in his chest. He dropped the scalpel. It clattered to the floor.

The dead woman smiled wider at the sounds Dexter was making. That smile flooded Dexter with a quick memory of shark fishing. The dead woman held out her arms and cocked her head to the side like a dog does when it hears something strange. Blood ran from her mouth in dribbles.

"Not real." Dexter muttered clutching at his chest.

Pain shot through his arms like electric needles he fell to his knees as darkness engulfed him.

The FBI is still looking for Wilma Turner's body. Some believe it was stolen. Others believe in something much different…

Eric Enck-
MARCH 2006
Midnight-

199

ABOUT THE ILLUSTRATOR

Robert Holsonbake was born on June 15, 1978 in Purcell, Okalahoma. He is a graduate of the Art Institute of Dallas with a degree in 3D Animation and Visual Effects.

Today Robert resides in Plano Texas and works as a Freelance Graphics Artists. His work consists of illustrations, photo manipulation, web sites, logos, print ads, video, and of course 3D animation and visual effects.

ABOUT THE AUTHOR

Eric Enck was born in Ephrata Pennsylvania in 1976, and some say so was his insanity. During a troubling childhood Enck discovered Stephen King and Clive Barker. He began dictating poetry at the early age of fifteen when he had to kill his beloved dog, Strata, based on the dogs suffering illness. Enck lived in a massive old house in the deep woods of the mountains in Ephrata, where at the mountains base a legendary haunted hospital remained in the tales of people residing in Ephrata. Ironically, the house was torn down when Enck left Ephrata in 1996. Enck moved to Delaware and discovered his agent Earlston Wansel and his most prized possession, his wife Johnna. Eric Enck has two children, Mason Edward, and Mallory Ann, both of which are the reasons he writes. Eric's official website is at **http://www.freewebs.com/ericenck**..

Printed in the United States
71966LV00006BA/18